DEATH LOGS IN

DEATH
LOGS IN

A Novel

E. J. SIMON

S/Z

DEATH LOGS IN

S/Z
Simon/Zef Publishing
243 Fifth Avenue
New York, New York 10016
For more information about this book and its author, visit www.EJSimon.com

Library of Congress Cataloging-in-Publication Data has been applied for.
Edition ISBNs
Hardcover 978-0-9912564-2-6
Trade Paperback 978-0-9912564-3-3
E-book 978-0-9912564-4-0

Cover design by Pete Garceau
Book interior by Catherine Leonardo

This edition was prepared for printing by The Editorial Department
7650 E. Broadway, #308, Tucson, Arizona 85710
www.editorialdepartment.com

Printed in the United States of America.

For Danielle, who every day shows me the special love
that only a daughter can bring to her father.

Chapter 1

Alone inside his wine cellar, Michael Nicholas pecked away at his computer keyboard, clicking the gold Byzantine Orthodox cross icon and then typing in the password his brother had set up ... just before he "died."

It was a year ago, but, for Michael, it seemed like an eternity. And for Alex Nicholas, it was.

Alex had been gunned down while enjoying a plate of sizzling veal parmigiana in a Queens restaurant. The shooter had been hired by Joseph Sharkey, an aging former Mafia hit man and certifiable psychopath.

Alex had been a bookie, a very successful one. He had owned one of the largest sports bookmaking and loan sharking operations in New York City.

Thinking back upon the wake when Donna, his brother's widow, asked him to briefly help settle Alex's affairs, Michael never could have dreamed that Alex's shadowy world would have drawn him in. But none of that compared to what he was about to do tonight—just as he had been doing all along—since his brother's death.

No matter how often Michael typed in the password, he always expected the screen to turn blank. And the moment Alex appeared on the screen, as he always did, Michael made a mental leap into an abyss, stretching any remaining sense of reason and rationality that he still retained.

Alex's image appeared, his powerful presence concealing his fifty-five years, just as it had in life—and, now, the fact that he was dead; his facial expressions, body movements and mannerisms were just as real as his gruff, deep voice which gave Michael the warning.

"You don't have much time," Alex said. "They've sent someone over from Rome just to kill you. I don't know too many details yet except that his first name is Frank."

Michael could feel his stomach tighten; he was falling, dropping quickly, and there was no net to break the fall.

"How soon?"

"Just days," Alex said.

"How do I find this guy?"

"Michael, I'm afraid he's going to find you."

Chapter 2

Michael recognized the voice. It was a call he'd hoped would never come.

"Michael, congratulations on your promotion."

He placed his hand over the receiver and called out to his secretary, "Karen, please close my door."

"You know, I don't know many CEOs or, what are you now, chairman? ... Michael?... Are you there? It's Johnny, Johnny Feathers."

Johnny had been one of his late brother's closest friends, a Queens bartender with a notoriously unsteady hand. Tall, fit and recognizable from a distance by his full mane of perfectly groomed white hair, he exuded a calm exterior except for that most recognizable characteristic: his trembling hands.

"Johnny, of course, I'm sorry. We haven't spoken since—"

"Yeah, since that time just before you took off for L.A. What, last July?" Michael remembered his annoying habit of interrupting people in mid-sentence.

"Oh, sure, I remember."

Michael felt sick. He looked out through the glass wall separating his large private office from the reception area and the desk of his trusted assistant, Karen DiNardo. For a moment, as he listened, he wondered whether she had any inkling of his double life, until Johnny Feathers' voice brought Michael back to the one he was hiding.

"Yeah, I don't think you forget things like that. I wanted to check in case you needed me to handle anything else for you."

"When you say, 'anything *else*,' what do you—"

"Jesus, there you go again, Michael. You know I loved your brother and I would have done anything for him. God rest his soul. Occasionally, he'd ask me to do some small favors. I'd always tell him, 'Alex, I can do a lot more for you.' But, he never liked to ask. You know what I'm saying?"

As Michael listened, his mind flashed back to scenes from years ago, Alex and Johnny hanging out together in Queens.

"Michael, you know what I'm saying?"

"What *exactly* are you saying?"

"Just that I know he'd want me to take good care of his little brother."

"Yes, I understand that part. It's the part about what *else* I might want that I don't understand."

"So, I'm hoping you're kidding here. You know, people are funny. I'm sure you're under a lot of fucking pressure, I guess they call it stress these days."

"I'm not trying to be cute, I just don't—"

"OK, you do remember your old friend, Apple Blossom?"

"You mean my old boss, Dick Applegarden?" Michael's anxiety level skyrocketed as he thought back to his dead boss. "Of course I remember but—"

"Hey, I'm sure you do. You got his job after we finished with him, right? My people did a good job, don't you think? I mean, weren't you fucking happy?"

"What do you mean?"

"What do I *mean*? What do I *mean*? Listen, my good friend, I don't like to discuss things over the phone. You never know who's listening, you know what I'm saying?"

Michael now remembered Johnny's other annoying habit, frequently ending his comments with, 'you know what I'm saying?'

"Absolutely, I understand. It's—"

"But don't tell me you believed that sleep apnea shit, Michael? I had my best team take care of this for you. And here I'm thinking you knew what the hell went on and you're probably gonna call and thank me, you know what I'm saying? I thought I'd have heard from you a while ago, to be honest."

"No, no—" Now Michael was hoping Johnny would interrupt because he wasn't sure what to say.

But Michael knew.

Although "Chairman Dick" Applegarden had hired him, Michael despised him and everything he stood for. For taking the company into the subprime mortgage business and gloating over the profits while everyone knew it wasn't a good business. For directing the egotistical but disastrous acquisition of numerous companies, resulting in the loss of millions of dollars and hundreds of jobs—and then hiring Michael to just "fix" it all—and attacking him when he couldn't do it quickly enough.

But he would never think of having him murdered.

"You told me that son of a bitch was getting ready to fire you, remember?"

"Yes—"

"You said you hated the guy. You said, 'I wish you could fix this for me' and I told you, 'Don't worry, Michael, consider it done.'"

"But, we were drinking—and joking around."

"Michael, you know that saying, 'there's no such thing as a joke. It was either Freud or Woody Allen. One of them said it."

Michael remembered the conversation perfectly. Of course, that alone told him something. It was over drinks—too many drinks—at the Black Rose bar in Queens Village late one night just before

Michael was to go to L.A. to deliver the speech on top-level management greed that he was sure would give Applegarden the excuse he needed to fire him.

Michael also recalled feeling a nagging doubt that seemed to build in his mind on his drive home that night. He wondered whether he had gone too far. At that point, however, he had no idea that his brother's good friend engaged in arranging professional hits. He'd thought about calling John and making sure there had been no misunderstanding. But he never did.

"Listen, Michael, murder, like every other vice, you don't need no motive, just opportunity. You know what I'm saying?" The word *murder* seared through Michael's insides. "It's just that most people don't have the opportunity."

And now that he had entered the business of his murdered brother, Michael had easy access to people who could "fix" anything. It was also, however, a culture of subtleties, where things unspoken were somehow clear, a world to which he was unaccustomed and a language still foreign.

Michael knew now that he had made an inconceivable mistake.

Applegarden's sudden death in his suite at the Peninsula Beverly Hills after a night at the bar had been attributed by the coroner to sleep apnea complicated by scotch and Ambien. But Michael always had a dark, uncomfortable suspicion that it was otherwise.

"Would these people—the ones who did this thing for you—"

"For *you*, you mean."

"OK, whatever, would they have any idea that ... you and I spoke ... or suspect who I am?"

"They're professionals; they don't want to know nothing from nothing."

"Did my brother ever have anyone ... you know—" Michael didn't want to say the word, as though by verbalizing it he would be taking another step closer to where he didn't want to go.

"Taken out? Ha, you mean 'eliminated,' or whatever they call it now?"

"Yes, I guess that's what I mean. Did he?"

"Not really."

"*Not really*? What the hell does *that* mean? Either he did or he didn't."

There was silence, then finally, "No, he didn't."

Michael felt at least a small token of relief. Not enough to wash away his angst over what had occurred. But at least he had a confirmation that his brother had not crossed a line that Michael would have found impossible to reconcile, the same one he himself had apparently, although mistakenly, crossed.

At least he hoped it was purely a mistake. As hard as he tried, he couldn't find that part of his soul that could shout at him *for certain* that it wasn't the outcome that he secretly desired.

"Michael, let me say this—he never had anyone iced, but …"

"But, what?"

"He should have."

"What do you mean, 'he should have'?" Michael asked.

"He'd be alive today."

Chapter 3

Westport, Connecticut

It all started right after Alex was murdered.

Michael knew that he and Samantha had drifted apart. Maybe it was his decision to take over Alex's business and the fact that he was home even less than ever now.

Or, maybe it was the elephant in the room: Michael had found his brother again and, although Samantha was aware of some communication with "Alex's computer software," as she liked to describe it, she clearly didn't want to hear any more about it. Whenever Michael tried to open up the issue, she would turn away, accusing him of losing his sense of critical judgment, or something worse.

"Michael, how did this all come about?" Samantha said softly as she turned her attention away from her novel, looking up from her bed, snugly surrounded by her down comforter and soft Frette sheets. Blonde, tan, and fit, she looked a decade younger than her forty-five years.

"Remember right after Alex was murdered, beginning at his funeral, I began getting these strange emails?" Michael said as he sat in his favorite chaise lounge, dressed in his soft, black cashmere sweater, tan although he was slightly chilly despite the evening's summer heat outside. Their bedroom thermostat was set at sixty-six degrees. They both loved a chilled—if not refrigerated—sleeping temperature; it was a quirk they shared.

"Yes, how could I forget? Someone sent you a picture of Alex on your BlackBerry while the priest was giving his eulogy, for God's sake. I was hoping you would have dropped this whole artificial intelligence thing by now. Not to mention that your brother wasn't exactly a computer genius."

"You're right, Samantha, but he had the smarts to find odd but incredibly smart techies to figure it out. You've got to listen to me. You know Alex was obsessed with his own mortality and he must have read about artificial intelligence somewhere—"

"And he wasn't much of a reader."

"No, you're right again—but he did read when he was on the toilet. But then—maybe from working with these geeks he hired—they came up with the idea of combining the artificial intelligence software with other advances like computer imaging and voice replication and recognition and, somehow, made a breakthrough."

"Oh, come on. It couldn't have been that simple."

"It wasn't. I told you, they spent hundreds of hours feeding Alex's history, his reactions to different questions, his voice, his images and his gestures, facial expressions, all kinds of things, into this system and then onto his secret laptop."

Samantha rolled her eyes. "And who told you about this *laptop*?"

"Alex had a mistress."

"What a surprise." Samantha said. "Was this the supposed 'hairdresser to the stars'?

"Yes, Jennifer Walsh."

"She does blow jobs—"

"Blow*outs*," Michael corrected.

"Oh, sorry, I remember her now. You told me about some of this with her but you never gave me the whole story."

"In the beginning, I wasn't sure I believed it myself. Jennifer never really understood what it was; she was thinking it was more of a record of his life. Then, as I realized what Alex had actually created, I knew you'd think I was crazy or obsessed or something, so I have avoided bringing it up. But it's part of what's separating us now. You have to listen, with an open mind."

"Michael, I love you but I do think you're either obsessed or maybe still grieving for your brother in such a way that you just can't let go, and I'm sorry but I just can't believe this …fantasy of yours—and neither would you … normally."

"OK, hear me out. Jennifer contacts me right after the funeral and explains that Alex had this hidden, secret Apple laptop with all this customized software that he'd spent millions of dollars on and that he'd created a 'virtual Alex Nicholas,' a *duplicate* of himself, on his laptop, which he'd hidden from everyone. She then told me where to find it—he'd had a secret compartment built into his closet where he stored it—and she gave me Alex's password."

"Michael, I can't even keep straight what you've already told me and what you haven't. I can't believe you're serious. What difference does this make? So what, you've got Alex's old password."

"It was the last thing I needed in order to find him."

"In order to *find him*? Michael, you *haven't* found Alex. He's dead."

He knew it was time to show her.

"Samantha, Alex is in our wine cellar."

Chapter 4

Rome, Italy

"I am a guest of Monsignor Petrucceli."

As he observed the reaction on the face of the maître d', Joseph Sharkey knew that he was still an important man.

He hoped that he was again being mistaken for the actor Christopher Walken; he knew that, behind his back, people had whispered about his uncanny resemblance to Walken, particularly in one of the actor's more demonic roles. Sharkey cultivated the attention—and the comparison. His pasty, pale skin tone and thick mane of white hair contrasted with his all-black attire.

Dal Bolognese's rich wood-paneled walls and gold-framed, illuminated paintings reminded Sharkey of the luxurious restaurants he would frequent in New York, when he was in his prime, a "made man."

While the maître d' grabbed a menu, Sharkey looked around hoping to catch a glimpse of his imaginary flame, Sophia Loren, whom the hotel concierge had assured him dined there often.

Dal Bolognese was filled with the elite of Rome on this Friday evening. From the deepest depths of his dark soul, Joseph Sharkey believed that he was one of them.

He immediately recognized the tall, young, dark-haired gentleman sitting quietly at his table. Dressed in a black suit and white Roman clerical collar, sipping a glass of Chianti. Monsignor Dominick Petrucceli was the special aide and confidant of the esteemed Holy Cardinal Lovallo.

"Good evening, Joseph." The monsignor's English was perfect.

"Yes, Monsignor. It's good to see you. I was hoping to see the cardinal too." As he sat down, Sharkey looked around, distracted by the voluptuous women at neighboring tables.

The Monsignor's face tightened, his voice lower, just above a whisper.

"You'll meet the cardinal in good time, but surely you understand that, under the circumstances, he cannot be here in such a public setting."

Petrucceli hesitated, seemingly uneasy, and began again, "For now, I'd like to be sure that we understand your situation so that we can best assist you. The cardinal has instructed me to provide you with all the assistance possible from His Eminency's offices."

Sharkey had met periodically with the monsignor as part of his protective arrangement, or, as he thought of it, payback; however, he'd yet to meet the cardinal. His contact with him had been over the phone or through the intercession of the monsignor. He understood now that this was by design.

"I appreciate the cardinal's consideration, Monsignor."

Dishes of crumbly Parmesan cheese and rich, marbled red slices of Italian salami were placed on the table. Sharkey's glass was filled with the deep red Chianti from the monsignor's bottle. The waiter, an older professional, was deferential to the monsignor but had a more condescending approach toward Sharkey as his eyebrows seemed to arch with disapproval whenever he looked his way.

"Joseph, let's look at the menu and order. Then we can discuss our business." Sharkey realized the monsignor wanted to get this over as soon as possible. He took a deep breath and concealed his annoyance. After all, Petrucceli and his cardinal were his only protection from arrest, extradition and an eternity in a high-security prison in Colorado.

The waiter reappeared, smiling and speaking to Petrucceli in Italian.

Once they finished ordering, Petrucceli got back to business.

"Joseph, all of your problems stem from the murder of this Greek-American, Alex Nicholas, and the subsequent kidnapping of his younger brother, Michael, by your associates, who, if my memory serves me correctly, are named Morty, Nicky Bats and Lump. You know, you don't make Italian-Americans look good with all of this difficulty and with these characters. And may I ask again why you found it necessary to have Alex Nicholas murdered?"

"It was to settle an old score. He screwed his first wife, Greta, out of money in his divorce."

"And what has that got to do with you?"

"She was a good woman. We became close. She's gone now, but that's a long story."

"I see. And now the brother, Michael? What is your issue with him"?"

"He's his brother."

"I understand that but why the need to try and eliminate him too?"

"He screwed Greta out of her rightful share of Alex's estate."

Petrucceli sat back in his chair. "And so, here we are."

"Monsignor, I don't like this situation myself. I'd like to be home in Brooklyn. But I didn't lecture the Church when you came to me twenty years ago when your high and holy Bishop McCarthy raped those two kids in his parish. I fixed that problem for you. I put myself at risk. Do you think 'accidents' like that are created by the good Lord?"

Petrucceli placed his right hand gently over Sharkey's arm. "We do not forget our friends. We will fix this problem and have already taken steps in that direction. I have just arranged for the release on bail of your friends with the odd names. They are under our protection at a Bronx parish. They will not represent a threat to you."

Sharkey tried to relax, closing his eyes.

"They're gonna testify against me."

"No, they won't. Not on this earth, anyway. I promise you."

But Sharkey never trusted a promise from a man in a collar.

"Allora, here are the three problems which we must solve. First, we have to ensure your three little friends do not testify. Second, you have mentioned this cassette tape that was captured with them and is now in the hands of the New York City Police Department. What exactly is on this cassette, Joseph?"

"Yeah, uh, it alludes to the Michael Nicholas kidnapping." He cleared his throat and this time looked anywhere in the dining room but at the monsignor. "It may also contain references to some prior, unrelated problems."

"Joseph, if I'm going to help you, you have to be truthful with me. What 'problems' are on the tape?"

"I've had to help others—just like I helped your bishop—with their … difficulties. There were some other disappearances, you might say, which I arranged. In those cases, I had my men play a tape to the unfortunate soul, wishing him the best in his new life— a personal 'going away' card or message."

The monsignor rolled his eyes, seemingly to the heavens. "So you recorded such a message for Michael Nicholas, too?"

"Yes." He paused, put his lips together, rolling them over. "We have to get that cassette tape or I'm screwed."

"I cannot begin to tell you how ridiculous all this sounds. Nevertheless, we will handle this problem. I am sure we can find friends within that police station who have access to the evidence room."

"I'm grateful to you and the cardinal. You mentioned three problems. What is the third?"

"The third is that we must eliminate Alex's brother, Michael."

For the first time since he entered Dal Bolognese, Joseph Sharkey was a happy man.

"I'm glad to see you finally got religion, Monsignor."

"Brace yourself, Mr. Sharkey—we are in for a bloody few weeks."

Chapter 5

Michael opened the heavy oak door to his wine cellar. The customized oak shelves containing hundreds of bottles filled the walls from the floor to the ceiling, casting a soft greenish glow throughout the room. A big, rectangular, black mahogany table sat in the middle of the room, surrounded by eight red leather upholstered chairs. It was a beautiful and cozy space.

Soon, Michael thought, Samantha would understand his recent obsession with this room. Yet, despite his excitement, he felt an odd sensation, more like he was entering a tomb.

Samantha was the only person he told about what he'd discovered on Alex's hidden laptop nine months ago. And tonight, he would finally reveal to her the miracle that he still didn't fully understand; a miracle that sometimes made him wonder if his life was a dream from which he would awaken.

He sat down and reached under the dining table, pressing a switch hidden on the underside. The recessed ceiling lights slowly dimmed, and a large projection screen began to lower itself from the ceiling simultaneously, unfurling and covering a full wall of wine shelves.

Michael swung open a series of wine shelves, disclosing a sleek, aluminum Apple computer connected to a series of black boxes taking up nearly a third of the wall hidden behind the shelves. Small blue indicator lights were blinking like Christmas lights on the boxes.

Michael began typing on the Mac's silver and white keyboard. He clicked on the icon, a tiny, gold, ancient Greek cross. As he did, he thought of Bob Dylan's song, "Knocking on Heaven's Door."

As Samantha entered the cellar, Michael watched her eyes widen, scanning the room.

"Oh my God, Michael, what is this? I know you had all this work done down here—but why do I get the feeling that this is more than just converting our wine cellar into a home theater or whatever I'm looking at?"

"Just keep watching," Michael said as the lights dimmed and a blue color filled the giant screen. Michael had plugged his laptop cable into an outlet under the table and was typing in a password.

Suddenly, the blue screen changed. A series of broken images, faces, flashed across the screen; some looked familiar to Samantha.

"What's going on? What are you doing?"

He said nothing, his attention focused on the laptop keyboard as he continued to type.

Samantha stared at the screen as her former brother-in-law, Alex Nicholas, appeared, larger than life, on the screen.

"Oh my God," she said. "Alex is dead. What is this?"

Alex, looking tan and healthy, if not fully alive, stared back at them both, smiling, his face lifelike and animated as though this were simply a video conference coming from another location, not the afterlife.

Michael wondered how Alex could possibly have gotten a tan, a thought so bizarre he decided to just let it go.

Samantha looked at the screen and called out, "Alex? Alex?" She turned away from the screen and looked directly at Michael, "Who—what—is this?"

Alex looked out from the screen, his expressions just as they had been in life. He appeared to be amused, as he so often used to be while watching Samantha. His eyes followed her. "Why's she talking about me as though I'm not here? Is this your worst nightmare, Samantha? By the way, when are you finally going to invite me to dinner, especially since I'm right downstairs now? Where the hell am I? Is this your wine cellar? You know I don't like wine. I hope you've got some Dewar's in here somewhere—"

Samantha turned away from the screen, her face appeared stricken, she spoke right over Alex, as though he wasn't present. Michael could no longer hear him as he turned his attention to her.

"I don't understand this. It's unbelievable, and not in a good way. Something's wrong here; this isn't right. I just can't believe what I'm seeing. Actually, I don't *know* what I'm seeing."

"It's no trick. Those guys that looked like they were teenagers who were working down here last month were actually big-deal tech consultants. They improved what Alex's tech guys had set up before he was murdered; it's a breakthrough combination of artificial intelligence, computer imaging, and voice replication and recognition technology. Samantha, you and I are the only ones who really know about this. I only let the guys who worked on it see the parts they needed to deal with."

Alex began to laugh, his image filling the screen with a wry smile. "I may be dead, but I can hear everything you're saying. I hate it when you talk as though I'm not in the room."

Samantha looked back at Alex, then back at Michael. "I'm sorry, Michael. But I'm not about to talk to this ... whatever it is," she said as she pointed to the screen.

Alex grinned, his eyes following Samantha. "You know, this isn't that much different from real life, Samantha. You barely talked to me anyway."

Michael, addressing both Samantha and Alex, said, "Listen, this is a lot—for both of you."

Samantha looked at Michael, her voice now rising to nearly a scream. "For *both* of us? Michael, are you crazy? There's only you and me in this room. You, me, and a pile of computer equipment."

Michael put his hands out, both palms up, as though to say, stay calm. "OK, just hear me out, let me finish. This technology is moving so fast." He turned to face Alex. "You've been enhanced with new vision and facial expression analysis software, more powerful than what you originally had installed—before, you know, you died. This will—supposedly—allow you to read other people's faces and then, to some degree at least, understand more than just the words that they speak. And, we've added emotion-sensing software."

Alex looked lost. "I wish I had that when I was alive," he said.

"Yeah, it'll be good for you. Maybe with that, your next marriage will last a little longer. We've also installed Bluetooth wireless capability. The consultants aren't even sure what it'll do here, but they said it's worth experimenting with. We haven't had a chance to play with that yet."

"Christ, I'm worn out already. Next thing you'll be sending me to some fucking gym to work out."

Michael looked straight into Alex's eyes. "To be honest, we don't know exactly what you're capable of at this point. It's a little frightening. With all the data you had loaded in while you were alive, and the new programs we've added—along with all this powerful new equipment—we're in unchartered waters."

Samantha stood still, looking paralyzed as she watched Michael and Alex parrying back and forth. She shook her head and turned to leave the room. "I'm sorry. This is too much for me."

"I'll be up in just a minute," Michael said as Samantha disappeared out of the cellar and up the stairs. "Let me finish up with Alex," he said now to the empty room and to his virtual brother on the screen. Michael understood the near-comedy of his words.

Alex looked at Michael. "She's not *my* wife, but you've got to loosen her up."

"Thanks for the advice," Michael said. "You've got two—three now—ex-wives and you want to be my new marriage counselor?"

"I only have two ex-wives."

"Oh, you're right, just two divorces—and now you have a widow."

"A widow doesn't count as an ex-wife." Alex looked serious.

"For most guys that die, it does."

"Well then, maybe I don't have a widow. How many widows' husbands do you talk to?"

"*Donna* thinks she's a widow."

"She wasn't the sharpest crayon in the box."

"That's true. Otherwise, you probably wouldn't have married her." As he said it, Michael wondered whether he'd gone too far. Nevertheless, Alex seemed to be comfortable with the give and take. Michael decided to leave his brother's choice of wives alone for now.

For a moment, everything seemed to stand still. Alex's facial expression changed; he looked serious, if not strained. "Michael, I'm worried about you."

"About me? What do you mean?"

"Well, we know that Sharkey was behind my murder. He's the one that hired that kid to shoot me, and he had those three idiots try and make you a concrete anchor at the bottom of Flushing Bay. He still needs to get rid of you. I told you, this guy Frank is on his way to kill you. I'm trying but I can't get anything more on him. How's your security?"

"Not good, not yet anyway. Don't forget, I have a 'day job' too. How do I explain to the Gibraltar corporate people that I need bodyguards without bringing more attention to this side of my life?"

"They already know about the attempts on your life, and they assume it's because you're my brother. They don't know you're running my business now. Have the cops said anything about capturing Sharkey?"

"Not really; there's all kinds of warrants out for his arrest, but they're not sure where in the world he is now. I can't exactly tell them that *you're* sure he's somewhere in Rome."

"Well, he is and well-protected and hidden by the Vatican. I can't get his exact location. He's been silent lately. "

"We've got to find him. As long as he's alive, Samantha and I will never be safe."

"And what do we do when we find him?"

"We turn him over to the authorities."

"What greater authority is there—especially in Rome—than the Church?"

"I thought you were an atheist."

"Yeah, atheism is easy when you're young. Not so much when you're dead though."

"You've got a point there." But Michael was just beginning to digest Alex's comment.

"I wish I was still in Queens. But this isn't bad …" Michael noticed that Alex's eyes looked away, "…although I'm not crazy about being in the basement or whatever you call this."

"It's a wine cellar." Michael said.

"Yeah, but it's still underground. I went to a lot of trouble not to be in the ground."

———

As he came up the stairs from the basement, Michael wondered what would await him. He knew Samantha was upset. He could see the bedroom door was open—which was, perhaps, a good sign. But before he reached the door, he could hear her voice; she was on the phone. He paused several feet away but out of sight, and listened.

"Angie, I am so scared. You won't believe what I just saw in our basement."

Angie Fanelli was Samantha's best friend.

"No, Ang, I didn't finally check the freezer and find the body of that nanny I fired several years ago. This is serious."

"No, it's not about Michael. It's about Alex."

Chapter 6

New York City

It was by accident that Michael had first seen her.

About a year ago, the night before his speech and Applegarden's murder, he passed her in the lobby of the Peninsula Hotel in Beverly Hills. He remembered her because of her striking good looks; she was exceptionally tall and fit.

Was this the woman he now saw before him? She reached out to shake his hand.

"Mr. Nicholas, Cynthia Scotto, I'm a financial reporter for the *Financial Times*. I heard your speech last year in L.A. and I'm doing a follow-up article."

Michael recalled his conversation with Karen, who said Scotto had called the day before and, due to an urgent deadline, pleaded for an appointment to interview him, promising a positive story.

"Ms. Scotto. It's so good to meet you." Michael looked into her cold grey eyes.

"Please, it's Cynthia—actually Sindy with an S—and I'm delighted to finally meet you. I must say, your speech took a lot of guts."

"First, please call me Michael. I guess I did cause a lot of uproar. I'm just glad I had the opportunity to speak my mind about all the damage these hedge funds and some of these Wall Street types are doing to good companies and the people in them."

"Well, the press certainly loved it. You've become a celebrity at the *Financial Times*."

He motioned toward a chair around the coffee table. "Please, have a seat."

She sat down while he seated himself on the chair across the table, opposite her.

"And then to have your chairman die in his sleep that night at the hotel. That must have been quite a shock." She stared into Michael's eyes; her smile had disappeared.

"It was a tragedy, no question," he said, now slightly troubled. *Financial Times* reporters didn't typically venture into the more human or sensational topics.

"Yet, as tragic as it was, it did open the door for you to move into his position."

"I hope this interview—and your story—will be about the substance of the business issue I spoke about and not the more unfortunate passing of our former chairman."

"Of course, anyway, we're not even on the record yet, as they say. Believe me, we'll move on soon."

He didn't want to acknowledge that he may have remembered her from the hotel the night before his speech but he was still curious to find out if it was really her. "So I hope—besides my speech—that you had a chance to enjoy L.A. while you were out there."

"Oh, I did. I've spent a lot of time on the West Coast, before I was a reporter."

"I'm curious, where does the *Financial Times* put up a reporter in L.A. on a trip like that?"

"Nowhere special, I can assure you. But I did get out to some of the hot spots and restaurants while I was there. I had a few really great dinners on that trip."

"I'm always interested in new restaurants. Where'd you eat?"

"Well, neither of them is new, but they're both excellent. I had sushi at Matsuhisa on La Cienega."

"I love Matsuhisa, actually there's a little place in Westport called Matsu that, I think, is right up there."

"I'll have to get out to Westport, it seems all you financial types live there... I also had a business dinner at the Belvedere, the night before your speech."

"Isn't that the restaurant in the Peninsula?"

"Yes, as a matter of fact—and what a gorgeous hotel. I wish they'd put me up there. I'll bet the rooms are beautiful."

He knew for sure now that she was the woman in the lobby, but something was wrong about her. Michael had been interviewed hundreds of times over the years; he'd learned to quickly read a reporter's personality. She didn't fit the *Financial Times* mold. She was much too social, too chatty. She was either trying to lull him into a false sense of security, or she was someone else. But Karen had checked out her credentials before confirming the appointment.

"May I ask, how long have you been with *FT*?"

She hesitated; he could see her thinking about her response.

"I haven't been honest with you. My name is Sindy Steele, and I'm not a reporter.

"OK ... who are you?"

"I'm the woman who's going to save your life."

"I didn't know my life was in danger."

"Dick Applegarden didn't die of sleep apnea, whiskey and Ambien."

This can't be happening, Michael thought. He knew he needed to sound firm, confident, despite the feeling that his world was imploding.

"I beg your pardon—"

But now *she* appeared confident, sure of her ground.

"He was murdered."

"What do you mean? How's that possible? They did an autopsy; the coroner determined it was—"

"I know what the authorities said. They're overworked and not always the brightest crayons in the box."

"And how would *you* know this?" he asked.

"My business is security. I'm a bodyguard, Michael. I've protected some very high-profile, very vulnerable people."

"But how do you know anything about Dick Applegarden's death?"

"I was on an unrelated assignment for someone whose name I can't disclose. He was staying at the Peninsula for a week, including the night your chairman died—or, as I believe, was murdered—in his room."

She looked at her watch. Michael checked his, it was nearly six o'clock.

"Listen, this is too sensitive to discuss here. How about if we continue this over a cocktail at Bemelmans at the Carlyle? I just need fifteen minutes or so here to take care of some things before I leave."

"Perfect. I'll go ahead and get a table. You look like you need a drink."

Chapter 7

Bronx, New York

"I understand that you're an undertaker, Morty?" Bishop Kevin McCarthy asked.

"You mean besides my work for Mr. Sharkey? Yeah, I suppose you could say that, Father. Actually, I drive a hearse for the D'Amato Funeral Home in Brooklyn."

"That is God's work too, my son."

"Yeah, I deliver them from evil."

Morty was starving. He looked at his two friends, Lump and Nicky Bats. They had just been released with him from Rikers Island, after seven months of pre-trial hearings for the kidnapping and attempted murder of Michael Nicholas.

"I appreciate you getting us out of there. You must have some pretty powerful friends," Morty said.

"The Lord takes care of its flock. I've invited a good friend of the Church, Frank Cortese, tonight for dinner. He was instrumental in securing those unfortunate cassette tapes and in arranging for your release. You will find him interesting, I promise."

"Hey, Bishop, I love the guy already. He got us out of that hole," Nicky Bats chimed in.

"No worries, my son. Sister Mary Margaret blessed us with her superb lasagna," the bishop said, gesturing toward the large well-worn pan covered with aluminum foil.

Morty eyed the familiar setting of this typical church basement. He had been in many of them over the years. A small stage on the left and the hundred or so old metal and plastic-cushioned chairs served as the auditorium for the parochial school next door, St. Joseph's Catholic. He could remember hearing the joyous sounds of children rising up throughout the building. There were the happy wedding receptions, immediately following the religious ceremony upstairs in the church, with bands or a simple boom box providing the music for the dancing and celebration festivities.

He knew that this same room had likely been the site of thousands of Irish, Italian, and now, more typically, Puerto Rican or Colombian wakes following the funerals held in the church upstairs.

A kitchen in the next room allowed for the preparation of whatever dishes the families and friends of the deceased wanted to feast on while the guest of honor, unable to attend, was either on his ascent to heaven or securely lying in a box in the cemetery, depending on the strength of one's faith. Morty laughed at the thought.

The rectangular white Formica table was set for five. Dishes of freshly grated Parmesan cheese, a small jar of crushed red peppers, bottles of oil and vinegar, and a large carafe of red wine sat next to the pan of lasagna. The five grey steel chairs were aligned near each plate setting.

It felt good to be free.

Bishop McCarthy stood by his seat in the middle of the table and began his prayer as his three guests were seated on either side of him.

"Bless us, O Lord, and these gifts, which we are about to receive from Thy bounty, through Christ our Lord."

Morty, Lump, and Nicky Bats indulged the bishop and faithfully bowed their heads in apparent prayer. Morty inhaled the smell of the rich tomato sauce and still sizzling ground beef and sausage from the lasagna while, with one eye half open, gazing first at the platter on the table in front of him. He was anxious to dig in.

As the bishop appeared to have finished his prayer, the three guests simultaneously but prematurely whispered, "Amen." But the bishop continued:

"And grant us,
Lord Jesus,
always to follow the example of Your holy family,
that at the hour of our death
Your glorious Virgin Mother
with blessed Joseph
may come to meet us,
and so we may deserve to be received by You
into Your everlasting dwelling place.
Amen."

Morty looked up at Bishop McCarthy, who returned the glance with a benevolent smile as he passed around the tray of lasagna." Morty looked around the room at the fifth place setting and the empty chair. "Aren't we waiting for our guest?"

"Frank often works late. I'm sure he'll be here shortly. Let's begin and enjoy Sister Mary Margaret's hard work while it's still warm. I know you three are hungry for a home-cooked meal."

The creamy, melting mozzarella cheese blended so sumptuously with the slick pasta, the rich tomato sauce, and the earthy taste of the crumbled sausage. It coursed through Morty's body with that instant feel-good effect of comfort foods.

After downing the first glass of dry Chianti, he began to relax. Until the basement door opened and Frank Cortese walked in.

Morty saw the same vacant look he had seen before, on the faces and in the eyes of the psychopathic killers he so often associated with. The same look he'd seen in the open eyes of the dead before they were shut. He looked for the exits. There was only one, it was the door through which Cortese had just walked.

He looked at Cortese's buttoned, dark green sport coat and noticed the familiar bulge where a weapon would be concealed.

"Have a seat, my friend." the bishop said, motioning toward the empty chair. "Let me introduce you."

Good, Morty thought, introductions are good, and he's going to eat.

But before Morty could even finish his next thought, Cortese in one quick motion had unbuttoned his sport jacket, pulled out a gun with a long silencer attached and put a single bullet each into the foreheads of Lump and Nicky Bats; the force of the hot lead sent them backward, and they fell to the floor still in their chairs, like ducks in an amusement park shooting gallery.

Morty knew that he was next, and in that split second, which seemed like an eternity, he stared at the strange, different-colored eyes of the man who was to kill him, and wondered, he knew for the last time, if there really was a God.

Chapter 8

New York City

Michael knew Bemelmans Bar in the Carlyle Hotel well. The legendary hangout of Upper East Side Manhattan socialites, cheating politicians, and celebrities seeking privacy, was a short ten-block walk from his office. He was running about fifteen minutes late as he entered through the hotel's side entrance on Madison Avenue and went into the dimly lit bar.

He saw her at the bar getting a drink. She had changed her dress. Even from a distance, she was captivating, very tall—nearly six feet tall in her stilettos—a stunning woman dressed in the shortest, sheer black dress exposing miles of her perfectly tapered, white bare legs. Her long black hair hung straight down to the small of her exposed back. Although almost slim, she was powerfully built. Her bare shoulders and back were toned in a way only possible from hours spent working out.

Michael was intrigued. But still, something about her was eerily off. He glanced again at those long, slender white legs, gently tapering calves, and thin ankles, and he knew someone—and something—ominous had entered his life.

They were quickly seated in a red leather banquette along the wall.

"So, what's going on here?" Despite his uncertainty, his tone was friendly, almost warm. He wanted to break the tension. Looking at Steele, he was curious. He felt an odd attraction—to her beauty, her strength. He wasn't sure, but he also sensed a certain vulnerability in her. On the other hand, he always thought he sensed vulnerability in people.

"I understand you're looking for a bodyguard. I'm one of the best in the world."

"So that's what this is all about? A job?"

"Only partly. I was attracted to you when I saw you pass by in the Peninsula. Then, when I attended your speech the next day, I couldn't believe that was you. And when I heard your message, I knew I had to find you. It wasn't hard, of course. But I admit I wasn't sure how to actually get in to meet with you. That's why I did the reporter thing. Turns out, there *is* an FT reporter whose name isn't that far off from mine."

"And you flew out to New York to meet me?"

She laughed, "No, I'm afraid not. I may be a bit obsessive but I'm not crazy. I'm here on other business. I spend several months of the year in New York." She sipped her drink, closed her eyes, appearing to inhale the vodka's effects. She finally looked back at Michael, and continued. "It just proves my point though."

"Which is?"

"If I can get this close to you this easily, anyone who wishes you harm can do the same."

"And why do you think anyone would want to harm *me*?"

"Come on, Michael. Your brother was murdered last year, your boss shortly after and you were kidnapped on Spring Street right after that. Need I go on?"

"My company has provided me with extensive security since those events—and I still don't understand why you believe Dick Applegarden was murdered."

"OK, first of all, your security stinks. I don't see anyone around you or watching you."

"I mean my home security—"

"Oh please, you've got to be kidding. You think some RadioShack system on steroids is going to deter anyone who wants to get into your house?"

"OK, I get your point. But what about Applegarden? How are you so sure he was murdered?"

"I was in the hotel bar the night he died. The power went off—just for a few minutes—but long enough to conveniently disrupt the security cameras and distract the staff. No one seemed to know why either."

"That's it?"

"No, of course not. I can't disclose everything I know, but let's put it this way, the protection world is a small one, particularly in L.A. I know the hotel security people very well. I was with them shortly after they discovered Applegarden's body. They're not convinced it was sleep apnea and drugs. They don't have any real conclusive evidence and … well, the hotel isn't interested in a scandal—especially after the coroner quickly ruled it an accidental death. Plus, they want to keep their job. That's all I can say, but I know enough to know it was a well-planned hit."

She appeared to be watching Michael for a response. He was careful, not showing any expression. "You know these things are usually guys who, you know, are involved in some criminal stuff or looking to get rid of their business partner, wives or a pregnant lover. But Applegarden was clean. He looked like a typical suit, a corporate type, not even close to anything that would involve being taken out. Same with you—until I read about your brother."

Michael felt a strange sensation pass through him as she looked into his eyes. Her probing stare and seemingly intuitive grasp of the new dichotomy of his life and, perhaps, personality, opened Michael's own eyes to his attractive yet unwelcome visitor.

"Alex and I never mixed much as adults. I stayed out of his affairs. Both his business and his wives for that matter."

"No one stays out of their family's stuff completely. Particularly in Italian families."

"My family's not Italian. They're Greek," Michael corrected.

"Please. It's the same thing."

"Keep going," he said.

"So then I was even more curious."

"So you decided to find out."

She took a deep breath. "I'm not sure what I decided."

"Sindy, what's going on here? Is there something you want? I don't know if I'm being threatened or courted. Are you a tabloid reporter wearing a wire?"

"God, I never actually thought of that. Of course you might think I'm wearing a wire. I can assure you, I'm not. In fact," her face brightened as though she had a great idea or was relieving herself of a heavy burden, "I'm willing to prove it to you."

Surprised by the turn of the conversation and unsure whether he was reading the situation correctly, he stayed noncommittal. "What do you mean?"

"Listen, wires are now fitted into our most private parts. There's only one way to know for sure that someone's not wearing one." She looked at Michael, paused, and said, "And I don't think you want me to show you here."

Chapter 9

New York City

Suite 801 at the St. Regis Hotel was a perk for the chairman of Gibraltar Financial. It had originally been purchased with the approval of the Gibraltar board for corporate entertaining and the periodic use of senior executives traveling to New York City. An exhaustive, fifty-three-page study detailed how the investment was cost-justified by saving the company money that would otherwise be spent on the rapidly rising Manhattan hotel bills. As absurd as that premise was, it paled in comparison to the actual purpose that the suite served. It became the exclusive pied-à-terre of the chairman who proposed the purchase in the first place, the late Chairman Dick Applegarden.

The extravagance of the suite while the company was under financial pressure had always been a sore point with Michael. Now it was his, at least while he was still at Gibraltar. He had intended to sell it off but had not gotten around to it yet. As he entered it tonight, he wondered if he ever would.

Steele had made herself at home on the sofa, her long, pale legs crossed. The top two buttons of her black silk blouse were unbuttoned. Michael recalled that only one had been so before she had gone to the bathroom shortly after they entered the suite. Her shoes were off, lying on their sides under the coffee table in front of her.

Michael had fixed himself a dry martini with two green olives. She had just downed her first shot of ice-cold Grey Goose vodka and was about to do the same with the second one he was pouring.

Questions still hung in the air, but at this particular moment, Michael didn't care enough about the answers. It appeared that she didn't either.

He poured a third shot for her and began sipping his second martini. As she downed her drink, he reached over and kissed her. She finally broke away and, gripping her blouse from her waist with both hands, lifted it over her head and tossed it onto the adjacent chair. He reached behind her, undid the black lace bra and gently stroked her breasts. She unbuttoned her skirt, allowing it to drop straight down onto the floor as she stepped out of it. She then gripped the back of Michael's head and moved it between her legs.

"This is what they call a landing strip. I hope you're not out of fuel."

Like a powerful drug moving through his body, he felt a rush of emotions, a swirl of the forbidden, exotic, and dangerous. So anxious to discover the magic that lay beneath those black panties—the look, the feel, the taste, and the scent he was already inhaling—Michael placed the twinge of guilt that had been speaking to him into a corner of his mind where, he hoped, it would leave him alone—at least for now.

It felt like an endless night. They finally wound up in the bedroom and, with little conversation afterward, fell asleep.

Turning over in bed during the night, Michael wondered about Samantha, the state of their marriage, and the naked woman sound asleep next to him.

Chapter 10

New York City

Michael didn't want to talk about what he'd just done and with whom—but he needed to reconnect with Alex. Unable to sleep, he finally got out of bed and, after quietly closing the bedroom door behind him, took his Apple laptop out of his briefcase and sat down on the suite's living room couch. His team of geeks had web-enabled Alex so that Michael could access him—literally virtually—on any computer. He clicked on the icon, typed in the password and, once again, was amazed to see his brother appear.

"I don't think I'll ever get used to this," he said.

"It's a bit of a change for me, too." Alex smirked. "I've got to figure out what I'm going to do with my life now. Maybe I'll start up an online gambling business."

"I just hired a bodyguard." Michael could see that he got his brother's attention.

"I guess I should have had one myself. I wouldn't be here right now if I did. What's his name?"

"It's a she, Sindy."

There was a moment of silence as Alex appeared to be stymied, as though he couldn't assimilate the thought.

"A woman?"

"Yes, that would be a she."

"Is she good-looking?"

"What's that got to do with anything?"

"If she is, probably a lot."

Michael proceeded to fill Alex in on most of the circumstances surrounding his hiring of Sindy Steele, excluding the part that occurred at the hotel.

"I'll check her out more thoroughly for you."

"By the way, she spells Sindy with an 'S.' "

Alex started to smile, "No shit."

"Also, I've got a plan to deal with Sharkey and his friends at the Vatican. I'm still working on the details, but I'm going to need your help."

It was time to change the subject. He wasn't prepared yet.

"Alex, are there others—like you—who have been able to do this? To duplicate themselves on a computer?"

Alex appeared to be annoyed; Michael wasn't sure why. Was it the question, the implication that, perhaps, Alex was less than real? And was he?

"Duplicate myself on a computer—I guess you could call it that. No, I'm not aware of anyone else who's done it. That doesn't mean they don't exist. There are a lot of connections I've still got to figure out."

"And where does this all fit with religion and everything? Do you have a clue?" Michael couldn't believe his own conversation. He also knew that Alex had always been quite critical of any organized religions.

"What, are you kidding? How the hell would I know? Don't forget, I didn't even create this computer thing myself—I paid my friend Russell and then he hired a bunch of geeks from somewhere. This is all over my head but I do sense now that there's something beyond what you can see. I never really believed that before. I thought the spiritual world was all bullshit, some fantasy. It's hard to believe something you can't see or touch or have any proof of. But the Internet and the cyber-world—and all this spiritual, religious stuff—are the same, you can't see them but somehow all these things happen and people show up. They may be connected. It seems like somehow the two worlds—the spiritual and cyber-world—have come together or intersected. Maybe the Internet gave the spirit the mechanism for a physical presence. That's the best I can see for now. But this is just the beginning."

"No one will believe this you know."

"Samantha didn't believe it—even after I was so nice to her." Alex said, his cynical nature coming through just as it always had.

"Maybe that's why she didn't believe it." Alex and Samantha never had the warmest relationship, just as Michael never appreciated Alex's wives.

"Well, we can't let this get out, at least not yet. If you think Samantha had such a bad reaction, you can imagine how others would see this. It'll be like when they tried those witches."

"You mean the Salem witch trials in the 1600s?"

"Whenever it was. I can promise you it won't be pretty. Whatever happened to those witches?"

Michael was surprised his brother even remembered that much history.

"They weren't witches, but they were hung regardless."

"Oh. You won't need to worry about that."

"Why not?" Michael asked.

"America's civilized now. They'll just shoot you."

Despite the knot in his stomach, Michael broke up laughing.

Chapter 11

"**N**othing good ever happens in a conference room," Michael whispered to himself as he sat at in the plush, tan leather chair across the long, rich mahogany table in the Gibraltar headquarters conference room.

Now that he had, ironically, been promoted to the late Dick Applegarden's position, he reported to the chairman of the board of the parent corporation. Richard Perkins was a Southern gentleman, a former military officer and Alabama highway patrolman. Michael often joked that when he met with Richard, he often felt the urge to offer his driver's license and registration. Fifty-four years old, tall and fit, soft-spoken yet commanding, he was a natural leader. Although Michael often disagreed with Perkins' business strategy, he respected him for his work ethic and his straightforward, no-nonsense approach.

Perkins' assistant—or "chief of staff"—was John Hightower. Michael's blood pressure rose whenever Hightower appeared. Hightower, in his mid-thirties, was an accountant whom Perkins hired to do the numbers analysis, which usually led to short-sighted, short-term decisions with long-term problems. Hightower had no business-operating experience but knew how to run his numbers and was quick to push cost-cutting solutions that showed the benefits of eliminating salaries—without any knowledge or appreciation of the long-term damage to the organization. He was British, with the haughty and superficial manner that underlined Michael's innate distrust and dislike of him.

Michael faced Perkins and Hightower across the table. He knew Richard had an agenda or, as he would say, a "mission" to communicate. Michael wasn't sure what today's news would be, but he suspected it wasn't going to be good.

Perkins was always serious, his eyes making searing contact when he spoke, echoing his inherent sincerity and determination in whatever he was discussing. He spoke in his gentle, velvet-gloved tone with a rich, mellow Southern accent.

"Michael, we need to make more cuts. For you, I know this is like running fingernails on a blackboard, but we're going to do this."

Michael looked over at a nodding Hightower who continued to bang away on his laptop keyboard. Hightower never made eye contact, even when speaking directly with him, or anyone.

"But Richard, we just finished a round of cuts. Revenue's on track. We're right on budget. Our forecast seems solid for the remaining months. There are no indicators showing a slowdown. What's happened now that you want to cut further? You know this'll mean cutting further into the muscle of the company—any fat was eliminated long ago."

He glanced again at Hightower, who immediately looked back at his keyboard.

"John," Michael said, "you've been tracking the numbers. Our employees are also aware of them. What would you have me say to them when I make these cuts and they ask why we'd eliminate these talented people now when our results are turning around and we need to rebuild from the loss of the experienced people we just laid off?"

Looking at Perkins instead of Michael, Hightower said, "I'd tell them to do their job and not try to sell us on their talent or experience, or their valuable industry knowledge. I'd tell them we don't care about it. We'll get new, cheaper, younger inexperienced people when we're ready. That's what I'd tell them."

Perkins, seemingly uncomfortable with the bluntness of his assistant's comments, put his hand up, signaling he needed to interrupt.

"Michael, here's what driving this action now. What I'm about to tell you is extremely confidential; it can't get out—to anyone. I'll have your head on a stake if it does. We have two prospective suitors who are trying to purchase Gibraltar. It's all very preliminary at this point, but now's the time to show the very best returns we can—however fleeting they may be prove to be."

Michael was surprised, not only at the possibility of a sale of the company but also at Richard's apparent willingness to allow such a takeover. Nevertheless, his first priority was to stop the elimination of more personnel from his organization.

"Richard, you know we've already cut out over twenty percent of our workforce in the two or so years that I've been here. Revenues have stayed steady over the last eighteen months. We've given up some critical functions and lost experienced people that'll be necessary long term to grow the company. Whoever buys this company is not going to want to find out that we stripped it to make the numbers look good."

Michael knew from Richard Perkins' expression—or lack of—that his arguments were going nowhere. Nevertheless, he continued, "Who are the suitors?"

"I can't tell you that yet. One is more solid than the other."

"Well, I guess that's encouraging." Michael said.

"But the other offer will be better for us, Michael."

"What do you mean?" Michael said.

Richard paused; he was clearly reluctant to go further.

"Richard, I know this is sensitive, but in view of what you're asking me to do, it would help me to have some more information."

"OK, Michael, listen, the deal we need to move forward with is going to be coming from Cartan Holdings."

Michael knew the company, a multinational holding company based in the U.K. It had been close to bankruptcy a few short years ago but had seemingly bounced back after a series of well-timed acquisitions, which included private security companies benefitting from the wars in Iraq and Afghanistan. Cartan Holdings owned two of the major private contractors to both the U.K. and U.S. governments. They had most recently been in the news for the alleged free-wheeling murders of Iraqi civilians.

"Jesus, Richard. That company will be a disaster for us. Why would we in any way favor them over the other potential buyer?"

"Because the other firm is already in the same businesses as we are. With them, you and I would be kept on—at best at our current compensation and in the roles we're in now. Even then, who knows for how long? They won't need us after the deal closes. Cartan's willing to put a huge package on the table for us if we favor them in this deal."

Michael began to speak, but Richard, his demeanor turning ice cold, cut him off. "Michael, don't be short-sighted now. Either way, people are going to have to be let go. That's going to happen and you'll either get it done or I'll get someone else to do it. The question is whether you and I survive this and how we will benefit. The Cartan deal can make us both richer than we can imagine."

Michael knew Perkins well enough to end the discussion. After some trivial pleasantries, Perkins gathered his papers, stood up to leave.

"Michael. This is a good thing. Believe me."

As Perkins, with Hightower in tow, reached the door, he turned around.

"Oh, Michael, one other thing. I've decided to add a new member to our board. It'll be a good public relations move for us right now. I'd like you two to get to know each other before the next board meeting. He'll also be able to help you with your plan to expand Gibraltar's services in Italy, too. You'll enjoy him; he's a priest, a Jesuit. I'll have John here set up a dinner for just the two of you sometime next week."

"Sure." Michael said, still thinking about Cartan Holdings "Who is he?"

"You may have heard of him. He's highly respected and a terrific man, too. One of our people from the Vatican Bank contacted us and offered his services. In return, Gibraltar is going to make a sizeable contribution to St. Joseph's Catholic School in the Bronx to help fund their program and build a decent auditorium for those little kids."

"What's his name?

Turning to leave, Richard said, "Bishop Kevin McCarthy."

Chapter 12

Westport, Connecticut

I t was after midnight as Michael walked into their bedroom. He was sick with guilt. The word may as well have been written in neon graffiti all over the walls. So this is what it feels like to have an affair and then come home.

After his previous evening's activities at the St. Regis, he was relieved to see that Samantha was sound asleep. He quietly hung up his suit and slipped into his robe. For a moment, he stopped and looked around at their beautifully decorated room; it seemed distant now, slightly off, as though he was looking at it from afar. The sense of serenity that he always felt here was somehow gone. Things had changed.

He left the bedroom and walked down the two flights of stairs to the wine cellar where, once the computer was powered on and the passwords entered, the large screen rolled down from the ceiling. After several seconds, Alex appeared, a virtual but life-size image.

Michael watched as Alex looked around the room at the dark wood shelves, filled with wine bottles. "It's a shame to be down here with all this expensive wine of yours and not be able to drink it. Maybe I'd acquire a taste for it now."

"Feel free to help yourself anytime. I can leave a corkscrew for you."

"By the way, what does this Bluetooth shit you mentioned last time mean?" Alex asked.

"I can only imagine what it could allow you to do. It might mean that you can now reach out and actually call me. If that's true, then you won't have to wait for me to turn on the computer and log onto you. I think so anyway."

"I've been trying to figure out anything I can about this guy Frank who's been sent to kill you, but I can't find anything. I've tried all the taps and emails I can get to—but nothing. Nothing. But, you know, I'm not sure what I'm capable of either."

"Well, there've been some new developments. Remember I mentioned that Sharkey's guys were out on bail?"

"Yeah, and I told you that once the Vatican got behind him, things would get dicey. They can't afford to be exposed and they need to be sure things get fixed quietly. These guys are worse than any organized crime. It's a joke. They've got the best racket. I should have incorporated as a religion. I could have run my betting business and been fully protected. I wouldn't have even had to worry about paying taxes. They make the Swiss bankers look like saints. You know, I'm not big on guys who wear robes outside."

"Well," Michael said, "It gets even more interesting. Sharkey's men were murdered the day after they were released. Supposedly some priest at a church in the Bronx fed them a big dinner the other night in the church basement. The priest claims he put them in a taxi after dinner to take them back to the home of some parishioner where they were to stay. The cab never showed up. Their bodies were found wrapped in plastic in the trunk of an abandoned car near the Bruckner Expressway. All three had been shot in the head, execution style."

Alex looked straight ahead. "Big surprise."

"And guess who the priest was?" Michael said.

"No ... don't tell me ... that Irish guy?"

"Yes, Bishop Kevin McCarthy, the original altar boy molester, the one whose problem Sharkey took care of."

Michael found himself fascinated not only to be having a normal conversation with his brother—but also with Alex's ability to grasp a rather complex situation.

"I'm not done," Michael continued. "Remember the cassette tape with Sharkey's 'goodbye' message to me, the one they played in the car just before they figured they'd be dumping me in Flushing Bay that night?"

"Yeah. Sharkey was known for having his hit men play a personal message that he had recorded for anyone he was having killed. He used to brag about it to me. He said it gave him some special satisfaction. He said, 'What's the point of having someone whacked if the guy didn't know *why* he was being whacked?' Kind of makes sense if you think about it. At least in his sick mind."

Michael cringed as he recounted his own chilling encounter a year ago, "I'll never forget it. I'm in crazy Morty's car, wrapped in duct tape. My feet are encased in a cement block. I'm still drugged up from the chloroform they used to knock me out. Then, Morty puts the cassette player up to my ear and I hear Sharkey's voice. His last words were, 'You always lose the final game. Goodbye, Michael.' Well, the cassette has disappeared from the precinct evidence room. With the three idiots dead, that tape was the last concrete, no pun intended, link to Sharkey for my kidnapping. Except for me, of course."

"That's right; they've taken care of everything else. Now if they can get rid of you, Sharkey can come back and the cops have nothing on him. And whoever owed Sharkey a favor for his help just made the first payment on it."

"One more thing," Michael added, "I just found out that the good bishop, of all people, has been placed on my Gibraltar board."

Alex interrupted him, "McCarthy himself? No wonder there's

so much sex going on with some of those priests—they do have some balls."

"Yes, Bishop Kevin McCarthy himself. But, don't forget, no one except his superiors in the Vatican knows what he did to those kids years ago. Without them, the investigation had nowhere to go. So now the Vatican worked out a deal to put this creep on the board so Gibraltar supposedly gets the PR benefit of a holy guy and the company's going to make a contribution to the church or school in the Bronx. It's unbelievable."

Alex laughed. "What a combination—a corrupt big corporation and a dirty bishop." He became very serious. "But this is their way of telling you that they can get you whenever they want. This is a power play. They've put this priest right into your backyard, your life. Your straight life. They'll know where you are and what you're doing."

"I know." But Michael didn't know yet how much information Alex could digest although it appeared that, as his computer consultants had predicted, he was getting smarter each time they spoke. The artificial intelligence program was designed to get smarter as more and more information was fed into it either through program uploads or the conversational interaction such as Michael and Alex were now having.

Alex stared hard at him, "Do you realize how deep you're in here? I was no saint, but you're into some heavy-duty business. Murder, the church, and at least one guy looking to kill you. Can you handle this?"

It was a good question. "I have a plan and I'm going to need your help to make it happen. I'll tell you about it soon enough but first I'm going to need you to help me find out exactly whom I need to get to in the Vatican."

"You mean the person pulling the strings? I already told you about Lovallo and Petrucceli."

"No, someone higher than that.""Like the Pope?"

"Preferably not the Pope. But you're getting closer."

49

"So, we're going to show Sharkey that artificial intelligence is better than no intelligence."

"Yes, if my plan works, Sharkey and his protectors will be in for a big surprise."

"By the way, you should be loading your own personal stuff onto an artificial intelligence software program because, at this rate, I'm going to outlive you—and I'll be talking to myself here."

"That's an interesting thought. I wonder, do you even exist if I disappear and no one else knows about you? It's a scary thought, isn't it?"

Alex laughed, then turned solemn. "You have no idea."

Chapter 13

Samantha Nicholas was an enigma to all but her very closest friends, who numbered no more than three. Yet that in itself was a mystery to those who knew her. It was a mystery to her too.

She was smart, a graduate of NYU, fluent in French, and had a good head for business. Before her marriage, Samantha had been a legend in the cutthroat world of high-end Manhattan real estate, using her intelligence, calm manner and astute evaluation of people to navigate successfully through the eccentric and egomaniacal personalities.

She was in great shape and, although in her mid-forties, could easily pass for someone ten years younger. She had a solid marriage for over twenty years, a successful husband and a beautiful and sensitive daughter, Sofia, in her second year at Notre Dame.

Angie and Fletcher Fanelli, in their early forties, were Michael and Samantha's closest friends, two tough and spirited characters with a young baby daughter.

Fletcher, the police chief of Westport, Connecticut, was one of the few people Michael could confide in as he moved from the strictly straight and narrow world of Gibraltar Financial to his brother's revitalized illegal business, now known as Tartarus. Fletcher could be trusted to be there when Michael needed him— and keep things to himself, leaving even Angie in the dark.

Samantha and Angie sat at a table in the cozy back room of Mario's. Samantha looked around; the restaurant, an institution in Westport, was filled with its usual combination of laid-back "townies" and the suit-and-tie commuter crowd returning from Manhattan.

"Michael loves this place. I swear I think sometimes he actually dreams about the meatballs. He says he'll never forget the day Tiger took him into the kitchen one afternoon to show him the meatballs simmering in the tomato sauce. I think they had to carry him out."

Angie laughed, "Well, Michael's the only person I know who remembers every meal he's ever had."

Once Angie and Samantha had polished off their first bottle of champagne and dispensed with the chitchat, Samantha turned somber.

"Something's happened to Michael." she said. "It all started when his brother was murdered. Donna, Alex's widow, pushed Michael to get involved, just to clean up Alex's affairs and that sort of thing. Up until then, he'd always steered clear of anything having to do with his brother's affairs. But I'm afraid once he got a taste of Alex's life, he liked it. He liked it too much."

"What exactly does that mean, Samantha?"

"I'm not sure exactly. We always talked about everything. We shared everything with each other. Not anymore. Michael's running Gibraltar—how, I can't imagine—but he's still doing that and not only heading up his brother's business but expanding it. With everything going on now, I hardly ever see him."

"Oh, Samantha." Angie said.

"Wait, there's more. But, Angie, I'm not supposed to tell this to anyone."

"Samantha, I know I can be a little ditzy at times but, you know, you can trust me."

"Angie, this is more than a secret. It's about what I said on the phone last night. This is about life and death—and maybe beyond that. I feel like I'm living in The Twilight Zone."

"My God, what is it?"

"Before Alex died, he got into some crazy artificial intelligence thing. He paid a good friend of his, who was a computer whiz, to purchase some combination of sophisticated artificial intelligence and computer imaging software. Alex wanted to live forever—or some type of nonsense—he paid a small fortune for all of this. Then he had these technology gurus load all kinds of personal data onto a secret Apple laptop that he'd had hidden away somewhere. Michael found it after Alex died. I think one of Alex's mistresses, some hot-shot hairdresser in the city, told Michael about it and then gave him Alex's password so he could log in."

"No wonder Alex didn't go to a regular old barber. With what little hair he had, it certainly wasn't for a blow-out. Maybe a blow—"

"Ang, seriously, it gets worse. I think this technology thing works, at least like some sophisticated computer game anyway. But for Michael—he thinks it's more than that. And now he's spent his own money on computer consultants and more hardware. He's set up a huge screen and computers hidden in our wine cellar. He goes down there now and talks to the screen—and thinks he's speaking with Alex."

"Samantha, I can't believe this. It's not like Michael, he's as down to earth as anyone I've ever known. I can't believe he'd get involved with Alex's stuff—let alone believe this voodoo artificial intelligence shit."

"He brought me down to the wine cellar last night, just before I called you. It was spooky. He presses some buttons and all of a sudden the giant screen comes down and Alex comes to life and they start talking to each other!"

"Oh my God." Angie said. "What did they say?"

"I had to leave. It was too much for me. It was Alex, big as life on the screen, big as life with all his expressions and quirky mannerisms. I must admit, they did a great job with that. But Michael actually believes he's speaking with his brother. It's crazy. Michael's crazy."

Tiger, Mario's venerable owner, looking out from his usual perch near the kitchen and seeing two of his favorite woman, ventured over to their table. He was a short, bald and lovable man, who looked like a cross between a bulldog and a teddy bear.

"I knew the noise level had gone up all of a sudden, now I know why. How are my two princesses doing?"

"Oh, Tiger, don't even ask. Men are just such freakin' idiots," Angie said. Samantha knew Angie considered Tiger to be a father figure.

Tiger, seventy-seven, divorced for over twenty years, with a wild streak and a stream of women he kept at a careful distance, thought for a moment before answering, "I can't argue with you there."

Chapter 14

The image reminded him of photographs he had admired from French *Vogue*. Michael glanced at Sindy Steel's long, white legs peering out from the high slit in her black silk skirt as she drove her powerful black Corvette over the Triboro Bridge. They were leaving glitzy Manhattan and heading for the gritty borough of Queens and Astoria.

As his new head of security, Michael knew that Sindy would be expected to be close by his side at all times. As they drove down Twenty-Eighth Avenue past the old stores and apartments, he thought of the many relatives and friends, mostly recent Greek immigrants like his own parents, that he would visit as a child. He noticed the old brick apartment building where his godparents, Jimmy and Erasmia Pappas, had lived. How quickly life changes, he thought, and it just keeps moving on.

Sitting in the passenger seat and approaching the restaurant and its waiting valet, Michael wondered how he had come to have not only a bodyguard but a mistress, all bundled into one extraordinary package.

"How do you want to play this?" Sindy said. "Should I stay outside with the car?

"No. Give it to the valet. Come in with me and sit at the bar while I dine with this dirtbag." Michael didn't know what to expect from Bishop McCarthy but he knew he wouldn't like him. "I can't believe this pedophile is still a bishop."

They walked under the red canopy through the front door of Piccola Venezia, entering into the large formal bar. The rich, wood-paneled walls framed the well-dressed, but tough, testosterone-fueled crowd around the bar, giving an old-world feel to the setting. It had that typical, solid middle-class, upper-end Queens restaurant aura—an appearance of dignified calm and alcoholic conviviality while, under the surface, percolated a macho-like volcano, waiting for the first show of disrespect for it to erupt in a free-for-all worthy of the alleys of Sicily or Baghdad. Nevertheless, the scene brought back many memories for Michael. He and Alex had eaten here many times over the years. Ezio—the paternal, dignified owner and maître d'—instantly recognized Michael and, eyeing Sindy by his side, greeted him with a broad smile and a firm handshake.

"Michael, it's so good to see you. How are you?"

"I'm very good, Ezio. I'd like you to meet my associate, Sindy Steele."

Gracious, but with a professional reserve, Sindy offered a firm handshake.

"I miss your brother, Michael. He was such a good man. Thank you for coming in, you are like family, you know. I have a great table for the two of you."

"Actually, Sindy is going to stay here in the bar. I'm meeting a Bishop McCarthy for dinner. I don't think he's arrived yet."

Ezio looked confused but he recovered quickly. Michael figured he had likely seen a lot of complicated situations involving men and their women, although perhaps not bishops. "Absolutely, Michael. We have a special seat here at the bar for the lady," he said, motioning toward a tall stool at the end of the bar, closest to the dining room. "And we will have a quiet table for you and the bishop in the dining room whenever you're ready."

"That's perfect, Ezio, thank you."

At that moment, the front door swung open and a man entered, dressed in black with a priest's white collar. He was of medium height and build, a red, ruddy Irish complexion and a large mane of curvy white hair.

"This must be your bishop, Michael." Ezio said.

"I've never met him but he sure looks like one."

Sindy Steele quietly slipped onto her barstool. Michael neither introduced nor acknowledged her in front of the bishop. He wasn't sure why. He hadn't planned or discussed that with her but they both seemed to simultaneously and silently agree that it was best that way. Ezio watched the scene unfold, curious yet with professional nonchalance.

Michael walked directly toward the bishop to greet him. Holding out his right hand, he said, "You must be Bishop McCarthy."

In the corner of his eye, Michael could see Sindy Steele observing them. Ever so briefly, his eyes met hers as he and the bishop walked right past her on their way to the dining room.

———

The bottle of Chianti was nearly empty. Michael had just finished his grilled calamari and was savoring his plate of *fusi alla grappa*, a homemade pasta with mushrooms, grappa and parmigiano. Despite the company, Michael was enjoying it. The bishop was eating a T-bone steak. Michael noticed the waiter wince when he ordered it "well done."

"So, how did you come to be on our illustrious board, Bishop?"

The bishop finished chewing, looked up from his plate and responded, grinning slightly. "I guess we have a mutual friend, Michael. John Hightower seems to be a very close friend of a monsignor at the Vatican, Monsignor Petrucceli. The monsignor and I have collaborated on spiritual issues for many years."

Michael tried to control his rising slow burn. He couldn't wait to tell Sindy about the connection with Hightower. He knew he couldn't afford to show the bishop any concern or displeasure on his part. So, instead, he played the congenial host, happy to have a member of the clergy on the board of the company he ran. But it was now clear that Bishop Kevin McCarthy was his mortal enemy.

"You know, Michael, I have no intention of interfering with your affairs at Gibraltar or challenging how you run the company. We just want you to know that we're there."

"That 'we're there?' " Michael challenged, his voice escalating, "Who's 'we'?"

"Michael, please. Relax. I am not here to threaten you. When I say 'we,' I refer to the Holy Trinity."

Michael chose to let the Holy Trinity response go unanswered. He had already revealed more than he intended and was annoyed with himself for letting his emotions show.

"God is with you, Michael. At all times." Bishop McCarthy smiled. Michael was sure that McCarthy had had his eyes done. A sure sign of divine vanity, he thought.

Later that evening, in the bar at the St. Regis, Sindy Steele sipped her Ketel One cocktail while Michael nursed his limoncello from a small, frosted glass. He filled her in on the ominous dinner conversation with Bishop McCarthy.

"The Vatican put him on the board to get to you. To play with your head. They want to show you who's boss, that you can't shield yourself from their influence," Sindy said. "He's as dangerous and as wicked as they come, Michael. Don't forget, after those poor kids were going to expose him for the pervert that he is, he pulled every string he had to have them killed. He's probably been put near you to do the same thing."

"I know, my brother said the same…" Michael caught himself. "Alex was never big on priests; he thought most of them were just holier-than-thou hypocrites."

"Your brother was right—and they don't get any worse than this guy."

"What did you do at the bar for almost two hours?" Michael asked, still thinking about McCarthy.

"Just watched the crowd. The bar was full most of the time. I saw a lot of characters."

"Anyone interesting?" Michael asked.

"Not really, but there was one guy who came in right after you and the bishop went to your table. He stayed the whole time while you ate. He seemed to watch everything and then got up just as you and the bishop were leaving."

"What did he look like?"

"He was in his mid-forties, trim and well-dressed in a too-shiny grey suit, blue shirt, gold cufflinks and a bright red tie. It's funny, I watched that pretty Russian bartender serve him his Campari. She seemed drawn to him but somehow but as she drew closer, handing him his drink, she suddenly turned away and never made eye contact with him again. And then, I stared at him more closely, trying to size him up, you know? It was then that I noticed his eyes—they were strange, somehow unnerving."

"What do you mean?"

"They were different colors; one a pale blue, the other a deep dark black. They were deep set. I can't quite put my finger on it except that he seemed to lower the temperature in the bar by ten degrees; that's how cold he appeared."

"Do you think it was just a coincidence that he was there?" Michael asked.

"Two things you should know. I don't believe in coincidences, and I will never forget those eyes."

Chapter 15

John Rizzo didn't like losing, especially when it came to his money. Today he had a plan to make it back.

Rizzo, a former cop, and Fat Lester, an old family friend of Alex's and now one of Michael's trusted bet-takers and collector, sat at the soda fountain counter of Irving's Luncheonette, drinking their morning coffee and watching while Irving Friedman waited on the morning's neighborhood customers.

Rizzo had just handed Fat Lester a wad of bills that Lester quickly counted and placed in his pants pocket, his large 250-pound frame perched uneasily on the luncheonette stool.

"That should even us up, Lester. Those fuckin' Mets are killin' me. By the way, how's Michael doing? I haven't spoken to him since that party you guys had last month." Rizzo suspected that Michael didn't like him. He didn't know why exactly, it was just a feeling but he knew his instincts were usually correct.

"He's good, man. He's good," Fat Lester said. But Rizzo could see that Fat Lester was not himself, he looked nervous, perspiring despite the unusual coolness of the summer morning.

"John, I want to ask you for a favor."

Before even hearing the request, Rizzo sensed an opportunity for himself. It was a sixth sense he had fine-tuned over the years while he was on the beat as a cop. He knew vulnerability when he saw it.

"Hey, sure, you name it."

"Nothing man, never mind."

Rizzo could see that Lester wasn't looking him in the eye but instead was glancing somewhere else, at the pinball machine over to his right.

Rizzo took his time, looking around also. He knew how to play people in need.

"You know, Lester, Irving's is one of the last of the city's luncheonettes. Remember, we used to call them 'candy stores' when we were kids? There used to be one on every corner. Not anymore. It's hard to even find a place to get an egg cream anymore." As he said it, Rizzo found himself with an urge for one of the unique New York City drinks, a concoction of chocolate syrup, milk and seltzer water from the soda fountain, briskly stirred until a perfect one-inch creamy head formed at the top.

Rizzo had been a cop; he knew when someone needed to talk.

"Lester, we've known each other for a lot of fuckin' years. I know you, buddy. You can trust me."

"Oh man, I can't go to Michael with this. He's OK, but he won't be able to understand this situation, this problem I got."

Rizzo put his hand on Lester's shoulder. It was his "good cop" routine.

"What 'situation?' What can I do? What do you need, my friend?"

"Listen, I'm gonna pay you. I don't want anything for nothing. I need to score some H."

Rizzo looked up and around, suddenly concerned that anyone overheard their conversation.

"Heroin?" Rizzo asked. Lester lowered his eyes and nodded.

"Jesus, pal, I thought you were clean."

"Listen," Lester quickly added, "Never mind. I haven't done anything in years. I don't know what I'm saying, you know?"

Rizzo looked at him. He knew already that he was about to "own" Fat Lester.

"Yeah, I know." Rizzo let several seconds go by, just enough, he thought, to make Lester sweat a little more. Make him wonder if he'll help him. Then he began again.

"Listen, maybe we can help each other. You know, so maybe you won't feel like you owe me or anything, or like you're indebted to me."

For just a moment, Lester's face appeared to loosen up. "What do you mean?"

"I mean we all have fuckin' problems. Nobody's perfect. You know what I'm saying?"

"I dunno, I dunno what you're saying. I dunno even know what I'm saying."

"Listen to me. You're gonna to be alright, OK? Listen to me. I got problems too, you understand what I'm saying? Since I've been off the force, it's been tough, the money. I mean I'm almost living off my damn pension. We can help each other out here."

"What are you talkin' about, what do you mean?"

"Lester, I can get you whatever the fuck you need. Let's start with that. But, here's the good part. Here's the fuckin' best part. You don't have to pay me for it. You just do me some favors. You know? Just some help."

"John, what are we talking about here? "

"It'd just be for a short time. Maybe just a couple of deals, you know?"

"No, I don't know what the fuck you're talking about. What do I need to do?"

"Let's say I make some bets, you know. But maybe you don't put all of them in. You understand?"

"I'm not sure …"

"OK, let's say I place four bets. Let's say I call you in the morning with bets on four teams, the Yanks, Phillies, whatever, it doesn't fuckin' matter, OK?"

"Yeah, so what, what then?"

"So," Rizzo continued, "maybe you don't give 'em to Michael until later in the day —after the games are over or maybe sometime after they're going. And maybe if the Phillies are losing, maybe you get rid of that bet. You just drop it; you forget that I made it. You understand what I'm saying here?"

"Shit. You mean 'past posting'—on Michael?"

"Yeah, whatever you want to call it. What difference does it make? Listen, you're confused. The way I see it, Alex was our friend, God rest his fuckin' soul. But you don't really know Michael. He's a suit trying to play Alex. You can't trust him, Lester. You understand that, don't you? Yeah, it's 'past posting' or whatever you want to call it, but, you know, you get what you need and I get what I want. Nobody loses."

"I can't do that. I just can't."

Rizzo didn't like that. He looked at Lester, "Then I can't fuckin' help you. I can't fuckin' help you, unless you're willing here to help yourself."

Lester was silent for a time. He looked away again. Rizzo looked also looked away. He knew that Lester would be the first one to break the silence. He'd been there before. The addict always gives in.

"I'll never get away with it." Lester looked even more nervous now, beads of perspiration formed on his forehead and under his nose, just above his upper lip. Rizzo noticed that Lester's hand was shaking.

Rizzo smiled. "If the only question is now whether you can get away with it, then we can do it, buddy. I'm tellin' you, we can do this. Just a few times, that's it. I get a little money. You get your dope. Then, we go back to the way things were and nobody knows from nothin'. That's it. It's not a forever thing. We both then forget about it. It never happened. You understand what I'm sayin'?"

Lester took a deep breath.

Rizzo continued, "And nobody, and I mean no-fuckin'-body knows about it except you and me. Not your skinny cousin. Nobody. You understand? That's the only way I'm in. It's the only way I'm doin' this for you."

Lester sat silent and finally shook his head.

Rizzo felt a familiar feeling of satisfaction. It was just like old times, and in a candy store, no less. He saw Irving looking up behind the counter.

"Irving, how about an egg cream—and one for my friend here. I think he needs a drink."

Chapter 16

New York City

"Michael, I know it's short notice, but why don't you join us for dinner at the Four Seasons?"

Michael and Sindy Steele were casually walking down Park Avenue on their way to their own private dinner at Fiorini's on East Fifty-Sixth Street when Michael answered his cell phone without checking who was calling. Annoyed and initially reluctant, he accepted the invitation after Steele's whispered insistence that it would be a good idea. "Michael, you have to do it. I'll have a drink by myself and take off."

Now he wished he was anywhere else but in the exclusive Pool Room of the Four Seasons restaurant. As though choreographed, Michael sipped his Blue Sapphire martini, Perkins his Knob Creek bourbon on the rocks, Hightower his Chivas Regal scotch and Bishop McCarthy his Chianti. It was an unlikely assembly of disparate characters made possible by Perkins' impromptu cell phone call ten minutes earlier.

From a table in an obscure corner of the restaurant with a

partially obstructed line of sight, Michael could see Sindy, sitting alone, watching the four men.

"Michael, I'm glad this dinner worked out at the last minute. Sorry for the short notice." Perkins clearly had an agenda to discuss with Michael.

"This was actually good timing, Richard. I had just finished my meeting and happened to be only a few blocks away when you called. I'm staying in the city tonight and I didn't have any firm dinner plans, so this worked out well."

Perkins looked around the table, seemingly comfortable with the apparent goodwill all around.

"Michael, things are moving quickly on our merger plan. Cartan has agreed to replace two of its board members with the bishop here—and myself—after the merger. John will continue in his current role reporting to me and we should soon have a confirmation on an expanded role for you—along with significant compensation bumps and parachutes for all of us. This is going to be a good deal for each of us and most of the Gibraltar executives."

Michael felt like an outsider. He couldn't tell whether this dinner was a carefully orchestrated attempt to persuade him to enthusiastically support the apparently preordained merger or whether Perkins was simply hoping to engender friendly camaraderie by bringing him together with his more trusted allies—or, perhaps more accurately, conspirators. He glanced slightly to his right. His eyes met Sindy's as she finished her cocktail.

He sensed the others were waiting for him to speak. "Well, this all sounds good. I must admit, you are obviously closer to this situation than I am. Fortunately, none of this has leaked out anywhere. I'm just trying to run the company, produce results and keep our people focused on their jobs."

John Hightower took this as his cue for what appeared to be a question he had been waiting to ask. "Speaking of our human capital, Michael, how are we doing on the headcount reduction plan?"

Michael fought the urge to attack, took another sip of his

martini and decided to attack anyway. "First, John, you know I don't use this bureaucratic doubletalk. I don't care what all the HR gurus call it today. It's not 'human capital'—it's people. Good ol' employees."

Hightower jumped in quickly, "Michael, the term human capital is being used to show that people are, just like our other assets, valuable and worth protecting. They need to show up on a balance sheet like a building or—"

Michael interrupted him. "Don't give me that crap, John. The part you like about making people an asset is that assets depreciate over time and then they're worth less so we can just get rid of them."

Bishop McCarthy and Hightower exchanged glances. Michael looked carefully at Perkins to see if, he too, had knowingly locked eyes but he didn't see anything that suggested such an obvious agreement. Instead, Perkins tried to calm things down, to play mediator.

"Michael, John, I don't care what we call it. People, human capital, employees, personnel. We just have to bring the numbers into line before this merger can get done," Perkins said.

Michael knew he had played his hand as long as he could without jeopardizing his own job. If persisted any further, he'd be gone and Perkins would replace him with someone who'd be happy to implement the carnage in return for a CEO position, a few million in salary and even more in stock options.

Ignoring Hightower and directing his words to Perkins, he retreated. "Richard, you know I'm not naive. I know what needs to happen. At the same time, I need to make sure I can keep things stable—"

Never one to want to hear a balanced discussion of pros and cons, Richard Perkins cut him off. "Michael, there's no 'at the same time'—you need to get this done. Get me the list of terminations and the effective dates. Have it to me within the week."

Michael knew the discussion was over. The issue was closed.

Just as he looked over again at Sindy, a small team of servers converged on their table carrying plates covered with silver domes. As the dome was lifted off his plate, Michael gazed at the filet of bison with foie gras and Perigord black truffles. On any other night, with any other company, he would salivate over the prospect of the first bite. Not tonight. He knew Sindy was having a better time, alone.

As they began to bite into their entrees, Richard broke the silence. "I do have some good news, Michael. Something that I think will ease your qualms." Then, looking at Bishop McCarthy, he added, "Perhaps, Bishop, you'd like to break the news?"

Bishop McCarthy swallowed hard on his bite of well-done filet mignon while a tiny amount of its yellow béarnaise sauce seeped out of the corner of his mouth. After two or three seconds, he recovered and picked up on Perkins' cue. "Yes, Michael. We are very excited about this. And, I agree with Richard, it will ease some of your concerns regarding how we treat your employees or, as I suggest we call them, 'the Lord's assets.' "

Michael looked over at Sindy's table, wishing he was sitting in the empty seat facing her and enjoying his tender buffalo steak. Instead, he knew he was trapped in enemy territory. He looked at the bishop, trying to conceal the sarcasm that he feared was betraying him. "I can't wait to hear."

McCarthy was anxious to speak. "As you may know, Gibraltar was going to make a modest contribution to St. Joseph's School here in the Bronx, my parish. Instead, in a bold gesture of genius, John came up with an even better approach. One that not only helps our underprivileged Catholic school children but will also improve the perception of our new, post-merger organization. At the same time as the merger is announced, we will disclose an even larger contribution—ten million dollars—by Cartan Holdings and Gibraltar Financial to build a new church and school on the lot adjacent to our rectory. So, you see, Michael, while we may have some negative publicity regarding the layoffs, many more needy children and parishioners will benefit from your generosity."

Michael was tempted to ask him right then and there about the dead kids, but he knew he couldn't prove anything and would only wind up prematurely revealing his hand—and his plan to bring an end to everything threatening him and his family.

Thankfully, the waiter approached the table. Looking at Michael he asked, "How is everything so far this evening?"

Looking around at the table, Michael simply smiled and said, "Everything is perfect, thank you."

He looked for Sindy, but her table had already been cleared.

Chapter 17

New York City

I t didn't take long for Michael to explain everything that had gone on at dinner. After all, Sindy observed most of it, and even though she couldn't hear the conversation, by closely watching the four men, their body language, their facial expressions, the glances exchanged and ignored, the food devoured or left in disgust, she had an excellent idea of everything that had transpired.

After several after-dinner drinks that Michael served in the living room of his St. Regis suite, they resumed their talk while sitting up, half-naked, against the large down pillows on the plush king-sized bed. Although he was feeling the limoncellos, he was still wired from the dinner discussions. He reached over to the side of the bed and, touching the control panel, dimmed the lights to create a soothing atmosphere.

"I've got a plan. Have you ever been to Rome?"

"Yes, a number of years ago. What's the plan and how soon do we leave?"

"I'm not sure yet. Originally, I was going to have Richard Perkins or some others use their connections to make some introductions for me with a cardinal and his aide, a monsignor; they're the ones protecting Sharkey. It was to be under the guise of a Gibraltar initiative. But I realize now that I've got to get higher, above them."

"Did you ever think that maybe you're being too slow, too corporate in how you're approaching this?"

"I don't have everything I need yet to go. Don't worry. I have someone watching them in Rome. I know more than they think."

"Who?"

"Let's just say someone I trust. I can't tell you yet and—I promise you—you don't want to know. "

"And what about Hightower and McCarthy over here? Not to mention this Frank—we don't even know what he looks like. They've got plans for you and they don't involve you sitting behind a mahogany desk. Actually, they may be thinking mahogany but as in a casket."

"Isn't your job to protect me from them?"

"As long as I'm with you, no one's going to get to you. You can relax."

"Thanks. I needed that."

"I have something else I think you need even more."

Loosening her bra and leaving it to hang loosely, unfastened, she pulled down her black lace bikini panties and turned over on her stomach. She turned her head back and, looking at Michael, said "Why don't you do something to me we've never done before? Maybe something that hurts."

Chapter 18

As she drove up the quarter-mile stone driveway to John Hightower's mansion, Sindy Steele could hear the tortured erratic breathing coming from the plastic wrapped and duct-taped parcel in the back of her FedEx truck.

His house sat atop a hill on a perfectly manicured lawn surrounded by tall trees. Steele knew that Hightower lived alone and that no one in Greenwich was likely to notice when commonly accepted delivery vehicles entered their neighbor's property. In any case, this driveway was hidden from any neighbor's view. So she felt assured that no one took note of the white FedEx truck with New York license plates making a late-afternoon delivery.

As she approached the set of four garage doors in front of her, she pressed a series of buttons on a calculator-like device, disarming the alarm system. Then, a stream of tiny red lights flashed until the garage doors all began to open. Three of the stalls were occupied with luxury cars, a black Mercedes, a silver BMW and a dark green Jaguar XKE. The fourth stall was empty.

She pulled the small truck into the garage and pressed the

buttons again to close the doors behind her. She knew that she had plenty of time before Hightower returned home from his usual night of Manhattan barhopping.

She laughed to herself as she proceeded to unwrap her package. This will sober you up fast, Johnny boy, she thought. And don't worry, there's no signature necessary, but first, some assembly is required.

John Hightower tightly gripped the leather steering wheel. He checked the orange glowing dashboard. It was 10:45 PM. He always hated driving at night, particularly in the rain. He knew he'd had too much to drink.

He exited the Merritt Parkway at the North Street ramp and, trying to stay focused on the road despite imperfect vision, an unusually dark, moonless night and a driving rain, he steered his navy blue Range Rover the two miles down North Avenue and, as he did so routinely now, turned right at his royal blue mailbox. As the rain came down harder, in sheets, thunder erupted and bolts of lightning streaked through the sky above. Hightower loosened his grip on the steering wheel. He was home and safe. He drove the last lap up his driveway and, as he approached the four garage doors, he pressed the clicker button above his windshield.

He was anxious to get inside, out of the storm and, as soon as possible, go to the bathroom. He knew he should have gone before he left the city. He wondered what had become of the attractive blonde who, he thought, had been so drawn to him at the Carlyle bar. They had spent three hours together drinking and laughing, when she suddenly checked her watch, excused herself, went to the ladies room and never returned. After sending someone in to look for her, he finally concluded that she had had second thoughts and simply left him. Hightower had chalked it up to the capriciousness of American women. It had been a long drive this evening.

The garage door didn't budge. When rushed, he often pressed the button prematurely, before he was within range of the remote-controlled sensor. He pressed it again, pushing down hard and holding it until he saw the door begin to rise, revealing a still-dark interior. As the door lifted, disappearing into the garage ceiling, the interior light attached to the ceiling brightly illuminated the space immediately in front of his Range Rover. Hightower stared mindlessly into the void in front of him. Once the garage door had completely disappeared from view, he placed his foot on the accelerator pedal. But, despite his scotch-induced grogginess, something he saw caused him to stop; something was out of place, terribly wrong. At first, it simply didn't register; as though his brain was unable to interpret what his eyes were seeing.

The interior of the garage was now like a theatre stage—flooded with the glare from the Rover's powerful headlights and the lights attached to the garage door opener in the ceiling.

With the car idling, he opened his eyes wider, hoping, perhaps, that the vision in front of him would recalibrate, reshuffle and then make better sense. But, as he sat staring ahead, it only became clearer.

First, he saw the dangling legs, attached to black shoes and socks, black trousers, hanging, as though suspended like a mobile in midair. He raised his eyes, following the legs to a torso, and a full body, hanging, and, finally, a head and face, unnaturally red and grotesquely twisted to the side and downward. It was moving—the motion of the rising garage door mechanism had apparently caused the body to swing, as though it was trying to escape.

Hightower couldn't move his eyes away from what he hoped he was imagining. Although lifeless, this dangling body was bizarrely familiar in its black jacket and white cleric's collar. Time froze as he continued to stare ahead at what appeared to be a perfectly staged panorama, until he was sure that what he was seeing was really there.

Finally, he looked down at his cell phone on the console near his seat and, with a shaking hand and trembling fingers, punched in 911.

The strong voice came through the Range Rover's speaker system, "Greenwich police, what is the nature of your emergency?"

"I've just pulled up to my garage. There's a man hanging from the ceiling."

Chapter 19

Flushing, New York

Fat Lester knew that his life was falling apart. He felt like he'd jumped off a skyscraper and was in a rapidly accelerating free fall. He knew he'd be meeting the pavement soon. His conversation with Rizzo made him wish it was now.

"OK, Lester. I'm coming off some bad weeks, so today I gotta hit it big. Then, we'll tone it down a bit, maybe even some small losses tomorrow so it all looks kosher, you know?"

Rizzo had kept his word and delivered the relief that Lester so badly craved. As he sat at his desk at Tartarus, speaking with Rizzo on the phone, Fat Lester knew it was payback time. Today there would be thirty-six major league baseball games. By late tonight, eighteen teams would be winners. Joe Rizzo would begin a winning streak by placing bets on seven of them while losing two others. The losing bets would simply lend credibility to the winning ones. Lester would record the bets, known in the trade as "past posting," only after the results of each game were decided.

"Lester, I don't care how the fuck we do it, but I need to collect two-hundred grand over the next two weeks."

"Jesus, Joe, how the hell am I going to pull that off? I can't do that much right away."

"You should have thought of that before, you know, when you were desperate for a fix. The way you're gonna be again in a few days when what I gave you runs out. Or haven't you thought about that?"

Fat Lester knew his torment had only just begun. For in return for his fixes, he knew that he was about to betray Michael Nicholas and, worse, the memory of Alex Nicholas and all he had done for Lester during the forty years of their friendship.

After today, he knew he would be stepping into the abyss. Rizzo would own him, forever.

As he sat at his desk staring at the list of today's games and the betting confirmation sheet he was about to prepare to ensure Rizzo's winning day, he knew he was about to lose the last shred of dignity he had left.

Chapter 20

Michael knew it would be a special evening. He couldn't wait to see the legendary French actress, Catherine Saint-Laurent and her young American lover, Jennifer Walsh. They were another part of Alex's life that he had inherited.

Jennifer had been Alex's mistress. A beautiful blonde in her early thirties, she was a downtown Manhattan beautician known as the "hairdresser to the stars." It appeared to Michael that Alex loved Jennifer as much as he loved any other woman. Michael soon discovered that Alex's liaisons with Jennifer often included Catherine Saint-Laurent.

He was even more surprised when he later learned that Catherine and Jennifer were lovers.

Michael had never met Jennifer until she contacted him after Alex's murder. It was over lunch and cocktails that she had revealed the existence of his secret Apple laptop and the passwords necessary to enter into the world of artificial intelligence and computer imagery that Alex had created. Jennifer was the only person Alex had trusted with his secret. Without her help, Alex would have truly died the night he was murdered.

Michael was impressed with Alex's mistresses. He often wondered why Alex married bimbos but had affairs with smart, impressive and accomplished women.

Few women were more successful than Catherine Saint-Laurent. In her mid-sixties, alluring and classically beautiful, she was a French Hollywood legend. Alex had agreed to help finance the movie she hoped would launch her revival. He died before the funds were ever paid out. Once Michael decided to take over his brother's enterprise, he immediately backed Alex's commitment, investing three-quarters of a million dollars in *Mirror Image*, the film now being shot in Cannes, starring Catherine Saint-Laurent.

He was already seated in Le Bernardin's main dining room enjoying a glass of rosé champagne and watching the parade of the glamorous—and sometimes gaudy, when he observed a buzz around him. The attention of the other diners turned toward the two women approaching his table. All eyes appeared to be focused on Catherine Saint-Laurent and Jennifer Walsh as they made their entrance.

Catherine was stunning in her simple, long, white sundress. Her smile, so familiar from the screen, endless magazine covers, and classic movie posters caused Michael to reflect on how incredible it was it was that this famous star was about to sit at his dinner table.

She began their conversation while she was still yards away. "Michael darling, Jennifer and I just saw a fabulous exhibit at your favorite gallery, Staley-Wise. I simply adored a Harry Benson photograph of JFK and De Gaulle in a Paris motorcade. It's such a classic image and, of course—being a French classic myself—I couldn't help but buy it."

As soon as Catherine sat down, she appeared to admire the mural of the tempestuous sea that dominated the room as though it were the ocean itself. Jennifer Walsh's face had never appeared in print, but she looked as beautiful as any movie star. As she moved to embrace him, Michael could smell her familiar Chanel No. 5 and felt the stirring and titillation that must have captivated his brother. The heat from Dr. Simonetti's perfectly sculptured breasts pressed through Michael's fine cotton shirt.

"You look terrific," Jennifer said. Sometimes I feel like I'm just looking at a younger version of your brother. He was so good-looking, when he wanted to be."

Michael turned to Catherine, whose gaze finally turned away from the ocean, "I'm looking forward to this movie."

"I hope you will be impressed and that you will see that your money has been well-invested. I am very pleased with what we have shot." Catherine's mood seemed to lighten. "And how did you know that I loved Le Bernardin? You know your brother would not like it here. The portions are too small and the people—let's just say perhaps too polite for Alex." Catherine appeared at ease, her thoughts of Alex creating a slight smile and a twinkle in her eyes.

Jennifer burst out laughing. "I really couldn't see Alex here. He'd be out of this place in five minutes. First of all, he only likes steak, lobster or spaghetti." Michael noticed her use of the present tense. "Alex has to have what he called 'a real lobster'—at least three pounds and of course, he only eats the tails."

"Also," Catherine added, "he would never have been comfortable in a French restaurant. The French and Alex would not be good together."

"Except, of course, for you." Jennifer said as she looked at Catherine. "Catherine was Alex's French exception."

As Catherine looked around at the other diners, who were trying to discreetly look at her, her expression changed.

"What's wrong, Catherine? What did you see?" Jennifer asked.

Michael began to turn around, but Catherine put her hand on his arm, "Don't turn around. It's someone I know socially from Paris."

Jennifer looked around at the other tables. "Oh, not him."

Turning to Michael, she explained, "There's this guy, Bertrand Rosen, at the table just inside. He's been staring over here but I didn't notice who he was until now. Catherine can't stand him. He talked about financing *Mirror Image*. We went to dinner with him three times in Paris and then, at the last minute, he backed out of the deal."

His name was vaguely familiar to Michael but he couldn't place it.

"Sometimes I wish I could have more privacy or at least not be so visible," Catherine said, clearly annoyed by Rosen's presence.

Jennifer gently touched Catherine's arm. "Oh, Catherine, just a few months ago, you were upset. You said you felt invisible. Now, you're looking for privacy again."

"I know, dear," Catherine said, "but you are young and American—and I am French. The French are filled with contradictions. French women even more and French actresses even worse. It is impossible to be happy. Perhaps it is not possible to be a woman growing old—and to be happy."

"Catherine, you look absolutely stunning. But your beauty transcends your looks." Michael was struggling to find the perfect compliment.

Catherine frowned. "You are sweet, Michael. Just like your brother—although so different—but I can assure you, no woman over thirty wants to hear that her beauty transcends her looks. We spend our youth wanting men to desire us for our minds or personality or whatever. But, we spend much of our mature years longing for the time when men just wanted us for our beauty, our face, our breasts, our legs or," her face broke out in a wide smile as she laughed, "perhaps just for our ass." They all broke out laughing.

The waiter poured the last of the Veuve Clicquot rosé champagne into Jennifer's glass. Michael signaled for another bottle and, just as the waiter departed, Bertrand Rosen approached their table.

Rosen appeared to be in his sixties, balding with grey hair and rimless glasses and a slight paunch. He was dressed in white trousers and a snappy blue sport coat with shiny gold buttons and what appeared to be a family crest embroidered on the breast pocket.

"Bonsoir, Madame," he said, looking right at Catherine with his arms spread wide as though waiting for a warm embrace, which, Michael knew, was not about to happen. Then, turning to Jennifer, "Jennifer, my dear, you also look stunning this evening."

Catherine looked at Rosen and nodded, leaving it to Jennifer to respond. "Good evening, Mr. Rosen."

Rosen, obviously hoping for more but sensing that any conversation with the two ladies was going to be limited, then turned to Michael. Holding his hand out, he said, "Mr. Nicholas. We met in Paris last year—at Ralph Lauren's new restaurant. You were having lunch."

Now Michael remembered. It was an unusual meeting. Rosen had come up to him and Samantha while they were dining at Ralph's Lauren's bistro on the Left Bank. Rosen had acted as though they knew each other, yet Michael couldn't really recall when or where. He was apparently the founder and head of the highly successful French investment firm, Rosen & Sons. His clientele included some of the most distinguished members of French society.

"Yes, it is good to see you again, Monsieur Rosen. You look well and healthy." Michael hated these types of meaningless encounters and the small talk that they required. He felt sure that Rosen had only come to their table in order to be seen with Catherine Saint-Laurent who, nevertheless, clearly had no desire to engage Rosen any further.

He was saved from further conversation by the waiters who were now circling their table with plates of barely cooked scallops in a brown butter sauce and baked snapper surrounded by charred green tomatoes.

"Perhaps, Monsieur Nicholas, we could meet here in New York

or the next time you are in Paris?" Rosen surprised Michael with his interest, let alone the meeting request.

"Of course. I'll actually be leaving for Paris in several days. That would be the most convenient for me schedulewise." Michael was suspicious but curious. He saw the disapproving expressions from Catherine and Jennifer.

"Perfect. Let me know when you'll be there. Where will you be staying? I will call you."

"I'll be at the Park Hyatt, at Place Vendome."

"Very well. I will be in touch. Bonsoir." And with a polite nod to no one in particular at the table, Rosen returned to his table. Michael sensed an increased chill in the air conditioning. Catherine and Jennifer were vying to be the first to speak. Jennifer won.

"Michael, besides being an asshole, that guy is trouble. I know he's wildly successful but I can tell you, he's a creep."

Michael looked at Catherine who said nothing but tilted her head to one side, smirked and pointed her eyes upward, indicating a discreet but total agreement.

"I admit there's something about him that seems off, but I don't know him. He's certainly connected in Paris. I'll be cautious, but I need to see what he's about. He may be able to refer some people to me as potential clients for Gibraltar—or, for that matter, for Tartarus. Maybe he has rich friends who like to bet on sports. Not that I suppose he's even aware of Tartarus."

After tasting Le Bernardin's yellowfin tuna and foie gras on the toasted baguette, Catherine gazed again at the mural. "This fish is so fresh, I feel like I am swimming in that ocean." Her gaze then turned into a laser focus. "Be careful with that man, Michael. He is what I would call, rough seas. Be sure you're a good swimmer."

Michael looked back over to Rosen's table and saw him staring back.

Two hours, another bottle of champagne and a fabulous chocolate mille-feuille later, Jennifer insisted that Michael join them in their suite at the Standard Hotel downtown for a "nightcap." We have the room stocked with all of Alex's favorite…"

Michael felt a stirring—and a sense that he'd already ventured too far out to sea.

"You must come, Michael."

"I'd love to, but … as appealing as it is … I just can't."

Catherine leaned closer, "Please, only to watch. I promise."

Chapter 21

As Michael walked down the rue St. Honoré, he glanced at the stylish Parisian women as they passed by, many in high heels and bare legs, showing off their tans gained from weekends in Saint Tropez, a live version of French Vogue. The summer heat kept the skirts short and the blouses tight.

It was the opening week of operation for Tartarus Paris, the first expansion of Michael's sports gambling and loan sharking business. It was the culmination of months of planning, recruiting, negotiations, and payoffs—all the activities of a typical business startup in a new city.

The new office, on the third floor of a townhouse located in Paris' posh first arrondissement on the rue Cambon, behind the Ritz, was staffed with a combination of traditional European finance and accounting expertise along with the best gambling and sports betting talent ever assembled on the Right Bank. Except for an occasional party for employees or clients, the office would serve as the back room or operating center. It wasn't open to the public. But location and the perception of success were still important.

Michael looked forward to finally walking into the facility and seeing the talent he had carefully assembled all together, answering phones, setting up accounts, taking bets, running to pick up and pay out euros and all the same illegal activities that had been going on for years in Flushing, Queens.

To make matters more intriguing, Sindy Steele would be accompanying him to dinner, even though Samantha would arrive in Paris late in the morning. He would spend part of the day shopping with her, but he knew she'd be too tired for dinner that night. Her plan, she said, was to stay in and order an early room service from the hotel and go to sleep. Oddly, she'd never asked much about the dinner with Rosen or exactly who else might be attending. It was unusual for her since, he noted, it was usually her first question.

Tonight he'd be alone in the privacy of his suite. He missed his brother.

It was nearly midnight. Michael looked out the large living room window of the Park Hyatt at the Place Vendome. A few couples were strolling through the beautiful perfectly proportioned and intimately lit square. It was perhaps those perfect proportions, designed three hundred years ago, that always gave Michael a rare peace of mind.

He opened up his Apple MacBook and clicked on the Eastern Orthodox cross. As Alex appeared on the screen, Michael thought to himself that all the money he had spent on the computer consultants and new hardware was worth it. For the first time, he was able to see his brother without using Alex's heavy old laptop or the big computer now in Michael's wine cellar. Alex, though dead for over a year, was now not only virtual but web-enabled.

Michael was momentarily startled as Alex's voice came through the laptop's speakers. It seemed that no matter how often he summoned Alex, it still shocked him each time he heard his voice, even more than seeing his lifelike image and expressions on the computer screen.

"Michael, where are we now?"

Michael thought the question was curious yet funny, and he laughed, "We're in Paris. The Place Vendome."

"The place what? Never mind. Paris is close enough for me. Has our new office opened here yet?"

"You remembered. I knew I mentioned it when we spoke in Westport, but I wasn't sure you'd retain it. Your memory is better than when you were alive. "

"Michael, I am alive. How the hell do you think we're talking to each other?" Alex looked agitated. It was clear that his artificial intelligence programs were, as Alex himself had predicted, gaining strength and learning with each new encounter.

"I'm sorry, Alex. Anyway, I need to tell you some things that are going on."

"Oh yeah, like what? Jesus, you're always doing something or something's happening. You know, as crazy as I was, my life—except for the broads—was pretty stable. Nothing seemed to happen. In fact, except for the night I was murdered, I was bored."

Michael laughed, "Oh yeah, well I guess Sharkey and this Rizzo and all these guys are a figment of my imagination. Not to mention your three wives, one of whom tried to kill me."

"I said except for the broads."

Alex's comment about his women hit a sensitive nerve for Michael. After all, he thought, until he had stepped into Alex's life, he'd never cheated on Samantha. Sindy Steele had changed that. He hoped Alex would fail to point it out. Nevertheless, as he observed Alex on the computer screen, it was evident that Alex's attention had moved on to another topic.

"Michael, you know both Lesters were my closest friends. They knew you from the time you were ten years old. I trust them both. Skinny Lester has the brains. His politics is all screwed up with his liberal garbage but he's smart. Fat Lester's not the brightest guy but he's got a lot of heart. And remember, he had a problem. Once someone's on heroin and whatever else he tried, they're always vulnerable. He was sick for quite a while. It can always come back. You've got to watch over him."

"I will, don't worry. I liked them both, even as a kid, and I'm relying on them to run the business."

Alex continued, "Also, I know she can be a pain in the ass, but don't forget about Donna and George. I know I can trust you to take good care of them."

Donna was Alex's third and last wife and now his widow. Thirty-six, sexy, street smart and, like all Alex's wives, highly manipulative. George, twenty-four, was Alex's son from his marriage to Greta Garbone, his second wife. George was basically a good kid who loved both his parents, although he recognized, like his father had, that his mother was toxic.

"They're both in good shape. Don't worry, Alex. They pretty much split the three million I found that you had stashed away. Donna actually invested a few hundred thousand in the business. I didn't really need her money, but it'll probably get a better return for her than anything else right now."

"And what about George? What's he doing? Is he going to school or working? You didn't just give him his share, did you? He'll blow right through it."

"Alex, you know George. He's still young, but, no, he's not doing much. He doesn't look like he'll ever go back to college and he's certainly not working. I didn't give him a lump sum, but he'll get a hundred grand a year from me for the next ten years. So, that should be just enough to get him in some trouble. He's a good kid; he's just got no direction, especially now that you're gone, so to speak. I think his life revolved around you."

"Yeah, unfortunately, I think the kid got the short end of the stick when it came to a normal family. Anyway, what's going on with you besides the office opening?"

Michael sighed, just thinking about the next day. "Well, to-morrow Samantha flies in and, two hours later, Sindy Steele. Then, at night, Sindy and I meet this guy Bertrand Rosen for dinner."

Alex grimaced, "Who the hell is he? I don't like his name."

Michael chuckled. "He owns one of the largest investment funds in France. He's very connected to a lot of money here."

"Oh yeah?" Now Alex turned serious, focusing. "Wait a min-ute—you and your mistress are meeting him for dinner?"

"Who said anything about a mistress?"

"You certainly didn't. I guess you're the last to know you have one. And what about Samantha? What's she going to do, waitress?"

"Samantha will be tired from her flight. She's going to stay in her room and get room service. She knows I have a business din-ner," Michael said, hoping he'd put the issue to rest, knowing he didn't.

"Wow, you've got some racket. I'm not sure I could have ever pulled that off."

"Pulled what off? She doesn't want to go."

"Does she know Superwoman is going?"

"She knows she's going, but I don't think Samantha suspects anything, I mean, Sindy's paid to be my bodyguard." Michael said, although he now felt some apprehension building in his psyche. "Anyway, it all just rolled out that way. When I first set up the din-ner with Rosen, I didn't think Samantha would be here but she decided to come in a day early. But then I knew she wouldn't want to go out to a business dinner the same night she arrives."

"You may want to check and see if there's an app you can buy with some emotional intelligence for yourself because I think you may need it. I can promise you, Samantha knows you're screwing around even before you do." Michael could feel his anxiety building.

"I don't know how the fuck you're going to pull off having your

Steele and this Bernie guy out to dinner without your wife figuring it out."

"It's Bertrand, not Bernie," Michael corrected.

"Whatever. Right there, it tells you something. He's probably really a Bert trying to be a Bertrand. And what role are you playing at dinner—the head of Gibraltar and those legal crooks—or loan shark and bookie?

Chapter 22

Michael had reserved his usual table in the front bar room of Chez Dumonet. But as their taxi approached and he glanced down at Sindy's long, stark white legs, fully exposed from under her short black skirt, he felt titillated yet nostalgic. He found himself torn between guilt over Samantha—and the attraction of the unusual Sindy. He wondered whether he should have selected a different venue for the evening's dinner.

As he and Steele stepped into the restaurant, they were immediately greeted by Nono and Guillaume, the waiters who had greeted Michael and Samantha here for over ten years. Although Michael felt self-conscious, neither of them showed the slightest recognition that something was different. After all, this is France. In any case, he reasoned—or tried to—this was simply a business dinner, not a romantic interlude, despite the fact that all the other patrons—men and women—were following Sindy's long legs with every step she took.

Chez Dumonet was buzzing with Parisians finishing their beef bourguignon or duck confit. The chef and owner,

Jean-Christian Dumonet, dressed in his chef's crisp, white jacket with his name embroidered on the front, was making the rounds to the tables filled with his regular customers. On the rue du Cherche-Midi in the sixth arrondissement, Dumonet could have been a Hollywood stage set for a French bistro: a large vase overflowing with fresh flowers, silver Champagne buckets and a dozen wine bottles sitting atop a dark mahogany and copper bar at the entrance, tin ceiling above, black-and white-checkered tiles on the floor, window panes fogged up from the kitchen's heat, and tables fashionably covered with well-starched, white tablecloths and crystal-clean wine goblets. Michael enjoyed the atmosphere as much as the food.

He was surprised to see Rosen already seated at the table.

And even more surprised when he heard Nono, who was standing behind him, greeting a new arrival, Ah, Madame Nicholas, Bonsoir!"

Michael turned around and was immediately greeted with a kiss on the cheek. "I hope you don't mind, dear. The room service menu looked dreadful."

It was Samantha, looking stunning in a red, high-neck, open-back Stella McCartney dress.

"You look beautiful, Samantha. What a pleasant surprise," Michael managed to say, his mind now spinning in a thousand directions.

"Oh, I hope you don't mind, I couldn't resist the dress, I'm afraid I had to put it on your Black Card." Samantha flashed Michael an apologetic smile that he recognized, knowing her, to signify anything but that.

The tension was immediate, at least for Michael, as the evening now promised to bring together a toxic combination of relationships, most of which, though invisible on the surface, were as real as the bistro's hearty *boeuf bourguignon*. He now wondered why he hadn't thought twice before arranging this evening and including

Sindy with Samantha in town. And how could he have trusted her protestations about not wanting to go out tonight.

After the formalities of the introductions, Samantha seated herself between Rosen and Sindy. When the waiters promptly served the table's complimentary Champagne, a momentary break in the conversation occurred. Michael cherished the silence, brief though he knew it would be.

Samantha didn't wait long to break the spell.

"Michael, it was so considerate of you to choose our favorite restaurant here for tonight. She turned and looked directly at Steele. "As I'm sure you've discovered, my husband is very sensitive. I knew he wouldn't feel right dining here tonight without me so I decided I just couldn't let him down."

Rosen seemingly slow to catch on to the situation smiled, raised his glass and proposed a toast, "To the most beautiful women in Paris."

Michael wanted to strangle him right there. This is the stuff of chick-lit books, he thought to himself, as Samantha continued her attack.

"So, Sindy, Michael has told me a little about you and your role, and I must say, after all our family has been through this past year, it is comforting to know that he will have full-time security."

Michael knew that, despite the apparent compliment, this was simply Samantha's opening volley, designed to set the stage for the intense grilling that she excelled in, like a pitcher who sets up his fastball with a slower changeup just before.

Sindy smiled and began to respond but, although her lips moved, before she could utter a word, Samantha continued, cutting her off in mid-breath.

"Although I must say I'm surprised that Gibraltar would hire a female security person for this type of assignment. And such an attractive one at that." Despite the fact that her remarks were directed at Steele, she actually looked at Rosen who seemed to be enjoying the show—and Samantha's attention. After all, Michael repeated again to himself, this is France.

Now Sindy responded, her tone ice cold, "And what type of assignment are you referring to exactly?" She looked at Michael, but revealed nothing with her eyes. Michael looked away.

Samantha pressed deeper. Michael could see that she believed she had Sindy on the ropes. "Well, I'm surprised a company would hire a woman to travel all over the world to protect a male executive."

Seeing the guillotine blade in slow motion beginning its descent, Michael jumped into the fray. "Samantha, it's no different than other executives, men and women, who have to interact and travel together. Now, how's the burgundy?" He smiled, held his glass of freshly poured white burgundy up to his lips and watched in the corner of his eyes while both Sindy and Samantha burned.

Not to be deterred from her interrogation, Samantha took a sip of her wine and resumed her water torture. "Have you ever lost anyone you were hired to protect?" she asked.

Sindy, turned, looked at Michael and said, "Not anyone I didn't want to lose."

All of this seemed to go over Rosen's head. He appeared to be more interested in both Samantha's and Sindy's plunging necklines. Desperate to break the tension and realizing he needed to involve Rosen in the evening's conversation, Michael directed his attention and his questions to the invited guest.

"Bertrand," Michael began, "I hope we have not been ignoring you. We're pleased you could join us this evening."

"I have wanted to meet with you for some time, Michael. Many people have spoken so highly about you here in Paris."

"Really? I'm surprised. I didn't know that Gibraltar Financial was that well-known here."

"It isn't—but you are becoming well-known. Word has traveled throughout Paris that you have provided the financial backing of

Catherine Saint Laurent's latest film. I am a good friend of hers—and her beautiful American friend, Jennifer."

"Yes, Ms. Laurent was a friend of my late brother. I simply carried through with a commitment that he had initially made to her."

"I see." He smiled, Michael observed, like someone who thinks they know something that they think no one else thinks they know.

"Bertrand, I understand that, despite the crisis here in France—and throughout the world—your fund continues to thrive. You must be very proud—and very smart."

Rosen's eyes—actually, slits—behind the thick, rimless glasses opened wider. "Yes, we are very pleased with our results and our returns. We have maintained a steady fifteen percent return to our investors regardless of the vagaries and difficulties of the markets. We have so many people trying to give us their funds to invest; we have to turn them down. It is a nice position to be in, yes?"

It was odd, Michael thought. Despite the circus going on around him—and the not-so-subtle flirtation by Samantha—Rosen acted as though he was answering an analyst's questions on CNBC.

Michael knew he wasn't a financial analyst or a hedge fund expert, but he knew enough to know that Rosen's results were incredible and well-documented, despite their implausibility. Yet, this tired-looking, oddly passive man sitting before him was an international legend. Government agencies had vetted Rosen and his funds. He had attracted and retained some of the wealthiest and most sophisticated investors. So, why, he wondered, would this man who made many wealthy people even wealthier—and who himself had to be rich beyond anyone's wildest imagination—find himself drawn to Michael Nicholas this night in Paris?

He would throw out a lure. "The next time you're in New York, perhaps you'd like to visit our offices there? I'd be happy to give you a personal tour."

Rosen's eyes narrowed, the right one twitching slightly as he proceeded. "Well, I must confess, although you first came to my attention through your role at Gibraltar, the reason I hoped to get to know you better was because of your new business venture, this Tartarus I believe it is called."

Surprised at Rosen's frank acknowledgement at the table, Michael continued, "Surely you don't need a loan, Bertrand?"

Rosen smiled, then let out a slight chuckle. "No, no, of course not. But I must make a second confession. I do not have many vices but one I savor is to place occasional bets—on horses, soccer, whatever. And, unlike in America, it is not that easy to do in France. There are many complications, you understand? I also have been assured of your discretion."

As they spoke, he looked closely at Rosen, looking for something in his face or his eyes that would either dispel or confirm his suspicions, his fears. He saw nothing.

"Bertrand, how do you do it? What's your secret? Every other money manager in the world has ups and downs, but you're so consistent. Are you just a genius?" Michael had researched Rosen's track record and it was uncanny, almost unbelievable. Despite the turmoil of the markets over the past twenty years, Rosen had, as he'd just said, consistently returned fifteen percent to his investors, year in and year out.

Rosen had obviously answered this question many times before. "We take positions in blue-chip stocks and then we also take a split-strike conversion, or what's called a 'collar' on them. So, typically, our position might consist of say thirty-five S&P 100 stocks with option contracts on them. Then we have the sale of out-of-the-money 'calls' on the index and the purchase of out-of-the-money 'puts' on the index. The sale of the 'calls' increases our rate of return while the 'puts' limit the downside."

Michael nodded but had long since checked out. "Well, this is beyond my expertise. That's why I don't manage my own money."

Rosen's face brightened. He looked pleased with himself. "Michael, you aren't alone. Even the most sophisticated investors—not to mention some of the idiots our respective governments call regulators—have been unable to follow or understand our strategy. It's complex. By the way, I rarely actually meet with investors because it's too frustrating. They try—but can't—understand the strategy. If everyone could understand it, other people would replicate it. So, it gets too frustrating for them and then too annoying for me to try to continually explain it to people who simply do not have either the brainpower or technical background to follow it. It is simply, and beneficially, a complex formula that can't be duplicated."

Michael was bored with trying to follow the investment strategy but intrigued with Rosen's ability to successfully solicit sophisticated investors who were, nevertheless, unable to understand how he invested their money.

"I'm curious, Bertrand. Why are people so willing to give you their money when they can't follow your strategy? Or, better yet, how do the government investigators do their job if they can't comprehend your strategy?"

"You would be amazed at how insecure some of the most intelligent people are. When confronted with something that is beyond them mentally—especially coming from an expert with my track record, reputation and connections—they don't want to acknowledge their shortcomings. I believe it actually frightens them to realize that, within their very area of specialization, they are actually inadequate. They don't confront because they realize they can't keep up intellectually."

Michael noticed that Samantha appeared to have shifted her piercing glare away from Sindy—and onto Rosen. He knew what she was thinking. Nevertheless, if Rosen wanted to bet, Michael had no intention of turning away his euros.

"I see that I brought our conversation back to your funds—instead of your interest in Tartarus."

"Yes, I hope you will allow me to indulge my hobby—my true passion—with you." As he spoke, Rosen pulled a sheet of paper out of the inside breast pocket of his suit coat. Without even unfolding it, he handed across the table to Michael.

Michael quickly looked it over. It was a neatly typewritten document with several columns detailing a series of sports wagers to be placed over the next several days.

"Bertrand, you know these are significant bets, huge gambles. If you are successful, this will mean millions for you. I'll actually lay off some of this action to others just so that I'm not that heavily exposed. But, if you lose big, say you lost on each bet, you'll owe me over a million euros. Of course, that's not likely but, you know, anything is possible. Usually, I'd require some cash or security up front to just go ahead with something on this scale."

Rosen was polite but firm, "Michael, I came to you because I was told that I could trust you and, with my high profile here in Paris, I cannot place these bets with local bookmakers. Surely the bigger risk here is mine. As you said yourself, if I win, it'll be tens of millions, in which case I'm trusting that you'll be able to make good on it. Your worst-case loss, which would only be if I disappeared suddenly from the face of the earth, is a million. And, I don't need to remind you of who I am, my credentials and reputation here in France—and in America, for that matter." He looked straight into Michael's eyes, "I mean, please remember, Michael, I'm not your typical client. I have been investigated and have been cleared by the financial regulators on both continents, our French AMF and your own country's SEC."

Michael thought of hesitating, and then he thought of the upside of having a client like Bertrand Rosen to jump-start Tartarus in Paris.

"OK. I'm good with this. I trust you, Bertrand, and I look forward to a long working relationship here." Michael didn't trust him but his actual risk was minimal.

Rosen was clearly pleased. "Michael, I also hope that you will also become a client of mine. I do not generally even take on new investors to my firm, but, since you have been kind enough to trust me, it's only fair that I reciprocate. Also, there are other connections, very valuable ones, that I can make for you."

"Really?" Michael was curious. He was certainly interested in growing his Paris operation's client list, particularly with well-heeled investors or friends of Rosen."

"To start, Michael, I have a close friend who is a banker at IBS, the International Bank of Switzerland. His name is Hans Ulrich. I want to set up a meeting for you."

"Does he want to place bets?" Michael asked.

"No, no, not at all. He is a banker; a Swiss banker. Very discreet. He can arrange for your money to be safely held and invested—but without it being reported to your American Internal Revenue Service. Therefore, no one asks any questions, you aren't taxed and it is all safe and legal. It's all done through the bank's offshore private banking services. The Swiss are beautiful, you know. They are experts at working the system."

"Bertrand, I don't believe that it's legal for me, a U.S. citizen. I've got to report that income, at least in some way."

"Michael, very rich and sophisticated Americans have been doing this for decades. It's still legal here and it is legal in the U.S. because there simply is no paper trail."

"Unlike most people in this business, my preference is to show the income so that the extent of my legal risk is simply the nature of the business. The authorities frequently don't enforce the gambling laws, or at least fail to prosecute anyone. Evading taxes, however, is a far more serious issue in the U.S. I see taxes as simply a necessary cost of doing business."

Rosen was not convinced. "Michael, listen to me. Speak with Hans. He will guide you. As one of your famous Americans, Leona Helmsley, I believe, said, 'Taxes are for the little people.' "

"Bertrand, in that case, I'm going to remain a 'little person.' Leona Helmsley went to prison for tax evasion." And the more Michael listened to Rosen, the more determined he became to limit his involvement with him—only allowing him to bet through Tartarus. He knew it was the one area where the odds would always be in his favor.

The ringing of Michael's cell phone attracted everyone's attention.

As he reached to identify the caller on his BlackBerry screen, Michael remembered that it was here a year ago while dining with Samantha that his brother called him from a restaurant in Queens. Michael had sat at this same table joking with Alex when he heard the shots at the other end that would silence his brother forever. Or so he thought then.

But tonight the caller was Karen DiNardo, the only person at the firm who knew of Michael's parallel career as head of Tartarus. Michael enjoyed her straight talk and sharp sarcasm, he sensed she would not disappoint this evening.

"Karen, I see you're working late?" Michael answered, seeing her name light up on his BlackBerry and also noting the time in New York had to be three in the afternoon.

"Very funny, boss. I hate to interrupt your dinner but you're not going to believe what's happened here. I just received a call from Richard Perkins' office asking me to get a message to you."

Michael paused for a second, "What is it?"

"A man was found dead, hanging inside John Hightower's garage."

"You're kidding? What happened? Christ, who was it?"

"Actually, that's close. It was Bishop McCarthy."

"No … when did this happen?"

"I was just told but it sounds like it happened last night. In any case, Richard wants you back home as soon as possible."

"But what about the meeting his people were going to set up with Cardinal Lovallo and the monsignor?"

"Michael—really? Don't you think your timing might be off on this one?"

In that split second, he realized how ridiculous the thought of a meeting with them right now would be. He had let his plan get in the way of his common sense. He was surprised at his own brief mental lapse.

"Yes, of course. You're right." Michael continued, standing now near the restaurant's front door, a short distance from his table but far enough not to be overheard. He watched Sindy Steele as he spoke. "Listen, I'm just curious, exactly what time was he murdered?"

Chapter 23

"Lester, do you think Rizzo is capable of murder?" Fat Lester asked his cousin as he devoured another of Locanda Verde's famous meatball sliders, more out of nerves than simply his usual hearty appetite.

Skinny Lester put down his fork and looked closely at his cousin.

"Yes, he's definitely capable of murder."

For a few minutes, neither spoke but instead exchanged quick glances at each other while they continued to eat.

"Isn't this place owned by De Niro?" Fat Lester asked.

"Yeah, just look around you, Lester. The place is filled with the slick hedge fund crowd trying to look hip and then these artsy, young downtown types. The artsy ones are all in black and the hedge fund guys are all wearing jeans and three-hundred-dollar shirts with fancy cuff links."

Fat Lester felt confused and impatient. "So where does that leave us?"

Skinny Lester looked up at his cousin, a wry smile on his face, and said, "We're in no man's land, Lester. We're here to eat. More precisely, I'm here for these meatball sliders, the charred octopus and the simple but perfectly prepared al dente spaghetti with the rich red tomato sauce."

"You sound like the freakin' restaurant reviewer at the *Post*. Anyway, that's it? That's all you have to say?"

"No, you're right. I'm also here for the Chianti. Sorry, I almost forgot that."

Fat Lester, abruptly put down his fork. "Aren't you going to ask my *why*?"

"Why, *what*?"

"Why I asked you if Rizzo could kill a guy. I mean, would he kill a man who backed out on a deal with him? You know, after the guy had given him his word."

"Well, you know he could kill, he's a former cop to start. And, on top of that, he looks to me to be a guy who may even enjoy blowing someone's brains out. So, why did you ask?"

"What if someone asked Rizzo to supply him with some drugs and then decided he couldn't do what Rizzo wanted in order to pay him back?" Fat Lester squirmed in his chair.

"Then, I don't think Rizzo would actually blow the guy's brains out."

"Really?" Fat Lester felt what he sensed was going to be a very brief sense of relief.

"Yes, because that would be too quick. For that, Rizzo would want the guy to suffer first. Real pain, you know like a slowly penetrating ice pick in your ear for starters. But, why exactly are you asking?"

Fat Lester felt sick to his stomach. "No reason. Just curious."

It was after the sliders but before the spaghetti that Fat Lester confessed to the reemergence of his old drug problem and the desperate deal he made with Rizzo.

"I gotta tell you, Lester," he said, "just telling you this—getting it off my chest—makes me feel better. But now we gotta figure out what the fuck to do."

"Les, what was it, ten years ago, when you fell off the wagon, Alex took care of you. He got you help and he protected you. He fixed everything."

"Yeah, but Alex's gone now."

"Les, now you've got to get to Michael and let him know what's happening. We've also got to let Rizzo know the deal's off."

Fat Lester already knew this, but hearing his cousin verbalize it gave him strength and filled him with trepidation.

"I know, but what's Michael going to say? He's never seen this side of me. Alex did, but I doubt Michael ever knew about it. Then what the fuck happens with Rizzo? I've taken his drugs already."

"Don't worry, Lester, we've known Michael since he was a baby. He knows you better than you think. Listen, Alex was his brother. First we've got to let him know what's going on. He'll get you help; you know, rehab to start. Then, we've got to hope he's as good at dealing with Rizzo as Alex was." Skinny Lester paused, took another sip of his wine, and added, "Maybe more than that, we've got to hope that, underneath the suit, Michael's got a heart like Alex had."

"Alex'd be pissed if he heard you talking about his damned heart. He didn't talk about that stuff."

Fat Lester twirled a forkful of sweet, tomato-coated spaghetti and, savoring its flavor on his tongue, drew comfort from its familiar taste. He wished he could just keep eating it forever and never have to put the fork down or get up from the table. He watched as, with each deliberate twirl of his fork, the portion of spaghetti remaining in the bowl dwindled, bringing him closer to the two calls he dreaded and feared.

He wasn't sure which one he feared more, the one to Michael or to Rizzo.

Chapter 24

R izzo knew that his Museum Tower neighbors wondered how a retired New York City cop could afford to live in their exclusive building. He suspected that only the building's maintenance staff knew the truth. He had once overheard the doorman joking to the handyman that "Mr. Rizzo" had been known as "The Nose" by those on his beat, for his ability to sniff out the vulnerable ones he then extorted during his thirty years on the force.

Riding down the elevator, he laughed when he remembered the faces of undocumented immigrants, landlords with illegal apartments in their basement, bookies, loan sharks and small-time drug dealers who had provided him with the riches a straight street cop could only dream about. As he saw it, he provided a service: protection from arrest in return for cash. Protection led to greater opportunities as he branched out into dealing the cocaine and heroin he regularly confiscated.

Rizzo silently thanked those faces that had allowed him to build up enough cash to retire after twenty-five years on the force, along with a full pension as an added bonus. It wasn't long after his retirement that he moved into his $1.4 million condominium in the tony Museum Tower, adjacent to the Museum of Modern Art on Fifty-Third Street. As he waited for the elevator to reach the lobby, he felt content for the first time in his life.

Rizzo looked forward to meeting Fat Lester and collecting the first installment on what promised to be a new and substantial annuity. He had arranged to meet him right outside his building and he expected to be riding back up to his apartment a few minutes later with thirty-eight thousand dollars in cash.

When the elevator doors opened, immediately, Rizzo saw something was wrong.

The lobby was empty. No one was manning the concierge desk and, even more unusual, the doorman was absent from his post.

As he exited the building through the revolving door to meet Fat Lester, he was startled instead to see Michael Nicholas and a stocky, well-built stranger, who introduced himself simply as Fletcher. Fat Lester was nowhere in sight.

His instinct for danger set off the old familiar alarms, the defensive safeguards he had not felt since his years on the force. He knew he was caught off-guard and unprepared. He knew right then that his ride back up the elevator would not go as he planned.

Chapter 25

"Michael, I didn't expect to see you. I thought you were over in France," Rizzo said, keeping a slight distance away and looking Fletcher over. "I was just expecting Lester." Getting no reaction or response from Fletcher, he turned back toward Michael. "You didn't have to come yourself."

Michael and Fletcher both quickly advanced closer to Rizzo. Michael spoke, "Let's go back inside where we can have some privacy." Fletcher started the revolving door with his hand and guided Rizzo in as he and Michael followed close behind. As they all entered the still-abandoned lobby, Rizzo looked around, his eyes rapidly scanning the entire area, looking for any sign of the staff.

Once inside, Rizzo looked again at Fletcher, trying to access his role in this encounter. Fletcher returned his gaze and slowly opened his sport coat revealing a black Glock 19 pistol securely tucked into his waistband.

Rizzo straightened up as he further sized up Fanelli. He then turned to Michael. "What the hell's going on, Michael?" Then looking back at Fletcher, "And who are you?"

Fletcher didn't utter a word, but Michael jumped in, "Fat Lester couldn't make it tonight, Johnny. But we wanted to settle accounts."

"Michael, what is this? I could have waited for the gift. And you didn't need to bring your girlfriend." Rizzo smirked, staring again at Fletcher.

"Listen, you asshole," Michael said in a hushed tone, "You're lucky my friend here doesn't have you pulled in right now for procuring smack for Lester."

Trying to keep his temper and his fears in check, Rizzo kept up an aggressive show. "What the hell—you're going to have me arrested? You gotta be freakin' kidding. I think you've got things a little confused." He turned again to Fletcher. "Are you a cop?"

Fletcher took a step closer, now nearly in Rizzo's face. "Don't worry about who I am." He then put his hand on his gun and motioned Rizzo toward the elevator.

Rizzo turned toward Michael. "So what the fuck do you want? What about my money?"

"Get in the elevator," Michael said, motioning toward the open teak-walled elevator.

Rizzo was unsure; he tried to analyze the risk in going up to his apartment. On one hand, he'd no longer have the safety of a public place. But he didn't really believe Michael Nicholas was capable of hurting him. Fletcher was the wild card. On the other hand, he knew his own pistol was loaded and accessible in his nightstand drawer. If he could shift the scene up to his apartment, he might be able to get to his weapon.

Rizzo led the way to the elevator, entering and then pressing the number for his floor. But before he could even turn around, Fletcher slammed him violently against the back wall of the car. He then felt a crushing blow to the back of his knees, causing him to collapse in a heap onto the elevator floor. Rizzo knew the drill. He had done it himself countless times to those who resisted his shakedowns or whose looks he simply didn't like.

"Are you guys freakin' nuts? You're out of your freakin' minds." In a matter of seconds, Rizzo's face was pushed into the floor and he felt Fletcher's knee pressing hard into his back. He suspected Fletcher was a current or former cop as he found himself handcuffed to the waist-high steel railing with his hands behind his back.

He watched as Michael waited for the elevator door to close and then inserted the key that closed the doors but held the elevator on the lobby floor.

"Where'd you get that key?" Rizzo grunted.

He could feel Fletcher's knee pinning him even harder now into the floor.

"People in this building hate your guts, Rizzo. It wasn't hard." Fletcher said.

Michael's face was emotionless, his demeanor calm and his voice low. He looked at Rizzo and instructed Fletcher, "Let's get his clothes off."

Rizzo laughed and, as Fletcher finally released his knee-hold, he looked up at the car's floor indicator lights, hoping for a rescue. But he knew the elevator was going nowhere. "You're crazy."

With that, Fletcher punched him, hard and low, doubling Rizzo over. "Shit," he gasped, trying to catch his breath.

Fletcher then secured Rizzo's ankles together using a plastic cord.

Michael said, "What do you think, John? You were a dirty cop. You're still dirty. You knew Lester was trying to stay clean. You didn't give a damn. You didn't mind maybe killing him with your drugs for a little money?"

"He asked me for help. He asked me to score the stuff for him. I was doing fatty a freakin' favor."

"Yeah, sure, at my expense. You think we're as dumb as you are?" Michael said.

Rizzo was breathing hard. Secured to the railing with both hands cuffed behind his back and his feet bound at the ankles, his eyes bulged out as he saw Fletcher pull out a hunting knife from his back pocket. He didn't expect this.

In three short, swift strokes of the blade, most of Rizzo's clothes had been slashed open. Fletcher and Michael easily pulled off the remaining shards and rolled up the ripped garments, including the remains of his underwear. Rizzo was standing, bound and naked in his own elevator but relieved when he saw Fletcher return the blade to his pocket.

A voice came over the elevator intercom, "Is everything OK, Mr. Rizzo? We've got some folks here waiting to go up."

Before Rizzo could respond, Fletcher spoke, "Yes, Harry, we're done. Be out in a second. Thanks." Michael turned the key and pressed the button to take them to the basement where, Rizzo surmised, Michael and Fletcher could exit through the service door.

The elevator door opened and Michael and Fletcher walked out, carrying Rizzo's shredded clothing and leaving him secured to the railing, standing naked facing the door.

On his way out, Michael turned around, holding the elevator door with his arm as the buzzer went off. "Just remember, I've got enough on you to get you arrested for dealing and maybe even eliminate that cop's pension you somehow have held onto. Next time you'll know better, Rizzo. You don't cheat your bookie." Rizzo watched as Michael then pressed the lobby button and exited the elevator.

As the door closed, Rizzo shouted out to him, "No, next time, Michael, you're going to die." Even before the doors reopened into the lobby, Rizzo began planning his trip to Westport, Connecticut.

Chapter 26

New York City

Just before he climaxed, Michael looked hard into Sindy Steele's dark, half-opened eyes.

Had she really murdered the bishop and hung him inside John Hightower's garage? Although he knew it was a little sick, the very thought of it was like an intravenous injection of Viagra.

Michael rolled over to Sindy's side. His next thoughts were near panic. The St. Regis suite, he realized, had become his second home and his lover was possibly a murderer.

The lights were off, but the blue light from the digital alarm clock illuminated the tiny beads of perspiration that glistened on her body. One long, slender, pale white leg dangled outside the covers over the side of the bed. She stared up at the ceiling, spent and satisfied, Michael hoped. Or, perhaps she was somewhere else. Somewhere he couldn't go, somewhere he was afraid to go. Somewhere dark.

"Sindy, where are you?" he asked, whispering into her ear.

Her eyes darted back to life. "What do you mean?"

"You seemed to be far away, somewhere else."

"I have something to tell you. It's a strange thing. It frightens me." She looked vulnerable.

"Is it about McCarthy's suicide?" Michael knew the answer even though she had already denied having anything to do with his death.

"Michael, do I frighten you?"

He hesitated. "Sometimes. To be honest, right now my whole life frightens me."

He tried not to think about Samantha. He knew Alex was right, that Samantha knew he was sleeping with Sindy. After the dinner in Paris, the chill between them had almost become a deep freeze. Oddly though, Samantha had yet to confront him over his relationship with Sindy. Worse, Samantha had no way of knowing that he didn't see this arrangement—or relationship, or whatever it was—lasting too long. To him, it was—almost—just business and, perhaps, something he needed at the time. And, speaking of business, he realized that, in view of his plan, he was not yet ready to part ways with Sindy.

Sindy was now an integral part of the second life that Michael had come to inhabit. Just as much, he thought, as Samantha was an integral part of the first one. Michael knew he had taken his ability to "compartmentalize" to a new—and very troubling—level.

But what really panicked him was that he knew he couldn't envision how it could possibly end, or end well. Now he wanted to change the subject.

"You mentioned once in passing that you'd gone to medical school. I've been meaning to ask you about it? What happened?"

"I did—Stanford—and I did well there, academically, at least. I only attended for two years.

"Why'd you leave?"

"I was young, immature. I was in love with this guy, another medical student. It didn't work out. I was heartbroken. That'll never happen again."

"Did he—"

She cut him off firmly. "Michael, in time I'll tell you every-thing." She stopped, catching herself and softening, she continued. "But, if you don't mind, I don't want to talk about that time in my life anymore right now."

"I understand." He had to ask her one more thing that couldn't wait. "One last question, not related to that period."

"One," she said, totally expressionless.

"What do you think—what are your feelings—about the bishop being dead?"

"It was poetic justice. Hightower is your enemy. He knows you don't like him. He's the one with some connection at the Vatican that resulted in McCarthy being presented to Gibraltar as a board member. Believe me, Hightower is scared shitless. You've neutral-ized him. He's not about to mess around with you again. Now he's afraid for his own life. He believes you had something to do with this. He doesn't know how you pulled it off, or even what exactly happened. But the image of seeing that pervert hanging from his garage ceiling, all lit up, as he was about to drive in—that's one he's never going to forget."

"And how did I pull it off?" He was watching her closely now.

"Well, the police actually believe it may have been a suicide and they're privately acknowledging that it looks like the good bishop may have been a jilted lover. They're speculating that Hightower may have rejected McCarthy's advances or affection and so he hung him-self in a place where Hightower was sure to be the one to find him."

"How clever of him," he said.

"You don't get to be a bishop without being clever."

After a long silence, she spoke again. "I looked up 'tartarus.' I wondered what it meant and why you decided on that name for Alex's business."

"It's a prison, where the Greeks sent the defeated gods. A dank, gloomy pit surrounded by a wall of bronze," Michael said softly. "It's the lowest region of the universe, the abyss, even farther away than Hades or hell."

"Is that where we are, Michael? I forget that you're Greek. This sounds so mystical, so old European."

He listened, then continued. "My parents were Greek. I was born here. But, it's in my blood, how I was raised. It never leaves you, good or bad. Tartarus is the abyss I feel like I've jumped into with Alex's world." He paused, gently redirecting her. "You never answered my question about the bishop."

"Which question was that, exactly?"

"The one about—let me phrase it this way—did you kill him?"

"Of course I killed him. You knew that. It was probably the nicest thing I've ever done for anyone."

Chapter 27

Michael realized how little he really knew about Sindy Steele.

The concept of a single bodyguard made sense but, in practice, it was appearing to be impractical. Michael enjoyed some level of privacy. Leaving his office after a day of wall-to-wall meetings, he headed alone down Madison Avenue toward the St. Regis.

His thoughts alternated between visions of Sindy between the covers and trying to imagine how she could possibly have arranged to kidnap and then murder the bishop—and still catch her flight to Paris. The timing seemed almost impossible. Was she really capable of murder—or was she simply playing mind games with him? When he had tried to probe further with her on her comment regarding the bishop, she remained elusive, then seductive. "Stop thinking so much and just bury your face between my legs," she said. It was a line he knew he'd never forget.

His thoughts were interrupted by the ringing of his BlackBerry. It was his assistant, Karen DiNardo. Her voice brought him back to the moment. "I meant to tell you—before you rushed out—that your schedule of employees to be terminated was delivered on time to both Hightower and Mr. Perkins, so they should be happy."

"Thanks, Karen but, believe me, there's more trouble coming. They're not through with us. Wait until the details of the merger unfold."

"Are *you* in trouble?" she asked.

"I don't think so. They can't afford to lose me right now. I'm still newsworthy after all the publicity around my speech last year attacking Wall Street. Plus, you know how these things work. Senior management makes out like bandits. We'll all get bigger jobs, more money and big-time golden parachutes. In the meantime, the shareholders pay for it and the line-level employees lose their jobs."

"Boss, you know the game. Please, whatever they come up with—just take a deep breath before you react. Those two would love to find an excuse to push you out."

Michael knew that Karen was right as always. He had been brought on three years ago to turn around the company that was collapsing under the weight of several ill-advised acquisitions. Now, after stabilizing and rebuilding the organization, it just wasn't possible to deliver the unrealistic profits that his former boss, Dick Applegarden, and his current boss, Richard Perkins, were demanding.

"And speaking of your speech last year, that meeting is coming up again in L.A. in two weeks. Fortunately, you're not speaking this time, but Mr. Perkins wanted to confirm that you'll be there. He's going—along with Hightower. Do you want me to book you into the Peninsula?"

Michael thought about last year's meeting. His big speech, how a furious, red-faced Applegarden went up to him after he left the podium, cursing and threatening.

"No, book me into the Chateau Marmont. I've always wanted to stay there."

"Perkins' secretary wanted to know where you were staying."

"Tell her nicely to mind her own business. I like my privacy."

He continued his walk to the St. Regis but had only gone one block when he felt his BlackBerry vibrating. After fumbling around, he pulled it out of his suit coat pocket and, while continuing to walk, stole a glance at the notification on the screen: "Alex Nicholas changed his Facebook cover photo."

His mind took off in a million directions. What was going on? He was anxious to get to his laptop in the hotel. He and Sindy were going to order room service in the suite for dinner tonight. He knew he only had a short time before she returned for the night.

He sat on the couch in the living room, facing the front door of the suite so he couldn't be surprised by her arrival. Michael logged into his computer and then signed onto Facebook. He then typed in "Alex Nicholas" in the box for finding friends. He hadn't checked Alex's Facebook page since his murder. Why would he, of course? How many dead people change their Facebook cover picture? Only Alex, he thought.

Sure enough, the picture on his page had changed. It was no longer the one of Alex and his son at his seats at Yankee Stadium, the one that had been his Facebook cover photo at least a year before his death and, as far as Michael knew, right up until a few minutes ago. In its place was the interior of a church, facing the altar with a large gold cross just above it. Michael leaned in closer to the screen; as soon as he did, he knew for sure. It was the Greek Orthodox Church in Whitestone, Queens—the one where Alex's funeral had been held.

Michael immediately signed out of Facebook and clicked onto the icon for Alex.

"I figured that would get your attention," Alex said as soon as he appeared.

"What was that about? Are you trying to bring attention to

yourself?" Michael was annoyed. The last thing he needed now was questions regarding Alex. After all, Samantha was the only one he had shown the virtual Alex to—and even she didn't believe it.

"You probably didn't realize it but that would have been the view from my casket—if it had been open. Actually, I just got bored. Maybe I don't want my friends to …" he hesitated. Michael noticed a brief and rare look of vulnerability on his brother's face. "… to forget me."

Michael softened. "I wouldn't worry about that. Not yet, anyway."

Alex appeared to regain his normal, tougher composure. "I have some news that you're not going to like," he said, his expression turning unusually solemn, although Michael detected the slightest hint of a mischievous smirk. "It's about your mistress."

"I didn't expect you were going to do a Google search on her."

"Michael, I'm discovering that I can access things here that you wouldn't believe. I don't know how this has happened but it's like I can go anywhere and get inside anyone's email and even a lot of corporate internal email systems. My power seems to be growing. Anyway, I found out some interesting things about Sindy Steele that I picked up from some confidential documents that a dean at Stanford had saved in his email files."

"Don't tell me—she dropped out of Stanford medical school after two years," Michael said, hoping he'd beaten Alex to the punch. He'd seen it in the online background check he'd done—right *after* he hired her. "She fell in love with another medical student and I guess got her heart broken and never recovered."

"You're right—but I don't think that would be the headline if I was a reporter or something."

"OK, what would be the headline?" Michael could see that Alex was enjoying the intrigue and maybe some attention.

"You mean if I was writing an article in like the *New York Post*?"

"Exactly. Or the National Enquirer, take your pick."

"Try this one: 'Jilted female medical student murders her ex.' "

"OK, what's this all about?" Michael felt as though his Alex was toying with him, enjoying teasing his little brother like they were kids again.

"Is this your first affair?"

"Well, yes, it's the first time—and it'll be the last affair for me. This one won't last too long, either. I don't know, maybe it's the element of danger that I seem to suddenly like—but this whole affair thing is too complicated and I'm not very good at keeping stuff from Samantha. We're too close. Or we were. *Damn it, what did you find out?*"

"How soon do you plan on ending it?"

"I don't know, exactly. I have to admit, right now she's very useful to me. Not just for the sex. *What is it?*"

"Good. If I were you, I'd take my time and think very carefully before cutting things off with her."

Michael was exasperated. "What the hell are you talking about?

"It appears that a few weeks after her boyfriend—a William McGee—dumps her, he's found dead in his new apartment. No cause of death was immediately apparent." Alex appeared to be reading from some document or other computer screen out of Michael's range of sight. "The coroner initially ruled that the healthy twenty-six-year-old student had died of 'natural causes.' The press reports the next day stated that 'no foul play was detected or suspected.' "

"So—where does *murder* come in?" Michael said.

"Several weeks later, the toxicology results showed some, and I quote, 'disturbing yet inconclusive findings.' The medical examiner believed—but could not prove—McGee had somehow ingested a deadly but impossible-to-detect poison. By the way, do you happen to know what Steele's specialty was in med school?"

"No, what?"

"Try medicinal chemistry and pharmacology. I found out that records of the death, as well as an agreement leading up to her permanent departure from Stanford, were sealed as part of a settlement negotiated by her attorney."

Michael heard the crisp click of the electronic key lock on the front door of the suite. He looked up and saw the handle turning. She was back.

Chapter 28

Rome, Italy

Monsignor Petrucceli checked his watch and looked out at the dining room, searching for a familiar face. It was eight o'clock and every table at the ancient Ristorante La Campagna was filled with Romans enjoying dinner. The scene was a controlled chaos, mostly traditional looking, well-dressed families—in some cases four generations — seated around long tables, enjoying a festive evening of cheeses, salamis, artichokes, pasta and, perhaps, a sizzling bistecca. Bottles of the house red anchored each table. The brusque waiters, all men, uniformly dressed in white shirts, black suits and bow ties, roamed the room without a smile and with an occasional expression of annoyance.

Monsignor Petrucceli was already on his second glass of the *Morellino di Scansano 414*. Beginning to feel the warmth of the robust red wine soothe his nerves, his anxiety returned as soon he saw Joseph Sharkey being led by the maitre'd to his table.

"Joseph, sit down," he said, motioning Sharkey to the seat opposite him. As they shook hands, he remembered how odd it was that such a seemingly tough, fearless character could have such a weak, limp handshake.

"Good evening, Monsignor." Sharkey said as he poured himself a glass of wine, looked around at the other diners, their plates, and settled his stare on a particularly shapely woman seated at the next table.

The monsignor, wanting to bring Sharkey's eyes and attention back to the ground, said, "Joseph, it's good to see you. We have a lot to talk about. There have been developments."

Sharkey was attentive. " 'Developments'—what does that mean? I'm aware that my three little friends are no longer a problem."

"Yes, Joseph, they have found, as we say, everlasting peace."

"They were good men."

The monsignor, marveling at Sharkey's obtuseness, smiled, "Oh, I'm sure they were worthy of sainthood, Joseph. We will certainly miss them."

Sharkey's eyes narrowed as he looked across the table. The monsignor knew he had tweaked his companion's temper but continued to steer the conversation. "Joseph, you should also be aware that our mutual friend, Bishop McCarthy, is also gone."

This clearly caught Sharkey by surprise, his head jerked upward. "Gone? What do you mean 'gone? Where the hell did he go?'"

"He had a terrible accident."

"Monsignor, who do you think you're talking to here? What do you mean, 'He had a terrible accident?' "

"Calm down, Joseph. Everything is OK. The bishop was, after all, a liability. If you have been reading the papers, you will see that our Pope Leo is very distressed over all these pedophile priest problems. The church has, as he said, been humiliated. There will be no more tolerance for such behavior. I'm afraid Bishop McCarthy could no longer be protected."

"It was no accident. Who ordered it?" Sharkey was inflamed, yet obviously struggling to control his temper.

"The police believe he took his own life. He was found hanging," the monsignor said, trying to keep his voice low and calm, hoping his tone might help settle Sharkey down.

"Who are you kidding? I'm not some rookie, you know," Sharkey persisted.

"That is all I know right now. You must understand, the Vatican is made up of many layers, many separate fiefdoms. I am not privy to all that goes on."

But as he listened to Sharkey's ranting, the monsignor knew that he himself was the most surprised at this most recent turn of events. He also questioned the "suicide"—in fact, he had come to doubt all suicides and deaths by 'natural causes' of anyone under ninety who had certain dealings with the Vatican. He knew too much.

He thought back to his conversation with Hightower, who expressed his own shock at finding the bishop dangling in his garage. And several days before, the bishop himself mentioned that Michael Nicholas had been highly antagonistic toward him.

Hightower had sounded nervous on the call. He said he didn't think that Michael was capable of murdering the bishop—especially in such a sadistic manner—but he was afraid of this new female bodyguard.

He turned his attention back to Sharkey, who, having no clue that the monsignor's attention had drifted, was continuing his rant.

"Jesus, I don't like this. And what about Michael Nicholas? Everyone else is dropping like flies, but he's still traveling all over the world. He's still out there. He can screw me if he talks to the cops."

"Yes, we know, Joseph. He is the final remainder of the problem. The only one left who can expose you and testify. He is your only remaining vulnerability. He will be taken care of. You have my word."

"Monsignor, once Michael is dead, I can leave Rome and go back to the states. They can't touch me then." Sharkey suddenly smiled, "And, look at it this way, once he's gone, I'm out of your hair."

Monsignor Petrucceli sighed, shook his head and said, "Believe me, Joseph, every night I pray for such a miracle."

Chapter 29

Astoria, New York

Skinny Lester couldn't help but stare at the empty chair at the head of the long rectangular table it. He kept waiting for Alex to appear. Everyone did.

For the last twenty years, the fourteen men seated around the table in the private room of Piccola Venezia had celebrated Alex Nicholas' birthdays. This year was no different, except that Alex would not be there.

Alex's friends and his only son, George, had gathered—just as they did when Alex was alive. The event symbolized a loyalty that Alex had engendered at a time when friendships were fleeting and relationships transient.

Alex's buddies included an assortment of characters with legitimate and illegitimate businesses that represented the commercial lifeblood of the colorful borough of Queens and the larger city beyond.

Among those present were Alex's lifelong confidants, the boys who became men together; Fat and Skinny Lester, Lenny, "the Engineer," Joe "Bodyworks" Di, Phillip "the Florist" Phillips, and

Frankie "the Bookie" Feinstein. Others, like Pauly T and Vinnie G, had worked for Alex and, like the Lesters, were now employees of Tartarus, working for Michael.

The more legitimate business owners were talented and successful entrepreneurs. Phillip Phillips, a Greek immigrant who came penniless to America thirty years earlier was now the largest artificial flower wholesaler in the Northeast.

Joe Di, "the plastic surgeon," had always been introduced by Alex as a doctor. A fit, good looking guy with an ever-present tan and black, slick-backed hair, a sharp dresser, always attired in custom-tailored slacks and sport coat, was not, in fact, a Manhattan plastic surgeon, but the owner of Flushing Bodyworks, one of the largest auto-body shops in the city.

The night rolled on. The banter about sex, age, sports, and ex-wives continued through endless platters of stuffed clams, fried calamari, fresh jumbo shrimp, grilled Italian sausages, blocks of parmesan cheese and several bottles of Chianti and Pinot Grigio. But now the main courses—the spaghettis, veals and steaks—were served, including a plate of sizzling veal parmigiana respectfully placed in front of Alex's empty chair, and the talk turned to the absent guest of honor.

Skinny Lester pushed his chair back and stood tall, lifting his glass of Chianti up, as though to the heavens. "Here's to Alex. Alex, you were fucking crazy. You were one of a kind." His voice broke slightly as he struggled to keep his composure. "I miss you and I wish to hell you were here tonight."

As Skinny Lester sat down, Frankie the Bookie rose. "Yeah, you son of a bitch. Even though you're not here, we've still gotta pay for your fuckin' dinner tonight."

Looking at Skinny Lester, Joe Di spoke, "Lester, whatever happened to that computer thing Alex showed you one night? What was it? Some artificial intelligence game or app? Remember? Alex thought he could live forever."

Before Lester could answer, Frankie spoke up again. "Yeah,

Alex just wanted to be sure that anyone that owed him money would keep paying—even after he was dead."

But Skinny Lester was quiet, lost in thought over Joe Di's question. Finally, he began, "It was a few months before he was shot. We were sitting in his den and had a lot to drink. All of a sudden, Alex says, 'I've got something to show you.' He pulls out this laptop from a drawer. Not his usual computer. He was, like, hiding it. He opens it up, turns it on and—I couldn't believe it—Alex appears on the screen. Just like real life. It was crazy, man. Then he starts talking to it. He's talking to himself! And then, with God as my witness, it talks back to him. In his own voice."

Frankie looked on, straight-faced, "How much did you guys have to drink that night? Must have been more than your usual half a glass, huh Lester?" The entire table, including Skinny Lester, broke out in laughter.

But Skinny Lester continued and, as he spoke, everyone else, in an uncharacteristic show of attention, listened in silence. "I don't think he meant to show it to me because, after a minute or so, after the thing spoke back to him, he quickly turned it off and shut the lid. Then he made me swear I wouldn't tell anyone about it."

"What happened then?" Frankie asked, more seriously now.

"What happened? What do you mean, 'what happened?' He was fuckin' shot and he died. That's what happened."

The table was silent.

"I didn't tell anyone—not even Lester here," Skinny Lester continued, "until after Alex died. Actually, the first person I told was Michael, one day at the cemetery when we went to visit Alex's grave."

"Did Michael check out the laptop?" Frankie persisted as the rest of the table listened. Skinny Lester noticed that almost everyone, at one point or another, stole a glance at Alex's spot at the table. Almost, it seemed to him, as though Alex was there, devouring his plate of veal parmigiana while the conversation about him went on.

Skinny Lester continued, "Yeah, he did. Actually, Donna and George found it first but couldn't figure out the passwords. I guess Michael did eventually."

Frankie, looking frustrated, started waving his hands, "Yeah, then what? What did he find? What happened?"

Lester just shook his head, "I don't think anything really happened. Michael said he opened up the program and it was kind of interesting but there just wasn't that much to it. That was it."

Frankie laughed hard as the rest of the table exploded in near hysterics. "You mean Alex v. asn't able to do what all the scientists and computer experts in the fucking world have been unable to do? Because if he's alive in one of those freakin' computers somewhere, it'd be a shame you didn't bring the stupid thing and put it right there at Alex's seat. Maybe he could even eat his veal. You know, we could feed it into the computer."

George finally came to life, "Don't worry. I'm going to take my father's dish home. I'll have it for lunch tomorrow."

"Hey, I gotta tell you though, " Frankie added, "if Alex can eat his veal, he's also gonna get the check." Again, everyone at the table broke out in laughter.

But now Fat Lester cleared his throat. Normally quiet, he commanded attention when he spoke. "It's not funny, Frankie. You don't talk like that behind his back. It's not right."

"Oh come on, relax. Loosen up. There's no such thing as behind his back when he's dead, it's more like over his dead body, you know?"

Joe Di said, "I hear that Alex's business hasn't missed a beat. Sounds like Michael knows what he's doing. I must've been wrong but he looked too straight for the business."

Skinny Lester appeared to reflect for a moment, and then spoke. "Well, Lester and I both thought the same thing when Michael said he was going to keep the business open. We said, 'How's he going to do it?' But, I have to say, it's uncanny. He seems to know what the hell he's doing and he's been in some pretty tough situations with that crazy Sharkey and then Greta and all trying to kill him, for God's sake."

Fat Lester spoke again. "Yeah, it's almost like Alex's still around."

Chapter 30

New York City

Michael had not seen his brother's widow for nearly three months. When she called asking to meet, he guessed it was to let him know she was getting married. Donna wasn't a woman, he thought, who would allow herself to be defined as a widow for very long.

As they exchanged friendly kisses, Michael took in Donna's familiar scent, Alex's favorite, Chanel No. 5. Oddly, the fragrance always reminded Michael more of his brother than of the particular woman wearing it since Alex purchased the perfume for each of his wives and any mistress he was involved with. It was a quick way of identifying any woman Alex had seduced and just like the smell of cigar smoke reminded Michael of his long-deceased father, Chanel No. 5 instantly conjured Alex.

Donna was still quite young, thirty-six, and attractive. Alex's three wives were quite similar in appearance: each well-built and shapely. All three had great legs, which they invariably showed off with killer high heels. The older Alex became, the younger he married.

Donna had taken great care of herself, despite a healthy appetite for vodka. Her breasts, always prominently displayed, had been beautifully enhanced by Alex's plastic surgeon of choice, Dr. Armand Simonetti. After a few drinks, Alex would refer to them as "HDTs"—high-definition tits. The uplifted, plunger-shaped breast on a woman was another trademark of Alex's since, as with the perfume, each of his wives and his long-term mistresses all had been patients of Dr. Simonetti. Alex would pay Simonetti in cash—peeling off hundred-dollar bills—as the doctor left the operating room after each "boob job," as he so delicately referred to them. Dr. Simonetti gave Alex what he called his "groupie plan rates."

Cafe Cluny was one of Michael's favorite downtown restaurants. It was a trendy bistro on a cobblestone corner of the West Village with a laid-back downtown vibe that was different than a lot of his other frequent dining haunts. Michael and Donna were on their second specialty house cocktail, "The Cluny," an arresting concoction of Ketel One Citron, fresh lemon juice and ginger. Donna picked at her grilled shrimp salad. Michael admired his burger, very rare, sitting open-faced on the plate, oozing a creamy gruyere cheese and resting on a toasted bun. So far, the conversation had been routine reminisces peppered with saucy anecdotes about some of their mutual acquaintances.

Michael suspected that Donna had a specific reason for getting together, one that she had not yet disclosed. As soon as he wondered when she would press the "send" button, disclosing whatever it was that she really wanted to discuss, her face tightened up and she began to speak. It was coming.

"Michael, you seem to have adapted amazingly well to Alex's business. I have to say, I'm flabbergasted. You always impressed me as being just so different from your brother. And now you're still doing your regular corporate job—and you're running Alex's business and expanding it at that."

"I can't say I'm not surprised myself. After all, before Alex died,

I never even thought about bookmaking and loan sharking, let alone running an operation."

"More than that, Michael. Don't forget, you kept your distance from Alex and looked down on his business."

"Actually," Michael objected, "I never looked down on it. I just never had any interest in it and gambling never had any appeal to me."

Donna's attention span, like that of all of Alex's wives was extremely short. "Whatever, Michael."

"Anyway, what difference does it make now? We're all making money. Aren't you happy with your returns on your investment so far?"

"Of course, Michael, I'm delighted. It's not that."

She gave an uncharacteristic pause. Donna usually spoke her mind before the thoughts even entered. "It's just that, you know, Alex was a funny guy. He was capable of anything. I mean, the man was fucking nuts. And, I got to tell you, people are starting to ask a lot of questions."

"Who? What kind of questions?" Michael couldn't imagine where she was going.

"People, old friends of his, are wondering how you're doing it. You know, running his business, working with the two Lesters, handling the jerks who bet with him, dealing with the bad guys, paying off the cops—it's like, how could you do that with just your background? I mean, I know you ran some big businesses and all that, but this, this is totally different. This isn't some white-collar company. These guys are rough, some of them are criminals. But now, it's almost as if you and your brother are the same. Yet, you were always totally opposites."

"Well, I'll give you that it's very strange, on a number of levels. First, I have to admit, I'm really enjoying this. After all the years in a corporation working for someone else, this business is exhilarating. Maybe it's just in my blood, but it's like being a cowboy instead of a bureaucrat. Also, on another level, the businesses are, strangely, not that different. Third, I've got to tell you, the people in Alex's world, may be on the edge of being criminals—or over the edge— but there's a dignity and certainly a loyalty that doesn't exist in my corporate life."

Watching her eyes wander, Michael was sure he'd lost her. He realized how silly it was for him to give her an answer with three different points, and even worse, to actually number them as if he was in a meeting. All he needed now, he thought, was a PowerPoint presentation.

"Michael, I don't know about all that crap you're talking about. This is where you always get too complicated for me. All I know is, it's strange how you seem to have fit in so easily."

He was perplexed. "So, what are you saying?"

"Here's what I'm saying." Donna hesitated, took a deep breath, and then looked right into Michael's eyes. "Are you sure he's dead?"

Chapter 31

Alone in his wine cellar, Michael poured a second glass of white Bordeaux. Although he was anxious to speak with Alex, tonight he needed a little extra buzz to loosen him up before the screen came down again. Though it seemed impossible, life was getting more complicated.

Michael logged on to the computer. Alex spoke first. "You missed my birthday."

Michael recalled that, in fact, Alex's birthday had just passed two days earlier. "So did you. But how in the hell did you know that?"

"I'm linked in to some type of online calendar. I wonder if my old friends still got together for it at Piccola Venezia like they did when I was still alive for my birthdays."

"Actually, it's funny that you mention it because they did. I had dinner last night with Donna and she told me about it. I only found out later."

"Maybe they didn't think to invite you because you rarely showed up when I was alive. It was the only time I'd get out of a restaurant without paying for everybody. Anyway, how's Donna doing? Has she remarried yet? She shouldn't have any problems finding a guy with all the money and the new tits I left her."

"She's doing OK. I think she misses you. Or, at least the part of you that got along with her. I was surprised myself; I don't get the sense that she's seeing anyone on any kind of a regular basis."

"Kind of like Sinatra's first wife when they asked her why she never remarried, she said something like, 'After Frank, who?' You know, who could possibly fill his shoes?"

The ease of the conversation and the second Bordeaux had loosened him up. "I don't know if it's exactly like that but there's probably some similarity." Michael laughed.

"So how's the business going?"

"It's going pretty well. Paris is off to a good start. It's been very active and now we just got this new client, Bertrand Rosen, he's one of the biggest money managers in France. He's placed some huge action this week."

Alex's appeared to be puzzled as the image on the big screen zoomed in on him. "How'd you find this guy so quickly?"

"I first met him in Paris last year. He came up to me in a restaurant and introduced himself. I wasn't sure how he even knew me. "

"Does Catherine like him? Did she vouch for him?"

Michael felt that sense of doubt that he had suppressed rising up to the surface. "Well, actually, she knew him but didn't like him."

"Michael, be careful. She's a good judge of people. She's a prima donna, you know, a big actress and all that. But, she's been around. Don't give this guy too much rope until you're sure you trust him."

His anxiety heightened, Michael wanted to get on the phone to the Paris office but he still had more to discuss with Alex. He thought again about his dinner with Rosen and that uneasy—or just uncertain—feeling he had about him.

Michael brought Alex up to date on the "suicide" of Bishop Mc-Carthy and the somewhat unresolved question of whether Sindy had anything to do with it.

"What the hell are you doing? This can't end well. She's nuts, maybe worse. Are you still screwing her?"

"Yes, she's also helping run the business in some areas. You know, things Fat Lester couldn't do. She's tougher."

Alex's face flashed in anger. "Of course Fat Lester couldn't do it. Michael, we never did this stuff. You're in a different league than the one I played in. The most we ever had to do was threaten; maybe Fat Lester scared the shit out of someone every once in a while. You're talking murder, for Christ's sake."

"Alex, during my dinner with Donna, she mentioned something."

Michael noticed that, unlike in real life, the artificial intelligence technology allowed Michael to shift topics and Alex would follow. If Alex had been alive, he wouldn't have allowed such a volatile issue to end without resolution. Michael suspected, however, that the program was still "evolving" and that, at some point, this too would be corrected. For now, however, he was thankful for the ability to guide the conversation where he wanted it to go.

"She said that some of your friends think it's surprising how your business is going so well. They know that I'm new to it. They're surprised I'm able to keep it going, let alone expand it."

Alex was listening intently, his face appearing motionless, which was how he appeared when he was listening and digesting complex new information.

Michael pressed on. "I'm not sure yet if it's a problem but they suspect something. Donna asked me if I was sure you were dead."

"What did you say?"

Michael threw his arms up, "What do you think I said? No, I speak with you at least once a week? Of course, I said you were dead. I kind of laughed it off."

Alex stared straight ahead. "But I'm not dead. You know that, don't you, Michael?"

Chapter 32

Hollywood was not Frank Cortese's type of town. The Chateau Marmont was not his type of hotel; too many people and paparazzi. Cortese didn't care much for movie stars, at least not any under fifty. He felt disoriented, out of his element.

He entered the hotel through the garage in his rented white Buick, immediately distinguishing himself amongst the BMWs, Jaguars and Rolls Royces.

He took the elevator up to the main lobby which was too dark for mid-afternoon, the staff behind the reception desk a little too cool, too gay. He also sensed a condescending attitude that reminded him of his penniless upbringing in Calabria. To add to his insult, as he followed the young, sliver-thin bellman through the lobby back toward the elevator, he was jostled by two models, both several inches taller than he and in varying stages of undress, who were cavorting while a photographer with a heavy German accent was snapping away. To Cortese, it seemed that everyone he disliked was here in the lobby of the Chateau: the too-cool, too young, too tall, and too thin, mixed in with a bunch of gays, and Germans.

"This is a fucking zoo," he whispered. The quick-stepping attendant moved just a bit quicker when he heard it.

Besides, Cortese could not be photographed, and certainly not in Hollywood on the day he was to kill Michael Nicholas.

As he settled into his room, he looked around and was surprised at the old, almost worn look of the room and its furnishings. "What's all the fuss about here?" he said to himself.

Although it was now time to acquaint himself with the hotel and its grounds—and to begin to orchestrate his assignment, he couldn't stop thinking about the scene moments earlier in the lobby and the photographs in which he feared he would appear. He would have to find that photographer.

Cortese knocked on the door of Room 48. He waited a few seconds and knocked even harder. He could hear some muffled cursing and then the lock turning. The door opened and Cortese looked up at the disheveled photographer, dressed in a navy blue robe, wearing traditional bedroom slippers, his long silver hair in disarray. Stein was an intimidating figure, clearly even more so when his sleep, despite the late afternoon hour, had been interrupted.

"Mr. Stein. I believe some of your photographs this morning may have included me in the background. I need to have them."

Stein squinted, looked at his visitor as though he was crazy and said simply, "Go fuck yourself."

Cortese's face tightened. "Stein, I need those pictures."

"You're an idiot. That's why you woke me up? You were in a public place. Leave me alone." Stein then abruptly slammed the door shut. Cortese stepped back to avoid being hit by the door that stopped inches from his burning face. As he turned back toward the elevators, he knew that his plans for the evening would have to change. Before anything, he'd need to get those pictures.

Chapter 33

West Hollywood, California

The first thing Michael noticed as he and Sindy entered the lobby of the Chateau Marmont were the gorgeous models. He purposely inhaled their perfumes, all mixing together as the girls passed near him, seemingly unaware of his presence. Handing over his black Amex card to the all-black-attired Chateau Marmont front desk clerk, Michael knew he would never come closer to the fantasy of Hollywood than the stage he had just stepped onto.

"Welcome, Mr. and Mrs. Nicholas, I see this is your first time staying with us," the clerk said, in an indiscreetly loud voice for the muted lobby. You'd think, in L.A. of all places, they'd know better, Michael thought. What happened to this being the most discreet hotel in Hollywood?

As he waited, he looked around the lobby, thinking of the endless parade of celluloid ghosts who had walked through there before him: Garbo, Gable, Harlow, Taylor, and of course, John Belushi, whom, he recalled, checked out early.

Unlike last year's global business and press meeting, Michael had no formal role. He was simply an attendee and planned on relaxing while he was here.

For Michael, the Peninsula Hotel in nearby Beverly Hills was no longer the happy place where he and Samantha would go to luxuriate and escape. So he and Sindy Steele entered Room 29 together at the Chateau. Tonight he would take her to one of his favorite restaurants in L.A., one that Samantha never liked.

Michael loved Frank Sinatra. Maybe it was the life; late nights, partying until dawn; the constant parade of admirers; the easy women, showgirls, mistresses and multiple wives; the ever-present Jack Daniels; Las Vegas casinos; punching out drunks and reporters. Actually, the more he seriously thought about it, since Michael didn't care for most of those things, maybe it was just the concept of Frank Sinatra that appealed to him.

He left his car at the curb with the valet and, with Sindy in tow, entered La Dolce Vita, one of the late entertainer's favorite Beverly Hills restaurants. Michael thought of Sinatra and how he must have felt, decades ago, walking under the same green canopy and through the restaurant's dark, stone, cave-like entry. He could imagine Sinatra might have felt like he was entering a secluded refuge from the prying eyes of celebrity watchers and paparazzi.

Once inside, they were seated in one of the red leather banquettes near the tiny marble bar. Glittering glasses and bottles reflected in the surrounding mirrors. The gold-framed oil paintings, soft lighting, and the arched, red-brick, windowless walls, reinforced a feeling of being sheltered, secure in an Old World, and safe from the dangers outside.

But instead of the dining room being filled with Sinatra's Rat Pack, it looked like a new Hollywood, mixed with those seeking to recapture the old one—one that would never return.

After a round of cocktails, he enjoyed his lobster *fra diavolo* as he watched Sindy twirl her spaghetti with salmon in vodka sauce. Suddenly, she seemed distracted, her head following something moving through the room. Michael tried to follow in the direction of her darting eyes. "What's wrong? Is there something over there?" he asked nodding in the same direction.

"It's probably nothing. I just thought I recognized someone. A man, he's gone now. He went by earlier, to the bathrooms. He looked vaguely familiar, but I really hardly saw him."

Michael could hear the low buzz of his vibrating BlackBerry. It was Skinny Lester calling.

"Michael, we just made a fortune this week. Your friend Rosen may be great at picking stocks but he stinks in this game. He's lost or is losing every game he took and none of the horses he bet on even showed. You'd have to be pretty unlucky to miss as consistently as he's doing right now. He's going to be in to us for over a million."

Michael took a few seconds before responding. "I guess this is good. I mean this is one of the biggest scores we've made but, I don't know, it's not the best way to start out with a new client. I'd prefer that the guy had *some* success. We don't want to spook him or leave a bad taste in his mouth right out of the box. Frankly, he's more valuable than a typical client who, over any period of time, is always going to lose. You know, giving us maybe a smaller but steady income. Not such a dramatic wipeout as this."

"I know what you mean. Anyway, the rest of the reports coming in from both New York and Paris are pretty good. We're going to have a great week. I'll have the final numbers later tonight."

"Sounds good, Lester."

Like the legendary television detective Columbo, played by Peter Falk, Skinny Lester had a habit of adding on to a conversation just when it appeared to be over.

"What do you think Rosen is up to?"

It was as though he had read Michael's mind.

Chapter 34

West Hollywood, California

The Paris Vogue shoot produced the images the magazine desired, a sexy, sultry collection of young women and high fashion. Despite his seventy-plus years, Herbert Stein felt like a young man tonight. An afternoon nap, a swim in the hotel pool and the warm yet invigorating California air made him feel twenty years younger.

The only blemish on the day was the man with the odd eyes who startled him out of a deep sleep earlier in the day. Stein wondered who he could have been—and what was he up to that made him want those pictures? Most likely he was having a liaison with someone other than his wife.

He took the down elevator to the garage. Stein lived at the Marmont for months at a time, so he always self-parked his car in the hotel's garage, a small frugality.

Although German by birth, he loved America—and Cadillacs, especially the newly designed models with their sleek style and state-of-the-art electronics. He unlocked the doors with the press of a button, sat in the soft, black, glove leather seat and watched as the dashboard lit up when he turned the ignition. As he prepared to back the car out of his designated space, he noticed a shadowy figure passing by behind him, visible in the corner of his sight in the rearview mirror. Before he pressed the accelerator to back out, he heard the simultaneous clicking as each of the four doors locked electronically, a feature he hadn't noticed before.

He maneuvered the car out of the garage and onto the short narrow driveway leading out of the hotel grounds. As he began the drive out, he was surprised to see the dashboard flash on and off, the electronic dials performing a glittering yet brief light show. He checked to his left and it was there that he saw the strange angry man who had confronted him earlier in the day. He was standing, alone, his cell phone in his hand. The man's eyes—he remembered them—were strange.

He felt a surge of power as the car suddenly lurched forward. He took his foot off the accelerator, instinctively switching to the brake pedal. Then, as though a bomb had gone off inside the car, he was instantly blinded by an unworldly white flash of light obscuring everything, as some physical force violently slammed into his face and shoulders, pinning him back against his seat, knocking the air out of his lungs. At the same time, he felt his seat belt lock further securing him, paralyzed, in place.

It took a few seconds for him to realize that the Cadillac's air bags had deployed. Momentarily relieved, the air bag quickly deflated, his brain recovering and his vision restored, he knew something in the car had gone wrong. After all, the car had lurched forward—the air bags must have deployed to keep him safe. The car slowed nearly to a stop. He was badly bruised but alive. Thank God.

He looked around him, outside his driver's side window. He saw some young men and women walking up the driveway. Momentarily frozen, they stared back at him, like himself, probably trying to digest what had occurred. They began shouting and appeared to be coming to his aid. He felt a sharp pain in his right arm; it was likely broken.

With his left hand, he gripped the door handle to open it. The door remained locked. He tried pressing the button on the door panel to release the locks but nothing happened.

The dashboard again lit up, its LED lights flashing wildly. He looked outside around him and once again saw the man who'd confronted him. They exchanged glances. Herbert Stein knew he needed help. He mouthed the words, "Help me, please." But the man smiled and appeared to turn back to his cell phone. Stein mouthed the words he hoped the man could read, "Son of a bitch."

He was relieved to see the young people from down the driveway finally approaching his door. The first young man was about to reach for to the outside handle when Stein felt the engine suddenly begin to race and, once again, the car thrust forward. He looked ahead—he was catapulting down the embankment in front of the hotel's driveway, heading toward Sunset Boulevard. As the car jumped the curb, he felt his head hit the roof. His foot pressed down hard on the brakes, but nothing happened. He saw the look on the faces of pedestrians who watched open-mouthed as he sped by, encased in his sealed Cadillac. The steering wheel was locked.

Directly across the street he saw the concrete wall. The car accelerated even more, beyond what he thought possible, the new thrust driving his head back into the seat and then knocked hard again into the roof as the Cadillac powerfully jumped up and over a curb. As the car bounced back onto the street, he glanced at the already deployed air bags lying limp around him. Herbert Stein knew he was going to die.

Chapter 35

West Hollywood, California

Sindy was still asleep. Michael, in his white terry cloth bathrobe, stretched out on the couch and looked out the large picture window to the city where dreams were made. His eyes caught the front page of the morning's edition of the *L.A. Times* on the table directly before him. The headline read, "Famous Fashion Photographer Dies in Car Crash." Stunned, he picked up the paper and read further:

"With the help of several eyewitnesses, the LAPD was able to reconstruct the last moments of Herbert Stein's life. According to the hotel guests who had been in the parking area of the Chateau Marmont, it appeared that Mr. Stein stepped into his car and, as he began to drive away, the Cadillac suddenly and violently accelerated, crashing into a concrete wall on the opposite side of Sunset Boulevard. He was alone in the car. Mr. Stein was pronounced dead upon arrival at Cedars Sinai Hospital. Police are pursuing two theories behind the accident, speculating that Mr. Stein may have suffered an incapacitating stroke, thereby losing control of his car and are also examining the vehicle for a malfunction in its acceleration parts, possibly caused by electronic interference with the car's advanced computer system."

Looking forward to his morning pot of coffee and hot croissants, Michael opened the door as the server rolled in the room service cart. As the aspiring actress set the table for breakfast for two, she saw the newspaper opened to the article about last night's death of Herbert Stein.

"Oh my God, wasn't that terrible?" she said, whispering after she noticed Sindy in bed through the open door to the bedroom.

"Yes, it's unbelievable. I saw him doing a shoot in the lobby when we checked in. I always admired his work." Michael said.

"That's not all, someone broke into his room right after and stole all his pictures and his cameras. Can you imagine? I mean, the poor guy's barely cold and you go and rob his room. I mean, what's the world coming to?"

She put the finishing touch on the perfectly set table, looked again at Michael and, after a sigh, said simply, "May I pour your coffee?"

Chapter 36

West Hollywood, California

Frank Cortese took his special cell phone in hand and headed down to the hotel garage. He knew his way by now. He'd already installed a GPS tracking device under the body of Michael's rented black BMW sedan.

Monsignor 007—the Vatican's equivalent of James Bonds' Q who headed up the MI6's gadget lab—had supplied him with his newest technological breakthrough, the "Car Crasher." Once linked through a Bluetooth connection to certain high-tech cars, like the latest model BMWs, the app allowed Cortese to cyberhijack and take over most functions of the car through his cell phone.

He knew that Michael and Steele were scheduled to be at the UCLA auditorium for the annual global business conference in the morning. Tonight, he would connect his device to Michael's car and, in the morning, wait for him to drive away, following him until he saw the proper location—either over a cliff or into a barrier at a high speed—to send Michael and his girlfriend into oblivion.

He knew that Monsignor 007 wouldn't be happy once he found out that he'd used the device for two jobs in the same city in two days, but the photographer had interfered with his plans. As long as the accident didn't occur too close to the Marmont, he felt any connection between the two was unlikely to be made, after all, the police were still convinced that Stein's car simply malfunctioned or he'd had a stroke.

Not seeing Michael's car as he entered the garage, he switched onto the GPS function on his phone. He looked closely at the screen waiting for the indicator to point him to the car. Thinking there was a mistake, he looked closer. The car was in a parking lot at LAX airport.

Chapter 37

"**W**e're being taken over." His words seemed to echo back to him inside the executive conference room at Gibraltar Financial's Manhattan headquarters.

Michael's statement wasn't news to Karen DiNardo, who had been privy to his conversations and correspondence with Perkins and Hightower. He knew that Maggie O'Brien had been down this road before. Like Karen, she had worked for Michael Nicholas for several years and, like Karen, she had been through corporate upheavals before. The only surprise was the exact timing.

"The announcement had to be accelerated, that's why Perkins and Hightower canceled their trip to L.A. and I had to come back early. Not that I cared much about attending the conference this year."

Michael appreciated the fact that Maggie had not come to corporate America through the usual channels. After graduating Trinity College in Dublin, she had been a nurse and a professional bartender, tending the famous curved bar, the same one James Joyce rested his glass and elbows on, at Davy Byrnes Pub on Duke

Street in Dublin. Michael had often thought that perhaps dealing with the sick and sometimes inebriated was one reason that Maggie had become so talented in her job as a highly successful senior executive of a major American financial institution.

Unlike Karen, however, she was not aware of Michael's venture into the underworld of his brother's business. Not that it mattered. Today's crisis had only to do with Gibraltar Financial, the legitimate firm that Michael led. The firm that was no longer bleeding millions each quarter.

Michael's sixtieth-floor office overlooked Fifth Avenue. He had a clear view of the rooftop pools, gardens and luxury offices and penthouses, a view that "makes you feel like the whole world is rich." Today, he thought, it seemed a fitting backdrop to the coming debate about the widely divergent fates of those in power—and those who are powerless.

"What does this mean?" Maggie asked, although Michael knew that she knew.

"Cartan's official line is, of course, that nothing will change," he said.

"Yes, the corporate takeover equivalent of 'the check's in the mail.'" Karen said.

"But, everything will change, of course." he said. "We're going to have to eliminate another two hundred jobs. And Cartan Holdings is going to leverage the purchase, pull several million in equity out of Gibraltar and finance our takeover with our own equity. So they pocket another ten million and add it on to our books as debt and then we have to meet these additional debt payments out of our earnings."

"Do they understand that once we make these cuts and add on the debt that we won't be that profitable?" Maggie asked. He could see Maggie's Irish temper flaring up. She was back in Davy Byrnes Pub.

"They know but they'll turn around and sell off Gibraltar before the shit really hits the fan."

Santana's "Black Magic Woman," coming from Michael's BlackBerry, interrupted the discussion. He knew it was Sindy and excused himself, quickly walking out of his office into the hallway. He made a mental note to change her ringtone.

"It's not a great time. Is everything OK?" he whispered into the phone.

"Not really. Lester was right. It's even worse than we thought. Rosen's bets were a wipeout for him. He's into us for well over a million. It's like a worst-case scenario. He's a zero with the ponies and the games."

Michael braced himself for the rest of the story. He glanced back at his office and the agitated Maggie O'Brien. He wondered which one of his two lives at that moment were the least painful. "Are we going to have a problem?" he asked.

Steele was all business, "He's told Skinny Lester that he can't pay right now."

Michael's voice was no longer a whisper, "You've got to be kidding. This guy is one of the biggest hot shots on the planet. What do you mean he can't pay right now? What does that mean? Not today?"

She cut him off, "Not ever."

Chapter 38

Paris, France

As Steele arose from the steamy depths of the Paris Metro, at the Ecole Militaire station, she couldn't help but admire the view. The River Seine was behind her, just feet away, while towering blocks ahead and dominating the sky, stood the grand Eiffel Tower.

But she was not there to sightsee. She walked slowly past the outdoor market, admiring the hundreds of French cheeses, some firm, others oozing a soft cream; fish of every conceivable variety, so fresh they appeared to be staring back; bright red filet mignons and racks of lamb; pink hams; dark red and white-speckled salamis; terrines and foie gras; and delicate rich pastries and custards; all on display for the passing pedestrians. It was a gourmet's delight. She walked the hundred feet to the Pont de l'Alma, crossed the Quai d'Orsay and proceeded down Avenue Bosquet until she reached the address she was looking for, number four, a well-preserved, ten-story apartment residence. She looked at the small directory with the names of the residents alongside a small black intercom button for each apartment. When she saw the listing,

"10F: B. Rosen," she pressed the button and waited to hear his voice and the buzzer signaling the unlocked lobby door.

Her stilettos clicked on the black and white marble floor. The elevator was small but looked like a delicate mahogany and polished brass jewel box. The ride up to the tenth floor was agonizingly slow despite the adrenaline rushing through her body. Finally, the elevator door opened and she pulled open the collapsible brass gate. An ornate spiral staircase was directly in front of her. As she passed it, she looked down to the lobby floor from which she had just arisen. Rosen's door was just a few feet from the elevator.

The front door was already open, and there stood Bertrand Rosen waiting for her, smiling, his eyes open wide. As she entered the apartment, he seemed pleased, if not incredulous, that she was there. She nodded, walked by him and through the opened door. With her high heels, she was several inches taller than him. She could feel Rosen's eyes following her, leering she was sure, at the back of her long slim legs and tight skirt.

"Madame Steele, what a pleasant surprise. And to what do I owe the pleasure of your visit?"

"Perhaps we could have a glass of wine?" she said.

"*Bien sûr*," he answered in French as he motioned her to the living room and headed to the kitchen to fulfill her request. She took a quick stroll through as much of the spacious apartment as she could see without causing suspicion. A large, rotund cat rubbed up against her, purring.

"May I use the toilet?" she called out.

After determining that they were alone, she returned to the living room and sat on the long white velvet couch, just as Rosen was entering with two Baccarat crystal goblets of Sancerre. To her surprise, he sat down on the couch too, just close enough to make it clear that he misjudged the purpose of her visit. Perhaps worse, she thought, he had clearly misjudged her.

He motioned as though to make a toast but she ignored the gesture and took a long sip of her wine. But she was certain that

Rosen had misjudged again. Looking into her eyes he said, "Don't be nervous. I'm delighted that you came."

But she wasn't nervous. Instead, she took her first sip, then looked around the room and began her mental calculations, assessing the physical surroundings and situation and comparing it to the detailed options she had run through in her mind before arriving.

She placed her glass on the coffee table. Rosen did the same. He looked into her eyes.

She clutched her Louis Vuitton handbag and inserted her right hand inside, gripping the silencer-equipped HK45 handgun, still out of sight from Rosen and, abruptly, stood up. He remained seated, clearly unsure of what was happening. She moved to the other side of the coffee table, thereby putting several feet between them.

"Bertrand," she said, dispensing with the formalities of French address, "this is not a personal visit. This is business, strictly business. Mr. Nicholas' business. You have a debt which must be paid."

His head jerked back ever so slightly, perhaps the recognition on his part that she was not attracted to him or his riches.

"But, of course, it will be paid. Very soon. Of course."

Something in the exuberance of his smile, a subtle hint of French or male condescension—or perhaps it was just her own intuitive sense from having dealt with people on the edge of desperation—whispered to her that he was lying.

"When exactly will you pay us?" she asked.

"In due time, in due time, my dear."

Still hidden inside her bag, she placed her hand on the pistol handle and inserted her right index finger into the trigger. "The money is owed now."

"But, madam, we are speaking of an extraordinary sum of money, over a million euros..."

She cut him off, "Had you won, you would have expected several times that from us—and immediately."

"Perhaps, you are correct. Nevertheless, I am not in a position to pay you at this moment." His smile was gone. His expression had turned from amusement to tension, even anger. "How dare you come here demanding money? Who do you think you are? My business is with Monsieur Nicholas, with Michael. Not with you."

"I'm leaving here with cash, a check or some negotiable instrument which I can take directly to your bank."

His look was incredulous. "Madame Steele, I suggest you leave my apartment."

She pulled the gun out of her bag and, with both hands, leveled it at him. If the appearance of the steel black pistol alone wasn't enough, she was sure the addition of the long silencer convinced Rosen that the threat was imminent and deadly. His mouth opened slightly, his eyes looked back into hers.

"Very well, I will do whatever you want. Or at least, whatever is possible." His face softened, appearing to relax or, perhaps, it was resignation. "I have little to lose."

"You have your life to lose," she said softly, wondering what he meant.

"I have no money, no money at all. And, therefore, perhaps not much life either."

"Who the fuck are you kidding? You manage billions. Maybe I'm imagining this place," she looked around at the Louis XIV furnishings, the Matisse and Picasso oils on the walls in their ornate, gold frames, the silk drapes, the large floor-to-ceiling windows. She continued, revving up her own anger, "Your villa in Cannes, your penthouse in New York. A million either way can't make that much difference to you."

He looked down, his eyes nearly closed, sad. "I cannot pay you. I'm sorry. I can't explain it now but it will soon be evident to you, to everyone."

"That's not good enough. You think I'm going to believe you?" Motioning toward the large window, she said, "Go over there and open the window."

He hesitated.

She lifted the gun, aiming it higher now, toward his head. "I don't think you're in a position to defy me. Move!"

"Killing me will not get you your money." His voice was soft, cracking.

"It doesn't look like we're going to get it anyway. And we can't stay in business allowing people to walk away from their debts. Go to the window and open it."

He shrugged and walked across the large living room to the wall of floor-to-ceiling, square-paned windows, opening two of the large panels. As she stepped several steps closer to him, he turned back toward her. "Are you going to shoot me or push me? What is it that you want?"

She smiled, "Maybe I'll give you the choice. But what I really want is our money, Bertrand. I would prefer not to kill you but I will if I have to. I think you know that."

"But, you see, I have nothing to live for," he said, calmly.

She wondered how that could possibly be. Was this a well-orchestrated bluff by Rosen? Either way, had she exhausted her leverage? No, there was more to this situation, more to Bertrand Rosen than she could figure out at this moment. Perhaps, she thought, she had made her point. He was certainly scared—but, oddly, appeared almost resigned, ready to die. Too ready. She was missing something. Perhaps he was stalling, almost as though he was waiting for something … or someone. Had he pushed a security alarm button without her seeing it? And, if there was any chance he would pay up, there was no point in killing him. Not now, not yet anyway. She'd push just a little harder; she had to find out what he was hiding. Then, she could reevaluate her next move.

The warm air flowed into the room, neutralizing the chill of the air conditioning. She could see a sliver of the steel side of the Eiffel Tower. The fat cat reappeared, purring and rubbing against her leg.

"Give me a portion of what you owe us, write the check right now, or my first shot will cut through your knee. Then, we'll work up from there."

He looked at her, laughed and said, simply, "Fuck you."

It was then that Bertrand Rosen, without even appearing to look, threw himself headfirst out the window. She rushed to the window and looked down just as his body hit the sidewalk. A dull thud carried up the ten floors. She immediately ducked back into the room, took a deep breath, gulped down the remaining wine in her glass, placed the glass in her bag and proceeded toward the door.

But just as she was preparing to turn the polished brass door handle to make her hurried exit, she heard the doorbell ring followed by the sound of a key in the lock—and then saw the handle turn.

How the hell could anyone possibly get up here so fast, she thought. Her mind was racing, she had seen that the sidewalk was empty when his body hit, so whomever it was, they had to have been on their way up *before* Rosen went out the window. They think he's here.

As the lock was turning, she ran several feet in the opposite direction from the entry hall and into what appeared to be a coat closet. She tucked herself securely inside, leaving the door ajar an inch or so. As she again gripped her gun, she hoped the person entering was not the maid.

She watched from her perch as the front door swung open. It was a woman but she couldn't get a good look at her face. "Bertrand, are you home? It's me. Are you on the phone? Bertrand?"

Steele knew the voice. All too well. Her heart racing, she watched as Samantha Nicholas cautiously entered the apartment, leaving the front door open as she proceeded down the long hallway to the living room on her left. And just as Samantha entered the room, Steele silently slipped out the front door, calmly removing her high heels and walking quickly yet silently down the ten flights of the building's ornate circular stairway.

Her high heels back on and clicking loudly now on the black and white marble floor, she exited the empty lobby. As she walked out the doors and stepped onto the sidewalk, she turned to her left, away from the direction from which she had arrived twenty minutes earlier and from the small group of men huddled over a body on the sidewalk to her right.

Chapter 39

Michael watched as Fletcher Fanelli took a heaping portion of the fried calamari and dipped his warm garlic bread with its melted mozzarella cheese into the bowl of Mario's famous red marinara sauce.

"I can do my daily duties as police chief in this town in about two hours. Our crime consists of shoplifting from Walgreens and a couple of DUIs each week. Once a year, a bunch of punks might travel up Route 95 from the Bronx figuring they can rob what looks to them like the 'small-town' Bank of America branch and then get back on 95 and return home with their loot. Just as often, one of my guys picks them up for speeding on their way out of Westport, making us look like J. Edgar Hoover."

"I know, since your promotion, you've seemed less excited about things. It's like something went out of you. Yet, you're the youngest police chief in the town's history. You should be pumped."

"The odd thing about my promotion is that now I'm bored to death. Half the time I'm working on budgets or appearing in front of some half-asleep committee. I'm frustrated and I don't have the patience for the town's politics. I guess I'm itchy for a little danger."

"Listen, I really need your help with this, but I don't want to put your career in jeopardy."

"I'm not taking any greater risk with my career than you are with yours. I didn't get into police work because I wanted to clean up the world. I became a cop because it was a good job, they were hiring and it paid well. I plan on remaining chief for a few years and then starting my own private security firm. In the meantime, as long as we're reasonably careful, I'm going to help you as much as I can and if I can make some extra cash doing it, it gets me where I want to be even faster. Angie spends it quicker than I can make it."

"OK then. It's nice to have someone besides Sindy watching my back."

"I have to be honest with you, that woman scares the shit out of me." Fletcher was afraid of very little in life. He sipped his Manhattan and looked around the restaurant at the early dinner crowd. "And now Bertrand Rosen lands on the sidewalk."

Michael frowned, "Fletcher, I hate to admit it, but she scares the shit out of me, too. But I'm not sure exactly how to deal with it. She swore to me she didn't push him. She went there to threaten him. She was shocked when he jumped out the window."

"So, she had nothing to do with it? It was just a coincidence that this guy with an incredible life decides to just commit suicide while, of all people, bingo, Sindy just happened to be visiting his apartment?"

"Life is full of coincidences. I only said—that *she* said—she didn't push him. She threatened him with her gun, told him to open the window, gave him a choice, asked him again for at least some partial payment and then he said 'fuck you' and jumped out the window."

"Oh yeah, that's very different. Don't forget she first said she hadn't touched that bishop either, or was it just that she left him hanging?" Fletcher sat back, laughing. "You must be in pretty deep with her."

Michael looked away, sighed, and said, "Deeper than I should be."

"Listen, what you do with her privately is none of my business. I don't care who you're screwing around with. It's murder that I'm worried about."

Fletcher went silent as Mario's owner, Tiger, pulled up a chair. "So what are you two rocket scientists up to?"

Michael answered, "Samantha's in Paris with Angie, shopping."

"Are you two crazy? You guys are strange. Next time, why don't you just give them an expenses-paid trip to the Short Hills Mall or something like that? Paris, Christ almighty."

Before Fletcher or Michael could answer, everyone's eyes moved to the front door of Mario's, which had just swung open. Chambers Galore, the famous '70s porn star and Westport native, accompanied by two younger versions in cut-off shorts and sneakers, walked in, tanned, toned and giggling, and approached the bar. Tiger squinted through his glasses and rose up from his chair, "Jesus, Mary and Joseph."

Chapter 40

I t was time to ask Alex again—the question no living person could answer.

Michael continued to be astonished at his brother's growing mental capacity—especially his reasoning and judgment. It was unquestionably Alex except—instead of the slight but steady deterioration of his mental capacity with his advancing age and the effects of unrestrained alcohol and tobacco use had he lived—now his mind seemed to get sharper each time they spoke. He knew he needed to engage Alex's help in tracking the people trying to get to him, but this was, after all, the biggest question of all.

"Alex, one time I asked you what it was like to be dead. You said you just didn't have enough information to answer at that point. But you've really grown over the past year. This is nothing like when we first started to speak after, you know, you were killed."

Alex looked back at Michael. His mannerisms were precisely as he remembered him in life, no matter how many times Michael saw him on the screen. It was still uncanny. "The system was designed to learn as it acquired more information and input. I told you, I'd eventually be smarter than I really was in life. And that's not easy."

Michael could see a new vibrancy, a spirit, in Alex's face that he had not seen for many years, perhaps before the inevitable disappointments of life and the stresses and wear from his three loopy wives.

"It's almost like I'm on drugs, on steroids. It feels good. I think I've finally got all the alcohol out of my system. Although I must admit, I miss a drink at times."

Michael paused and looked back at Alex. "Alex, what's it like? What's it like to be dead?"

Alex stared straight ahead then shut his eyes. Now he looked to be in pain or just lost in thought. Perhaps this question, Michael thought, required an extraordinary amount of time for Alex to assimilate, or compute. He worried; had he overstressed Alex, or the software? Was the gravity of the question an overload?

But Alex came to life. His eyes opened wide. "I don't feel dead. I'm not dead. I feel like I did before but, it's different in some ways. There's no time."

Michael could feel something happening. He felt a wave of something, a surge of feeling, of emotion, pass through him. "What do you mean, 'no time'?"

"I don't know how to explain it. It's different though. It's like time stands still. Or there is no time. Without it, everything's different. It's like I know what I did yesterday, I know what I'm doing now, but I also know what I'm doing tomorrow. Except, there really is no breakdown of time like that. It's all one, although it's not like I can tell you which horse is going to win the Preakness."

"That's too bad." But as intriguing as Alex's last comment was, Michael had bigger questions on his mind.

"Alex, is there a God? I mean, have you met him—or her? Have you seen *anyone*? Another person?"

Michael wasn't sure himself whether he was being serious or joking. He knew the entire situation was surreal yet it was happening. His brother was on this computer screen and they were carrying on a conversation much like they did before Alex left this earth. Except for the subject matter.

"Is there a God? How the hell do I know if there's a God?" Alex looked at Michael with the sarcastic expression he would often show when he wondered if someone was simply crazy. He was agitated. "I exist because you see me. I'm not here until I hear from you. Yet things seem to go on. But, it's not like there's some hotel up here that I'm staying at with people and angels—and Saint Peter's not at the front desk."

Alex paused and seemed to be thinking. Michael stayed silent, sensing Alex had more to say.

He started speaking again, his mood seeming to shift. "It's like I said. It's different. I'm alive, I'm here. But there's no order, no sequence to things. It just *is*—when it is at all. I don't know how to describe it."

Michael sensed that their common language couldn't accommodate what Alex was trying to communicate. "Alex, don't worry about it. Anyway, one reason I brought all this up is because both Lesters want to go to the cemetery tomorrow. I said I'd go with them."

Alex's face took on an expression of confusion. "I've never thought about the cemetery."

Michael was intrigued. "Do you know where you're buried?"

Alex paused, then answered, "Saint Michael's in Astoria."

"How did you know that? Do you remember the burial?"

Alex laughed, "No one can remember their own burial. It's like your own wedding—the whole event just flies by. What are you guys going to do there anyway?"

"What does anyone do there? You know, I don't generally go to cemeteries but I think both Lesters miss you. I guess it's their way of feeling closer to you or something."

"Tell them it's a waste of time. No one's there."

"What do you mean, 'No one's there?' Your body's there."

Alex, expressionless, said simply, "If you say so."

Chapter 41

Astoria, New York

I nside Saint Michael's Cemetery, Fat and Skinny Lester and Michael surrounded the white marble gravestone, each of them looking down at it as though expecting some response to their words, perhaps their prayers but, at the very least, their stares.

Michael focused on the inscription:

Alex Thomas Nicholas
Aged 61 Years
"Going, going, gone."
R. I. P.

"It's always so strange to see the name of someone you know–" Michael quickly corrected himself, "ah, knew—etched in stone." Michael had been to this cemetery many times before; he remembered the same feeling when he'd seen the names of his parents on their gravestones.

Years ago Alex had joked to Michael that he wanted his grave epitaph to be the signature home run call of the late Yankees announcer Mel Allen, and so it appeared. All who knew Alex well agreed it was fitting, not only because of Alex's love of baseball but for the subtle sarcasm on life and death that it represented.

"I still can't believe that he's down there, in that fucking box." Fat Lester said. He looked grizzled and rough, wearing baggy khakis and an old wrinkled and worn sport coat.

"I don't believe he's there either," Michael said, thinking, *if you guys only knew* ... Then, out of the corner of his eye, he noticed a man, in the distance, walking swiftly between the gravestones. He was heading in their direction.

Both Lesters turned and looked at Michael. He looked back; wondering what they were thinking.

"I'm only saying that I don't believe that what's buried matters very much. It's just symbolic. If there is anything after someone dies, I doubt it's in their grave."

But as Michael looked again for the figure he'd spotted, a black sedan drove slowly up the gravel, oak-tree-lined road. It stopped and, to everyone's surprise, a tall man in a flowing black and gold embroidered robe stepped out of the passenger side and walked the short distance to meet them.

Michael had not seen Father John Papadopoulos since Alex's funeral last year. A large man, in height and girth, made even larger by his ornate, billowing holy robes and his long grey beard, he brought a haunting yet Hollywood-like presence to a graveyard. He knew it was crazy, yet Michael sensed there was a greater possibility of God's existence when he saw Father Papadopoulos. They all watched as he approached.

"God's here," Fat Lester said.

Father Papadopoulos reached out and embraced Michael.

"My son, how are you?" he said. He then looked over at the two Lesters as they introduced themselves. Michael was amused as he watched the two atheist Jewish guys looking in apparent fascination at the odd embodiment of another time, another world.

"I'm good. It's good to see you again." Michael said. "What brings you here? Did you know that we were going to be visiting?"

"No, I was doing a visit with another parishioner here," he said, motioning back to the car with its driver still behind the wheel. "I saw you as we were passing and wanted to stop and give you my good wishes." It sounded plausible but Michael was dubious.

A short distance behind the car, Michael again saw the stranger. Like an apparition, he thought. But the stranger turned around and walked in the opposite direction. He was leaving. Perhaps, Michael thought, the presence of the Greek priest with all his black robes and crosses frightened him off. Or was it just someone keeping a respectful distance.

Looking over toward Alex's grave, Father Papadopoulos said, "And how is our brother Alex?"

Fat Lester coughed, Skinny Lester cleared his throat as Michael shot them both a stern glance.

"He's quiet," was all Michael could muster in response. Yet he felt an urge to confide in the priest who perhaps could help him reconcile the ancient world of the Scriptures with this new technology that had somehow brought Alex back to life. He wondered if Papadopoulos' rigorous Greek Orthodox religious training, his connection to thousands of years of theological thoughts and beliefs, would allow him to accommodate this new technological phenomenon as a further evolution of the holy philosophy. With all his own assumptions about life and death now in disarray, Michael longed for the childhood comfort that the church provided with its all-knowing view of life and eternity. The one comfort he wanted back more and more, the older he became.

But he knew better. Just as abortion threatens the devout living, immortality through technology would threaten the dead, challenge the concepts of the hereafter, of heaven, hell and, perhaps worst of all for the pious, of consequences and redemption. No, Father Papadopoulos might not be a receptive ear.

Papadopoulos moved slowly to Alex's grave. He first stood

directly above the headstone, folded his hands in prayer and then, as though speaking to God, looked up while continuing his whispered words, appearing certain they were being heard. He finished and came back to Michael.

"May I speak with you alone for a moment?"

Michael leaned in close to Papadopoulos. Fat Lester looked on; he seemed suspicious of the priest.

"Michael, is everything OK with you?" Papadopoulos looked concerned.

What in the world is he asking? Michael thought. Is this about Samantha, his marriage, Tartarus? Or, perhaps ... "What do you mean, Father?"

"I mean, how are you handling Alex's passing? I believe he's in a good place, a better place but I know, for those of us here or those of us who, at times, question our faith, it's not always easy to see this."

Michael didn't know where to start. "Father, first, of course I question my faith. But, listen, I question everything. Unfortunately, to me, almost nothing is certain. I live in the grey, for better or worse. I know a lot of priests who tell me that even *they* question their faith at times. So, of course, I do too. I miss Alex. How can you not miss a big brother? He's the last link for me to my parents. Everyone else is gone. It's like a small piece of them still lived here as long as Alex was alive. Now, they only live in my mind, my memory, or my imagination."

Michael looked at Father Papadopoulos but couldn't determine if what he had just said had gotten through. Michael couldn't read what he was thinking. It seemed to be true for a lot of people with whom he was communicating lately, he thought.

"Father, is that what you meant?"

"Not exactly, my son. I called upon your sister-in-law, Donna the other day. She confided in me, some fears, some concerns, perhaps rumors. She told me that she has already spoken to you about them."

"Yes, she did speak with me over dinner. She asked if Alex was really dead." Michael's tone was curt yet he was actually confused. After all, Alex was dead, at least in the sense that everyone understood death to be. Yet Alex was very much alive, as only Michael knew. But everything was turning grey.

He continued, "No one knows better than you, Father, that Alex's body—dead body—was in his casket. You helped close it yourself at your altar at the church."

Father Papadopoulos looked at Michael, his face brightened, "Yes, I know. But the Lord works in strange, miraculous ways."

Chapter 42

It was the first night out for Samantha since her shortened shopping trip to Paris. Dinner with Angie Fanelli in the familiar comfort of Mario's seemed like the perfect antidote to the horror she had just left on Avenue Bosquet.

As they began their evening's voyage with champagne cocktails, Tiger dropped by their table.

"So, how are the desperate housewives tonight? And where's the chief and mister president?"

"The chief's at the station, or so he says." Angie said, laughing. "Probably watching the Yankees on the television in his office."

Tiger looked at Angie with his own sly smile. "What does the chief do with that gun he carries anyway?"

"He cleans it," Angie answered, totally serious. "Regularly."

Tiger turned his attention to Samantha, who had finished her drink in record time.

"And where's your boy?"

Tiger was just what Samantha needed to lift her spirits, at least until the vodka did its job.

"He actually went to the cemetery this afternoon with some of his brother's friends, the Lesters. He might be joining us before we leave." Samantha knew as soon as she said it that it was doubtful. "Although I haven't heard from him since earlier in the day."

As Tiger moved on to another table, Samantha knew she had to tell someone. And there was no one better to tell than Angie. She watched the disbelief on her friend's face as she told her the story. The way Samantha had unlocked the door of Bertrand Rosen's apartment—with the key he had offered to her just the day before. The way she turned the lock and slowly opened the door …

"Samantha. Tell me more."

She continued her story, seeing everything in her mind as though she was still in the apartment on Avenue Bosquet.

"It was so eerie. I walked in, into the living room. I called out his name. Nothing, no one answered. Then I saw it. One of the big windows in the living room was open. The curtains were gently rustling. The little breeze I had felt was coming from the window. I walked all the way in, still calling out, 'Bertrand, it's me.'"

Angie Fanelli sat, speechless, her hands covering her mouth.

"So I walked over to the window. But, I knew. I don't know how I could have or why I would've assumed anything like that, but, I knew. I knew he'd jumped."

"What did you do?" Angie asked.

"I went to the window and I, I didn't want to look down but I knew I had to. So, I leaned on the windowsill and stuck my head out. I looked down. It was like ten stories. I looked and I could see something on the sidewalk. I couldn't tell for sure, I was too far up but I could see it, him, on the sidewalk. Then I saw some people below. They were frozen. Everything seemed to stand still for a second. It was like a dream, a nightmare. The world just stood still for whatever period of time it was. Then, like ants, they started moving toward him, running." And then Samantha just stopped speaking, her eyes gazing off, somewhere else.

Angie was on the edge of her seat. She reached across the table and took Samantha's hand, rubbing it. "What happened then, what did you do?"

"I'm so ashamed. I turned around and walked out of the apartment. I was so paranoid, I could swear someone was watching me, but as I was walking toward the door, I looked around. There was no one there. So I left and took the elevator down and walked out of the building. There was a whole commotion not too far from the door. I knew it was him. I walked the other way. I didn't want to look. I couldn't be seen there. I just walked away and walked all the way back to my hotel. I threw the key in a trash can. I … was just trying to get back … at Michael."

"Are you going to tell him?"

"No, not ever."

Samantha finished her drink and watched as the patrons of Mario's went about their business of eating, drinking, talking and dreaming. As her eyes scanned the dining room, she saw a man enter who appeared to know no one and whom no one appeared to know, which was rare inside Mario's. Her eyes followed him as he took a seat at the bar. She wished she wasn't driving home alone.

Chapter 43

Donna Nicholas, formerly Donna Finkelstein, was, to Michael, the least objectionable of his brother's three wives.

He arrived on time at Campanile, an old and aging restaurant on East Twenty-Ninth Street, and sat, alternately sipping and admiring his Blue Sapphire martini with its two green olives in the simple but elegant, classic martini glass.

Michael watched as the front door swung open and the eyes of the waiters, busboys and bartender turned toward the slender, tanned woman with perfect, uplifted breasts, a short skirt, inches above her perfectly proportioned knees and slender thighs. Making immediate eye contact, she strolled right over to his table and kissed him on both cheeks. He remembered the days following Alex's death when Donna begged him to help her sort through Alex's life and finances.

Donna sat down, ordered her Grey Goose cosmo, looked around her at the near empty dining room and, probably disappointed in the absence of potential admirers, exclaimed, "Well, Michael, we'll certainly have a quiet dinner tonight, won't we?"

As soon as they placed their dinner orders, he decided to get to the point.

"I just wanted to follow up on our discussion the other night at Cafe Cluny. You know, your question about Alex?"

"You mean the one about whether he was really dead?" Donna smiled and laughed lightly. "Michael, I know my crazy husband is dead. I'm not some nutcase. I know how you think."

It was typical Donna, he thought. One minute asking serious questions and the next, laughing them off. He made a mental note to check her medicine cabinet for OxyContin the next time he went to her house.

"No, come on, that's not what I meant at all. Listen, I went to the cemetery today with the two Lesters. Cemeteries never meant much to me but they wanted to go. It's funny how these two guys are so sentimental."

Donna interrupted, "You're trying to tell me that Fat Lester of all people is sentimental? Michael, that guy doesn't even think. He just grunts and eats. Jesus. And Skinny Lester, I mean, he's supposed to be some kind of genius. Alex thought he was so smart. He looks to me like some old, drugged-out, burned-out hippie. These two were Alex's groupies—his male ones anyway."

Michael could see he would have to fight to keep the conversation on point.

"Maybe I thought the same about both of them too until I started working with them on a daily basis. But Skinny Lester *is* very smart. He's a genius at assessing odds. If he was twenty-five, he'd be at Goldman Sachs trading derivatives. Anyway, he's smart. And Fat Lester is a gruff, tough guy on the surface but, you know, that works well in this business. No one wants to cross him. People pay their debts knowing he's around. The reality is he's almost harmless. He's a softie underneath—most of the time. And he really misses Alex. Don't forget, he had no other friends."

Donna's eyes were wandering.

"OK, let me get back to what I started to say. While we were at the cemetery, Father Papadopoulos drives up."

Donna broke in again. "Do you remember, at my wedding reception, how he came in his big robes and hat and all that, and put his hand on Alex's shoulder while Alex was eating. Which, by the way, was his first mistake. That's like messing with the dog when he's eating. Anyway, he said something to Alex like, 'God bless you son.' It was pretty funny. Alex, he's still swallowing, puts his fork down and turns to look over his shoulder at him—this Holy Father, you know—and said, 'Get your fucking hands off my shoulder.' You could hear a pin drop. I thought my parents—and yours—were going to die. It was funny, though. Alex had no patience for pompous people."

Michael had to laugh. "Yeah, it was classic Alex. I guess it's what we all loved about him—but what was also frightening at times. He was brutally honest."

"But you were always different, Michael. You were more respectful. I think in some ways your brother always admired that about you."

"Maybe, who knows?" Michael had exhausted any further desire to reminisce. "Father Papadopoulos took me aside and said he'd spoken to you. He said you had concerns about whether Alex was really dead."

She seemed to be taken aback. "Michael, please. Yes, I did speak with him and I brought up that question. I was confused. Maybe I just wish, in my heart, that he somehow really was still alive. I know it's crazy. I'd just spoken to a bunch of his old cronies after, you know, that birthday party that they just had for him. He wasn't there, of course."

Michael interrupted, "*Who* wasn't there?"

Donna was getting frazzled, "I meant Alex—the birthday boy—wasn't there. Jesus, I was kidding, Michael. Lighten up, will you? This is like talking to your brother. I loved him—some of the time—but he was a pain in the ass. Especially if he'd had a drink or two. Or ten."

"So what was the rest of your conversation with Father Papadopoulos?"

"As I was saying," she continued, rolling her eyes, "I told him that some of Alex's friends thought it was spooky how you, his straight little brother, who less than a year ago didn't know how to buy a fucking lottery ticket, was now running Alex's business without skipping a beat. Forget about the fact that you've made it even bigger than Alex could ever have imagined."

"Yeah, so what was the point? I mean, where were you going with it? Do you think I had a brain transplant or something or that we really dug Alex back up from the grave? Or, that somehow, we faked his shooting and death in front of a restaurant half filled with cops that night?"

"No, of course not. But one of the guys at dinner mentioned that Skinny Lester had talked about that computer that Alex had hidden. The Apple with that 'live forever' software or something on it."

"You mean the 'artificial intelligence' software?" Michael corrected.

"I don't know. I don't understand any of this myself. I think the priest got a little offended or, at least, annoyed. After all, he's the one who gave the eulogy. He buried him, for God's sake. You know, this whole artificial or virtual life thing, I had the feeling from him that it's like we were messing in his area or something. Frankly, he and Alex never got along. As I was saying, Alex never really liked priests."

As the waiter placed a seemingly delicate, paper-thin veal cutlet parmigiana sitting atop a delicate tomato sauce on the table, the restaurant erupted to the music of Billy Joel's "Uptown Girl." It was Michael's BlackBerry ring tone for Samantha. Looking at the phone and then Donna, he said, "Excuse me. I wouldn't take this except it's Samantha."

"Send her my love," Donna graciously offered.

He pressed the "Accept" button and, turning away slightly from Donna, put the phone to his ear. His wife's voice was low, she was whispering, or, was she crying? Michael knew something was wrong, very wrong.

Chapter 44

Florence, Italy

Cardinal Angelo Lovallo and Monsignor Dominick Petrucceli shared many secrets together; none more damning than their relationship with Joseph Sharkey.

After an exhausting day of academic meetings examining the spiritual implications of Brunelleschi's dome, Cardinal Lovallo looked forward to enjoying a quiet evening with his confidant, and eating the classic Florentine, charcoal-grilled steak at his favorite restaurant, Trattoria Omero, tucked inside an old stone farmhouse high up in the dark hills overlooking Florence.

He sipped his glass of 2004 Antinori Nobile di Montepulciano and listened as the young monsignor recounted in painful detail the "accidental" deaths years ago of the young men who were about to testify against the pedophile Bishop McCarthy; the murders of Morty, Nicky Bats and Lump in the basement of St. Joseph's Catholic Church; the garage hanging of the esteemed Bishop McCarthy; and, now, the aborted attempts to kill Michael Nicholas. But he took comfort as he looked out the trattoria's tall windows at the lights twinkling in the hills and the city of Florence. He inhaled the aroma of the steaks searing over the open charcoal oven nearby.

The cardinal spoke, his eyes still gazing out at the black hills, his mind seeming to drift to another time, "Dominick, it was here, very close to this trattoria, that the Church, Pope Urban VIII, banished Galileo for promulgating the theory that the Earth revolved around the sun. It was heresy at the time. He lived here under house arrest for ten years until his death."

The cardinal paused, his attention shifting to another thought. "Dominick, when will this be over?" he finally said, speaking softly in between bites of his first course, a golden, quill-shaped pasta in a rich red meat sauce.

Petrucceli appeared momentarily confused over the question, then answered, "Soon, I believe. We must consummate the mission regarding Michael Nicholas. He has been unusually elusive or fortunate so far. Mr. Cortese had expected to be back in Rome by now. I won't burden you with those details."

"I can imagine, Dominick. I can only imagine." The cardinal was tired; he was worried about this matter but he was hesitant to show Petrucceli how deeply it troubled him.

Petrucceli continued, "Frank just followed him into a Queens cemetery, but it appears that divine providence stepped in and, of all things, a Greek Orthodox priest unexpectedly presented himself, joining Nicholas and his friends, again making the assignment too risky to complete."

"Yes, my friend, the last thing we need in all of this mess is trouble from the Greeks. They are almost irrelevant—even in Greece—yet they believe the heavens are their exclusive domain."

The waiter placed a sizzling steak for two on the table, swiftly dividing it between the two clerics' plates. No words were exchanged; he nodded and went about his business.

"Tonight, Dominick, I feel all of my seventy-two years, perhaps more." The cardinal could see his young protégé watching him. He wasn't sure if what he sensed was fatigue—or fear.

"Angelo, you are like a father to me. Please, I have a difficult question. You need not answer it if you are uncomfortable."

"What is it, my son?" the cardinal asked, but he knew. He knew the question that was coming. He could read it on Petrucceli's face.

"Are you concerned that, as we proceed with what we believe to be the work of the Church, that, maybe, the times have changed, that, more to the point, perhaps the Holy Father seeing this change has altered his position? Perhaps, he no longer believes that men—men like Bishop McCarthy—need to be protected for the good of the Church. And if that is so, then all that we are doing to shield Sharkey and his crimes may no longer be valued by our Pope. All of these nasty deeds which I have just described to you—and the forthcoming elimination of Michael Nicholas—all of this has been done to pay back and protect Sharkey, who did us a favor by eliminating those unfortunate boys that McCarthy abused, and to protect him from arrest and exposure which would come right back to the Church."

His protégé had spoken his worst fears for him; its implications seared through to the pit of his chest. Angelo Lovallo sat back in his chair, as though simply taking a break from his meal.

"My son, I don't think there has been a substantive change. I am privy to many internal discussions, as you know. The pressures on Leo are enormous. Nothing is hidden from the eyes of the masses today. It is a different world. Our Pope must adapt on some level."

Petrucceli lowered his voice to a whisper. The cardinal struggled to hear him and moved in closer. "He has met now with victims, he's accepted the resignations of the bishops from Miami and Dublin. More are to come. Are you not concerned that our actions now, should they ever come to light, may no longer be quietly sanctioned by the Holy Father? Is it possible that we are alone in this endeavor?"

The cardinal reached across the table and gently grasped the younger man's arm.

"Dominick, we are never alone. We are doing God's work. As in war, actions are acceptable which would not be proper in peacetime. So it is today, with us. The Church is under siege—spiritually, morally, financially, socially—and extreme measures have to be undertaken. It is normal, it is right to question. But our mission is a holy one and it is understood at the very highest level. I promise you, my son."

With that, the cardinal released his grip, lifted his knife and fork and proceeded to finish his steak. "So what is the latest news on our plan to remove Mr. Michael Nicholas from this world?"

Monsignor Petrucceli's face brightened. "The New York Yankees will be playing the Boston Red Sox over the American Memorial Day weekend coming up. Michael will be attending the game, sitting in the box his brother Alex owned for years. It will be the season finale for him."

The cardinal listened and sighed, "It's a blood sport, this game of baseball, isn't it, Dominick?"

Chapter 45

L eaving Mario's, Samantha waved good-bye to Angie and breathed in the unusually cool air of the late August evening. It was eerie weather, she thought, just before a storm. A major thunderstorm had been predicted for later in the evening. Samantha had just enough to drink to enjoy a buzz and still be able to safely drive home, just across the narrow little bridge over the Saugatuck River inlet.

As she approached the house, she was thankful to be getting inside before the storm. She wondered, as she did on so many nights now, if Michael would be joining her, or, would she be spending the evening alone. Until a year ago, when Alex was shot dead and Michael entered his brother's world, Samantha and Michael spoke constantly, each knowing exactly where the other one was almost at any given hour. It was different now. They were together only by accident or for carefully orchestrated trips abroad.

She thought back to her dinner in Paris with Michael, Bertrand Rosen and Sindy Steele. It was then that she knew for sure that Steele had entered her marriage. Now, Steele had become a constant presence in Michael's life. Was Michael in love with this woman or was she a convenient, attractive and available mistress? But Samantha knew one thing for certain: she needed to deal with it—and that loomed over everything.

As she lay in her bed in the large house, she could hear the repetitive crack of the thunder, still far in the distance. The bedroom was dark except for the flashes of light preceding each clap of thunder, erratic strobe-like sparks bringing a brief but crisp clarity to the bedroom, the empty bedroom.

Tonight she hoped that she would hear the soft rumble of the automatic garage door opening, the brief buzz of the burglar alarm and then feel Michael's presence, distant though it had become, in their bed.

She turned over in the bed, but her thoughts began to win over her desire to sleep. She remembered the terrific bottle of very fine aged cognac sitting on the table in their wine cellar. She got up from her bed, turned on the lights and headed downstairs.

The door to the basement steps was slightly ajar; Michael always closed it, she habitually left it open. She must have been the last one to go down there, although she was unsure how that could be given Michael's regular trips down there for wine ... or to "play" with his computer.

No sooner had she reached the bottom of the steps, the power went out. Despite its rich-town reputation, Westport seemed to be losing power with each snowstorm, hurricane or thunderstorm. She only had several feet to go to reach the wine cellar, simply grab the bottle of cognac and head right back to the bedroom where they had stored the candles and flashlights.

Just as she turned the corner at the foot of the stairs, she was relieved to see a glow of light coming from the half-opened door of the wine cellar. It would make the rest of the way a lot easier, she thought.

Until she took her first steps and she saw the man from the bar at Mario's.

The door to the wine cellar was open, his large flashlight illuminating the room. He was holding two bottles of wine and staring at Michael's computer. She began to turn around and head back upstairs when she heard Alex.

Chapter 46

Westport, Connecticut

Rizzo guided his powerful searchlight around Michael Nicholas' basement. He had disabled the backup power system and activated the cell phone signal disabler. Samantha would be unable to communicate. The house was his.

But to his surprise, he heard the ring of his own cell phone. "What the hell?" he whispered, now regretting he had purchased the cheaper, Chinese cell phone disabler. He pulled the phone out of his pocket, looked at the screen identifying the caller, and decided it was one call he wanted to take.

"What's the matter, buddy, trouble sleeping?" he said softly into the phone while continuing to look around at the different parts of Michael's basement that were illuminated. "She's asleep upstairs. I've got their alarm system disabled and all their power off. There's a big thunderstorm here so even if she notices, she'll think it's from the storm. Hopefully, she didn't hear my phone go off. It's not the best time for a fucking chat, you know."

He opened a heavy door and flashed his light into the room.

"Shit, this guy knows how to live. You should see the wine cellar he's got here."

"Actually, I sleep very well but I figured this would be good timing and I didn't want to miss this moment," Joseph Sharkey said.

Just days ago, Sharkey had called him. For years, Officer Rizzo would take envelopes stuffed with cash to overlook Sharkey's various activities. For years, they knew they both shared the same bookie, Alex Nicholas, but this call quickly led to the realization they both had a common enemy, Michael Nicholas. Sharkey told him that Michael would soon be taken care of but getting Samantha first would be a way to ensure that he suffered before his own demise.

"John, don't get sidetracked down there. Take care of her," he said. Rizzo could feel his old friend's familiar insanity.

"Hey, stop worrying, partner. I'm just going to grab a few bottles before I leave. I think this is expensive shit here. We can drink them when this is over and you and I celebrate."

"Listen, you stupid fuck," Sharkey was screaming now. "Forget the booze, get the job done. And I want you to send me the pictures. Don't forget."

But Rizzo continued to look around, fascinated. "There's a lot of computer stuff down here too. I wonder what he needs all this for?"

Chapter 47

Rizzo knew he was pushing Sharkey's buttons and enjoyed knowing that his new partner—with a temper much like his own—was thousands of miles away and helpless. "Hey, Joseph, I'm thinking maybe I should take some of this computer equipment he's got here. I know some guys who'll pay—"

"Rizzo—are you nuts? Who the hell wants his computer crap?" Sharkey was hollering again.

"Maybe there's something good on it? Who knows what—" But Sharkey wouldn't let him finish. Rizzo placed his hand over the phone to muffle the sound. He laughed, "Relax, you crazy old man." He knew that would really get him fired up. "Why won't let me get Michael at the same time. I could just tie *her* up and wait for him to come home and do them both; her first so we still get the maximum benefit, you see what I'm saying?"

"John, I'll come there and kill you and her myself if you screw this up. Tonight just get rid of the bitch. Then wait for Michael to come home. These priests here are so fucking afraid of being caught; I don't know what the hell they're doing. I'd have finished him off a long time ago if I was there myself. Once he's gone, the cops can't touch me, they've got no one to testify about anything. I've got to get back, I'm going totally nuts here."

Rizzo was hardly listening and, instead, was looking for a bag or box in order to put aside some of Michael's wines. There was no way he was leaving without some wine.

"Don't worry man, I won't touch the computers," he said, deciding to just leave some bottles of wine out on the floor. He'd come back downstairs after he finished his work upstairs.

"OK, listen. I'm going to take care of things now and call you later."

He knew it was time to head upstairs but he saw something—a trace of light near the computers. He moved in closer and saw an Apple laptop. It was partially open; the screen flickering on and off. Perhaps Michael had left it on or forgotten to properly shut it down. It must be on its battery power, he thought. He opened it up and began poking randomly at the keys.

Alex Nicholas appeared on the screen.

At first he thought it was a computer photo album. "Hey, Alex," he said, laughing while speaking directly at Alex's image. But, just as he continued to leave, Rizzo could swear he heard Alex's voice.

"Rizzo, what the fuck are you doing in Michael's basement?"

He turned back and put his face close to the computer screen. "Alex? What the ..."

"I said, what are you doing in Michael's basement?"

"What is this, a fuckin' joke? Are you hiding somewhere? Where are—"

"Never mind where I am, you asshole. I'm more alive then you're going to be."

Alex looked so real, his voice, the way his face looked, his expressions. But Alex was dead. Or had he faked his death to hide for some reason. Yet, something was slightly different, a little off. He couldn't put his finger on it.

"Hey, what happened, Alex—did you owe out a lot?" Rizzo was laughing.

"If *you* want to stay alive, get out of my brother's house. Now..."

Rizzo kept laughing, but it was now a nervous laugh. He didn't know what to make of this, except he needed to finish what he'd come to do.

"Alex, just stay right where you are. I'll be back." No longer laughing, he turned to leave, but he heard Alex, still speaking.

"...And put the wine back."

Chapter 48

Westport, Connecticut

The only light was from the sporadic bolts of lightning, preceding a house-shaking clap of thunder. She moved back around the staircase, hiding herself from the intruder's view. She pulled her cell phone out of her robe's pocket and pressed 911. "Call Failed" lit up on the screen. And with the power out, she knew the house's phone system would be dead too. She could feel an impending panic attack battling her survival instincts.

She peeked back around the corner of the stairway, watching the man whose face appeared to be glued to Michael's computer. Although there was no power for the projection unit, the laptop had an internal battery.

She was afraid to move, afraid to make a sound now. She gripped the handrail and looked again, staring at his face while he appeared to be mesmerized by the computer screen. Was he seriously speaking to Alex—just as Michael had done that night? Is that why he came to their house? Or had he simply stumbled on the computer while doing whatever he was doing in the basement? And why did he have two bottles of wine in his hands. Was this a simple burglary?

She heard Alex's voice again—and the man laughed and quickly turned to leave. She saw his face more clearly. He was definitely the man she saw at the bar in Mario's.

She stared a moment too long: he had seen her.

She had to get out of the basement. She turned around and quickly took the first step back up the stairs. Samantha and Michael had built the house ten years earlier. She knew every square inch, every step, but it was different in the dark. Turning to her right, she reached for the familiar feel of the thick curved oak handrail and began her cautious climb to the first floor.

As she reached the last step, she again fought the urge to panic, to just crumble onto the floor. But she had to keep going, through the blackness, aware that her imagination—in addition to any real intruder—was her tormentor, able to strike without warning with each step she took.

She had a slight head start on him, he wouldn't know which way she'd turned at the top of the steps. It was her only advantage.

Now on the first floor, she turned to her left into the hallway that would take her to the breakfast room and then into the kitchen. On her way there, however, she would pass the door, on her right, to the powder room. It was always shut.

She placed her hand along the wall on her right as she moved. Her mind flashed back to scenes from the old movie thriller, *Wait Until Dark*, and she was the blind Audrey Hepburn, desperately trying to evade her own intruder. She reached out into the void, expecting to feel a body, a person, perhaps a muscular arm patiently waiting to grip her own. But she felt nothing until her hand, trembling, touched the partially opened powder room door. Who had opened it? Had this man actually gone to the bathroom when he arrived? Could there be more than one? She quietly continued along her way; the breakfast room was just ahead.

She reached out and grabbed the edge of the dining table, then the backs of a series of chairs, as she made her way through the breakfast room and toward the kitchen.

She could hear him coming up the steps. She turned around and could see an erratic spiral of light from his flashlight coming through the open basement door several feet behind her. He seemed to be playing it cautiously, not rushing headfirst and full speed after her. She had a chance.

A flash of lightning hyper-illuminated the kitchen ten feet in front of her. Another clap of thunder shook the house, vibrating her already-brittle nerves. She could feel her cell phone but she had no time to stop and look at it, even if it did work. She pressed a button without even looking, hoping something, maybe Michael's speed dial would work. She tried to stop crying.

She finally entered the kitchen. And then she heard him again. The creaking floor, a sound she swore in her mind that she could actually feel, as though the plank flooring beneath her feet were carrying the vibration right up her spine. She had to keep going. Standing still wasn't an option, not here, not in the dark. Where to now? The garage. The car. Lock the doors, press the electric door opener, and drive? But what was waiting for her between the kitchen and the car? Even if she made it to the car, she still had to get in, lock the doors, and try to back out while this man might be smashing her car window to get to her. She'd seen it in countless movies—and her worst nightmares. No one ever got away.

Another bolt of lightning silently flashed through the room, followed by thunder. But the light reflected onto the nearby black granite kitchen counter and in that split second, she thought she saw something amiss. The incongruity entered her brain before the visual image itself could appear in her sight, in the internal movie playing out on the darkened screen in front of her.

As she stepped forward, she moved her hand to the butcher block where the sharp knives were stored—and saw the empty slot where the largest knife should have been. Then the room went dark again.

She thrust her hand forward and gripped the first handle she could find, removing a weighty knife from its slot. She knew she had to keep moving. The mudroom and the back door leading to the patio and swimming pool were just ahead; the dining room and the main entry hall leading to the front door were behind her. Oh, God, this was no time to have to choose; she couldn't afford to pick the wrong door.

The back door would lead to their secluded yard and pool. She feared the attraction of the black pool water to her killer. She visualized herself again; this time being trapped, in the dark, unable to see the face of her pursuer. No final flash of recognition or understanding. A motive she'd never discover, even in the last moments of her life.

The path behind her, to the front door, she thought would be her best bet. But, as she turned, she heard a noise, the light creaking of the floor. He was getting close. It was time to go the other way, to the mudroom and out the back door. She started and suddenly felt a blow, she'd hit something hard, knocking her feet out from under her, her knife grazing her thigh as she fell. At first, fearing it was him, she tried to scream, but no sounds came out. She felt her own warm blood dripping down her leg. She realized she'd run into two cases of wine that had been recently delivered and were still stacked on the kitchen floor.

Now he'd know exactly where she was.

She got back to her feet and bolted out of the kitchen. Now she had to get out of the house. With the butcher knife still in her hand, she willed her legs to move. She knew the distance by memory—six or seven large, quick steps through the last room, the mudroom. She made it to the door and reached for the doorknob—but the door was wide open. Was this how the intruder came in? She had no choice, she had to keep going. She could feel him behind her, closing the short distance between them. No matter what, she said, I'm going to hurt him, scar him. He may kill me, but they'll be able to find him.

She stepped quickly out the back door, the cool night air focusing her. She was outside. Another sharp clap of thunder and a sequence of flashes. She could see the reflection of the swimming pool to her left and outlines of the patio furniture straight ahead. And then dark again. She felt he was behind her, but was no longer sure of how far. She could feel the goose bumps across her back. Was he somehow already *outside*, waiting for her to literally run into him? The lightning struck again. She saw no one in front of her. Nothing was moving, but the shrubs were tall and thick. They could hide anyone. The sliver of moonlight and the brief disconcerting bursts of lightning were all she had—both combined to illuminate fragments of life as she always knew it: the green manicured lawn, bluestone patio, Brown Jordan chaise lounges, the gas grill, the dark blue swimming pool.

She knew it was strange yet all she could think about at that moment was how much she loved her backyard.

Chapter 49

As he searched for her, Rizzo pictured Michael seeing his wife's body—just before he too was to die, slowly, regardless of what Sharkey wanted. Michael had humiliated him, leaving him nude, handcuffed to his elevator railing, for all his neighbors to see. Now he would pay.

But he couldn't help wondering what he'd *really* seen on that laptop downstairs. He was anxious to tell Sharkey. How had Alex—no, the computer—known to call out his name? He kept hearing it in his mind, "*Rizzo*, what the fuck are you doing in Michael's basement?" And how did he know about the wine? It had to be something with a camera—but where was Alex, if it was him at all?

He entered the mahogany, book-lined library. His flashlight traced the numerous books, the leather-framed family pictures. He knew he was in Michael's private sanctuary. *That*'s his fucking problem, he thought, Michael reads too fucking much. Through the French doors leading from the library to the dining room, he could see the winding staircase leading to the second floor.

He heard footsteps. She was still in the kitchen, the room he had just left. He tightened his grip on the butcher knife. A crack of thunder shook the house, followed by a flash of lightning briefly and bizarrely illuminating the spines of the hundreds of books surrounding him.

He heard her again. He needed to move quickly now, before she could get out of the house or get help. He saw her shape, her shadow, a hint of blonde hair, as she moved through the kitchen and into the mudroom. She'd be through the back door and outside in just seconds. But he knew the house was secluded and the backyard, with its high, thick hedges, was insulated from view to anyone nearby.

He now knew how he'd kill her.

Chapter 50

Rome, Italy

oseph Sharkey couldn't sleep. Sitting in his upholstered chair, looking out at the city, he wondered how he had let Michael Nicholas get under his skin. How had this businessman gotten to him? How had Michael been able to embarrass him, disrespect him? Ten years ago, Michael Nicholas wouldn't have lived through the week. Yet now, Sharkey sat in his luxurious but lonely room in the Hassler Hotel, forced to flee U.S. authorities because his own trusted crew had been unable to successfully eliminate Michael. And now he was relying on his friends in the Vatican to get to Michael and finish the job. But their "professional," the guy they had working on it, was too cautious, too slow.

In the meantime, Sharkey would extract some measure of satisfaction for the way Michael had treated him. Samantha Nicholas would soon be dead.

Sipping a limoncello, Sharkey was surprised when the hotel phone by his chair began ringing. It couldn't be Rizzo; he would only call on the cell phone.

"Joseph, it's Monsignor Petrucceli."

Sharkey quickly shifted gears in his head. "Monsignor, what a surprise this late at night. I'm just looking out at the Spanish Steps. It's so beautiful and peaceful at this hour."

The monsignor ignored the small talk. "We need to talk. Let's meet in the second-floor bar downstairs. I'll be there in ten minutes."

Before Sharkey could even protest, Petrucceli had hung up. Maybe something had happened.

The bar was empty. They sat a small, quiet table. Monsignor Dominick Petrucceli looked nervous. "I've been asked to provide some information."

Sharkey jumped on the question. "Information? What kind of information? Who wants information?"

"Never mind *who*. I need for you to tell me again exactly how we reached this point regarding the need to take care of Michael Nicholas."

"Monsignor, are your people having second thoughts? It's a little late for that, you know. When you needed something fixed ten years ago in the Bronx, I didn't come back and ask you for a report, did I?"

"No, you didn't. But things here are more complicated. There is, as you say in America, a new sheriff in town. The Holy Father sees things a little differently than some of his predecessors. There are new pressures that have come to bear. You read the papers, don't you? The Americans have been relentless for several years and now the Irish have allowed this whole sexual abuse business to escalate."

"What does that have to do with me? I'm not one of your clergy and I never abused any kids, remember?" Sharkey's temperature was rising. "I'm a saint compared to some of your guys."

"Yes, of course. But your involvement with us, indeed the debt we owe to you, was a result of the indiscretions of our friend, Bishop McCarthy, who, of course, is no longer with us after his unfortunate accident in Connecticut."

"Listen, Dominick, Monsignor, whatever, you guys needed a favor. A big favor, ten years ago. That bishop abused those kids and they were ready to blow the whistle. I took care of things for you. Now, your new guy with the big hat thinks maybe you guys need to stop protecting everyone. It's about time. But, let me tell you something, Mister Monsignor, that doesn't change anything about *our* situation. Do you understand? Because, it wouldn't be so good for people to find out what I did for you. Do you understand what I'm saying here?"

There was a brief silence before Petrucceli spoke. "Joseph, calm down. Believe me, I understand. I understand better than you think. I just need to answer the questions, to retrace the steps, as to how Michael Nicholas is linked to all of this."

"He's not linked to this except that you owe *me*. Do you understand? You owe *me*. Michael's brother, Alex, and I had a problem. It had to do with one of his wives. Anyway, I did her a favor, out of love, you know. So Alex had an unfortunate end last year. His brother, Michael, now enters the scene. He and I don't get along. Some associates of mine—a Mr. Bats, Nicky Bats, Lump and a legitimate mortician, Morty—were caught trying to dump Michael in the bay in Queens. Before they did, the New York police caught them. Now, your guy takes care of them in the church basement in the Bronx. So, the only person left who can finger me is Michael Nicholas. Once your guy Speedy Gonzalez takes care of him, I'm home free and I'm on my way back to New York and out of your hair."

"I see," Petrucceli answered.

"You see? What do you mean, 'I see?' What is that supposed to mean?"

Sharkey could feel his temper gaining control over him. He thought about the sequence of events that made it so necessary that

Michael Nicholas suffer and die. It was a little more complicated than the version he had just given Petrucceli. As with most crimes, he thought, there was a woman behind it.

It started with Michael's brother, Alex, a tough guy, but not tough like the men from the "family" that Sharkey knew. Alex would never kill a guy. It wasn't his type of thing. No, Alex was an outsider and he was smart. He wasn't Italian, either. Greek, not really even that. He was born in the U.S. But he ran a good business. Always paid off, on time. Made good on everything. No, it was Greta Garbone, Alex's ex, that started it all. Sharkey fell for her that night in the bar at Piccola Venezia. She was the one who convinced him to have Alex killed, to hire that kid from South Carolina to shoot him in his old restaurant that night. She figured she'd get a lot of his money. They surely knew the place would be filled with off-duty cops—many of them Alex's friends—and that the kid would never make it out alive either. Then, when Michael took over Alex's affairs and wouldn't give Greta the money she needed from the estate, and secret cash everyone knew he had, she convinced Sharkey to go after Michael too. He didn't mind that as much since Michael wasn't like Alex. No, he was a punk. He didn't grow up in the business. Too straight. Thought he was better than everyone. But Michael had escaped from the clutches of Sharkey' guys as they were dumping him in Flushing Bay that night. Then, when Sharkey's men were arrested, they fingered Sharkey. Hence, he had to flee the country and here he was, a secret guest of his old friends in the Vatican, his new protectors.

"Joseph, are you listening?"

Sharkey had tuned out. Back again, he looked up, "Yes, of course. But, Monsignor, you're making me nervous. When will your man complete the job?"

"Soon, Joseph. Very soon. I assure you."

"If your man can't get it done, I may have to take matters into my own hands."

The monsignor tilted his head slightly, his right eyebrow now raised, "Joseph, be careful, my friend. You are placing yourself in a precarious position. We are on top of this situation. Don't do anything that could endanger our operation. I am your advocate within the Vatican. You must not jeopardize my own support with the powers above me."

Knowing Petrucceli was looking for a sign of agreement, Sharkey looked away, his eyes following an attractive woman in a long formal gown crossing the room.

But Petrucceli persisted. "Joseph, you have already given me your word that you will take no action on your own toward Michael Nicholas. You must honor that. Do you understand me?"

Sharkey finally looked back at the monsignor but said nothing, while trying to weigh his options. He knew too well that he didn't have any. "OK, you have my word. I already told you I will not touch him—"

Petrucceli interrupted. "Nor will you authorize or hire anyone *else* to do so."

"Whatever. What are you, some kind of lawyer? You have my word. I won't touch him."

"I'm sorry if I disturbed you tonight. I have the information I need and I can make my report. There will be no problem. The cardinal needed to answer some questions, and I wanted to refresh my own memory on the facts."

"There are no facts, Monsignor. Only debts and obligations." Sharkey smiled. As they stood up to leave, Sharkey wondered if Samantha Nicholas was dead yet.

Chapter 51

Samantha looked out into her backyard. The trees were still. A ray of moonlight ever so slightly illuminated the shimmering swimming pool.

And then she heard him. He was right behind her. She bolted forward out onto the patio but, just as she did, she could feel his hand on the small of her back as he grabbed the elastic of her panties. She began to scream, "Help—" but his powerful arm took her around her neck, his hand covering her mouth. Her cell phone and the knife fell to the ground as he lifted her off her feet.

She couldn't believe his strength. It overwhelmed her. His strong arms held her entire body in place. In a split second, she was overpowered and immobilized. Who was he? She could smell his cologne and liquor. He'd been drinking too, she thought. Then her eyes were nearly completely covered by the pressing flesh of his hands against her face. Any thoughts of a struggle or even a scream were a fantasy. She knew she could never shake his grip. He held her from behind but was forcing her to the left, toward the swimming pool. The water was just a few feet away. She knew his plan.

She was choking for air before she even hit the water, his grip still firm as she went under, her lungs convulsing, desperately seeking whatever air was in her body. Briefly, she was able to bring her head back up, above the water. "We're almost through, you little bitch," she heard him say as she felt her body being thrust again below the surface. She knew she had only seconds of consciousness left. She opened her eyes under the water. It was black except for what appeared to be a mass of tiny colored lights, twinkling. She had seen them before, she thought, when she was a little girl and had pressed her fingers against her closed eyes. It reminded her of Christmas lights. Was this what dying was like? Visions of Michael and Sofia flashed before her. Where were they, she wondered? These thoughts had distracted her from her pain; she was no longer choking. No, now she was relaxed. Was it over? Was she waking up from a bad dream—or had she gone over to the other side, the place with the white light?

But as she opened her eyes again underwater, she saw his white pants and a glimmer of light miraculously reflecting onto the partially exposed steel zipper. Her mind was so oddly clear now. She remembered from somewhere about the best way to defend against a male attacker. They were there for the taking.

She reached over through the water and cupped her hand under Rizzo's balls and squeezed. Hard. Then harder. He released his hold on her, and she shot up to the surface. He was bent over, clearly in pain. She was free.

But before she could even turn away, he pulled up, stood upright in the waist-deep water and pulled out the large kitchen knife tucked under his belt. "You fuckin' bitch. Now we got to get the water all bloody."

She tried to swim away, diving into the water away from him, but no sooner had she made her move, she felt his hand tightly grip her ankle, pulling her swiftly back to him. As soon as she reached him, he changed his grip from her ankle to her throat. As she choked and began to feel her life slipping away, she saw him raise the large variegated silver blade in his right hand. She hoped she'd die before she felt it in her.

And then everything turned black. There was nothing to see but she could feel the warm water taking her. For a second, she remembered the feeling of being put to sleep before a surgery; that ever-so-brief split second before the anesthesia made everything go away.

She was on the surface again, her head above the water. He was gone. She waited for him to strike again.

She headed to the edge of the pool and then she felt something in the water brush up against her. She jumped back. A clap of thunder erupted and the sky lit up from a distant bolt of lightning. He was there ... his lifeless body on its way to the bottom.

Chapter 52

CEOs are just like everyone else. They want to be liked by their boss. Richard Perkins was finally going to meet the one man he was in awe of, Jonathan Goldstein, the chairman and the largest stockholder of Cartan Holdings

As soon as Cartan's takeover of Gibraltar Financial was closed, he would be working for Goldstein. Now, regardless of how tough Perkins was, he hoped Goldstein would also be his mentor.

As he and his chief of staff John Hightower entered Goldstein's private office, he caught his first glimpse of the man he had thus far only spoken to on the phone and read about in the press.

There were troubling rumors though. Perkins had read the reports on how Goldstein had dumped his wife of almost forty years after approaching a thirty-something woman at the takeout counter of a Chinese restaurant, slipping her his business card and whispering in her ear, "Google me," before walking out. On the other hand, how many people do you meet in the Hunan Delight who *are* worth a billion dollars? The young woman evidently fell in love with Goldstein, signed a pre-nup and married him as soon as his divorce papers were dry.

As Perkins and Hightower were led by Goldstein's attractive young secretary toward chairs facing Goldstein's desk, Perkins received the first indication that the meeting might be less than he'd hoped for. Ignoring the two visitors, she announced to Goldstein, "Hans Ulrich is on line three."

"Tell him I'll call him back in five minutes," Goldstein said, still not having made eye contact with his visitors.

Perkins, a former military MP, walked confidently over to Goldstein's large desk, held his hand out and, expecting a firm handshake, was surprised when Goldstein simply nodded, never offering his hand in return. Had he read somewhere that Goldstein was petrified of germs and rarely touched strangers?

"The deal will close on Monday. I want the new budgets on my desk first thing on Tuesday." His eyes were deep set, seeming to be placed far back into the hollows of his skull. His stare was vacant and cold. Goldstein's face looked even older than his seventy years. His skin was pulled back and his eyebrows unnaturally arched, a sure sign of a face-lift. Despite his riches, Goldstein couldn't turn back the clock. Apparently, too, even the best plastic surgeon money could buy, could only do so much. To Perkins, Goldstein looked like a corpse, albeit a living one with a billion-dollar portfolio.

He remembered what the investment banker had told him about Goldstein, that he surrounded himself with those who spent their careers executing his formula. There would be no emotion, no vacillation, no doubt. Real power would go to those with financial and accounting skills, strictly numbers people, not those with operating knowledge or organizational pride. Visions had no place here. Those who hesitated would be gone. But, for those who could spend their days under the gaze of his cold, lifeless eyes, Jonathan Goldstein would make them rich, very rich.

Chapter 53

Michael and Fletcher had settled into their familiar table by the front window of Mario's.

"I can't tell you how much I appreciate the security firm you arranged. It brings me some peace of mind knowing there are guards there. And, thank God Angie offered to stay in case Samantha woke up. I do hope those drugs Dr. Horn gave her help her get some sleep…she's obviously still unsettled, we all are—to say the least." Michael took a deep breath, "Fletcher, Thank God you showed up when you did."

"As soon as I saw the message, I rushed over to your house. When I pulled into the driveway, I heard Samantha screaming from the backyard. He was holding her down in the pool and was about to stab her when I put a bullet in the side of his head. I doubt he ever knew what hit him." Fletcher shook his head.

"That's too bad." Michael said.

"I didn't realize it was Rizzo until later when he was dragged out of the water."

"I was worried you wouldn't get my voicemail."

"What voicemail?" Fletcher looked puzzled.

"I tried your cell but when you didn't answer, I left you a voicemail. Isn't that the message you were talking about?"

"No, I never got it."

Michael realized that Fletcher was right, he hadn't left any message but had simply hung up and dialed 911. "Then how did you wind up at my house so quickly?"

"Listen, I don't want you to think I'm going off the deep end or something, or that I'm suddenly clairvoyant. I was leaving the Black Duck, I'm off-duty and I'd probably just had one too many and don't remember everything perfectly—"

"What do you mean?"

"Well, as I said, I'm just finishing up at the bar at the Duck when I get this instant message on my cell. It says something like, 'Samantha's in trouble. Go to her house asap.' So I'm heading to your house when I got the call from police dispatch about a problem, which must have been as a result of your call. But this instant message had come to my cell several minutes beforehand. If I hadn't gotten that, I'd have been too late."

"Did you save the message? Can I see it?"

"That's the first thing that was so strange. After it was all over, I went back to my messages—but it was gone. Nothing else had been deleted, but that message had just disappeared."

"OK, but who sent it?"

Fletcher finished his drink. "That's the other thing. The way it was worded, I could swear it said it was from *Alex*. Obviously it wasn't Alex—but *someone* sent me that message. Unfortunately, in the rush of things, I must have deleted it."

Both of them were silent. Michael knew who sent it, but he wasn't ready to tell Fletcher that Alex—or some version of him—was still alive. Not yet, especially after watching Samantha's reaction when he tried to show *her*. To break the spell, he looked around the restaurant. The bar was packed tonight and the restaurant's tables were filling up as the dinner crowd was filing in.

Still lost in his thoughts, Michael glanced up at the television monitor above the bar. A familiar face caught his attention. He pointed to the monitor, directing Fletcher's attention also to the newscaster's report:

"And now, breaking news from Paris that the global financier, Bertrand Rosen, who committed suicide on Tuesday by jumping out of his tenth-story Paris apartment, was about to be indicted for what is allegedly a massive Ponzi scheme. It's reported that the scale of this fraud may exceed seventy billion dollars. Investors from all over the world are in danger of losing all or most of the monies being held by Rosen's firm, Rosen Securities."

"How the hell did we miss that?" Michael said, shaking his head. "It was all a 'Hail Mary.' He was betting big to try and get some cash. The odds were against him. He figured it was his last shot to get some cash. If he won, he'd have enough to make it for a little longer. It would have bought him some time, although not much. If he lost, so what? We could get in line with everyone else he screwed. And now we have."

"I suppose it now all makes sense. But it's too late, you'll still never get the money he owes you." Fletcher said.

Michael thought about that for a moment. "The funny thing about this business is that, even though Rosen owes me the money, it's not like I'm out of pocket in any way."

"I guess you're right. You just don't get paid your winnings. It makes Sindy's account of what happened a little more credible. Maybe she *was* the final straw that made him realize he'd reached the end of the line."

"I hope so. She's been very coy about the whole thing, playing with my head. But, in any case, I've got to do something about her. I'm in much too deep, and I've got to start somewhere to repair my marriage. We've built so much—what the hell has happened to me?

The other night with Rizzo scared the hell out of me. ... It's all my fault ... I just worry it may be more difficult to extricate myself from Sindy than I imagined."

"Oh, you'll be able to extricate yourself. But if you do break up with her, I wouldn't let her mix your drinks."

As Michael was still digesting Fletcher's comment, Tiger rushed to their table. "Holy cow, do you guys believe this?" he said, pointing up to the television over the bar. Christ, the whole world's full of these rich crooks. I heard he cheated everyone he knew, his family, his friends. He had all their money. He must have been some piece of work." Tiger looked back up to the television monitor, which displayed stock footage of Rosen with his silver-grey hair, dressed in dark suits and formal dinner jackets, making speeches, benefit appearances and even testifying before a U.S. congressional committee.

Fletcher looked back at Michael, "And how did our government, the French, and all the regulatory agencies miss this all these years?"

"He exuded success." Michael said, thinking back on his dinner with Rosen in Paris. "He had this arrogant but low-key demeanor, like he didn't have to flaunt his intelligence or his brains. His reputation preceded him and he knew it. It allowed him to create a silence around himself. You had to fill in the void yourself. Who could challenge a guy with that kind of track record?"

Tiger turned his head away from the monitor again and, looking first at Fletcher and then to Michael, said, "Michael, you knew this guy?"

With a perfect poker face, Michael said, "No, not really. I did a little business with him. He owes me a million bucks."

"Jesus, Mary and Joseph. It shows you something, doesn't it? People have a much better chance pulling off a scam when they do it big. You can't screw smart people out of a hundred bucks. But, when you're talking about millions or billions, all these supposed geniuses believe it's got to be legit. Just the size of it makes you think it's got to be kosher. Shows you—you've got to think big."

"Gee, thanks, Tiger. You really have a lot of wisdom there. Maybe you should go down to the federal prison over in Danbury and offer your services as a motivational speaker," Fletcher said as he almost choked on his Manhattan.

Tiger looked back, squinting slightly through his eyeglasses, and said, "You guys are so smart. Enjoy your drinks because I'm going to start watering them down for you. We'll see if you ever catch on even now that I warned you. I mean, if that Rosen guy can pull the wool over your eyes for a million bucks, what's a few dollars more in booze?"

But Tiger wasn't finished. "All these guys come right in here after a day of work in the city. You know the type, in their forties maybe. They all dress in jeans and then a fancy, two-hundred-dollar shirt and a thousand-dollar sport coat. Their wives run around in Escalades or Range Rovers and work out with their trainers all day. These guys make huge money sitting behind a computer, they're traders or whatever. I can't figure it out. I'm no saint but I made my money the old-fashioned way—I worked my ass off. One meatball at a time."

Tiger paused again, smiled, and said, "Maybe *I will* call one of my old buddies and see if they need a speaker at that prison."

Chapter 54

"You sent that message to Fletcher, didn't you?" Michael said, placing a chilled glass of rosé on the table of his wine cellar.

"Yeah, I had to reach someone, especially since you were busy having dinner with *my wife* in the city."

"How the hell did you know that?" Michael said. He wondered now if he'd ever be able to do anything or be anywhere without Alex knowing.

"Michael, the world's about to change. There won't be any privacy—for anyone—ever again."

"I think that time has already come." Michael's mind was spinning. Tonight, he felt it was all too much.

"Rizzo's such an idiot, first, he sees me on your computer screen and he actually says hello. So I asked him what the hell he was doing there. He looked stunned for a few seconds, then he just stared back at me like a dumb fuck and walks away—*with* your wine. I think I may have given him something to think about though. I could tell he didn't know what to make of it."

"He's not going to make anything of it now. He's dead."

"I know."

"Alex, how do you know about so many things? Can you see whatever you want?"

"I can see a lot, but it's mostly through data, images, and sounds passing through the Internet. I'm learning to make certain connections. There's so much out there. You have no idea how much is flying through the ether each moment. And I'm only working on *private* communications—people's phones, their Wi-Fi, computers, some cameras. One day I'll figure out how to tap into what some of the *government* surveillance programs are doing. I can already see that the Chinese, the Russians, the French, the Israelis are doing a lot of electronic spying. Of course, I don't understand Chinese, Russian, French or Hebrew—although there's software to translate it."

"So everyone's spying on each other?"

"Michael, I can't access it yet but I've got a headache from it all. It's been going on forever but the computers and other devices are so much more powerful now. Eventually, I'll figure out how to get inside these government networks—"

"God, Alex, I'd rather you didn't. I think we have our hands full already."

"Maybe so, but it's just a matter of time until someone does. It may as well be me. Michael, I need you to do something for me. It's important."

"Sure—what is it?"

"You need to arrange for backup systems—in case we lose power, and in the event my software gets corrupted or deleted. I'm afraid of a power failure or, worse, someone coming in, finding out about me and ..."

"What?"

"Killing me *again*. Wiping out my software."

"Why? Are you expecting more visitors?"

"It's no joke. I'm working on making sure I'm not vulnerable."

"What do you mean?"

The picture was momentarily frozen. It had happened before. It reminded Michael of when a video feed into his computer periodically stopped, as it caught up or recalibrated when digesting something new. It was as if Alex was *buffering*.

"I'm putting myself in iCloud and I've ordered a commercial software backup—but none of that will help if someone who knows what they're doing really wants to eliminate me again."

"Alex, I don't understand. How do you even do this?"

"When my geek friends programmed me originally, they told me they designed everything so that, just like any animal—or human—I'd do whatever was necessary to survive. I automatically seek out anything to make sure I can't just disappear or that no one can pull the plug on me."

"You mean like HAL, the computer in *2001: A Space Odyssey*?" Michael remembered the movie—and the computer who fought back when the astronauts tried to disconnect him. It didn't end well for the astronauts.

"I never saw that movie. What are you talking about?"

"And who do you think could be trying to attack you?"

"I don't know. There are hackers trying to invade my systems. I don't know where they're coming from—but if they get in, it could be bad. I'm probably susceptible to viruses."

"It's just like you're alive, isn't it?"

"I may be alive."

Michael could see the slightest trace of what he was sure was a smile, almost as though Alex was suppressing it.

But Alex froze again, his eyes locked in position, he appeared almost ... *dead*. Michael felt a chill as he looked back at his brother. For a moment he feared someone had been successful in getting inside—inside what, Michael wasn't even sure—but Alex wasn't moving. The screen became scrambled, random lines appeared, flashing on and off. The screen went blank. There was nothing.

Michael looked at his keyboard. His brother's life was

disintegrating in front of him. He was at Alex's bedside, watching the monitor, watching him slip away as the line went straight.

Maybe he should try the *escape* key—or turning the computer off and then on again? Frozen himself now, he was afraid to do anything.

"Alex, can you hear me? Alex … Alex—are you there?" He began pressing the keys—first *ESC* then *return/enter*—and then he hit virtually every key.

Michael stared at the black screen.

Six minutes later, drained, he was sitting back in his leather chair when a flicker of light appeared in front of him. He looked up and quickly leaned in, inches from the monitor. The lines reappeared, accompanied by an Emergency Broadcast System alert-like sound, but unlike any that he had ever heard before. He looked closer, as Alex's inert image reappeared.

"Alex—are you there? Are you OK?"

Alex opened his eyes, wide. "What happened?"

"I don't know you … I lost you. You…"

"I passed out, that's all."

"I guess you could call it that." Funny that Alex used such a mundane, earthly term for what appeared to be a computer or Internet malfunction.

But Alex appeared to be back to normal, whatever that might be.

"If you lost me before—it could have just been my software duplicating itself or myself, so that if anything did happen, there's a copy of me, a backup."

"So—that would be a backup to the duplicate that you created when you were alive. The same duplicate that I'm speaking with now, right?" Michael felt like he was entering a maze from which he might never exit.

"No. Now you're speaking with *me*. There's only one *duplicate* now. It's the one I just created—and it's stored in my hard drive—and in iCloud. Just in case."

Michael took a deep breath. The truth was he was more confused than ever. "So this means—"

"It means … I will never die."

"*Never?*"

"Never, Michael. Even after *you're* gone."

Chapter 55

New York City

S indy had never told Michael that she saw Samantha entering
Bertrand Rosen's apartment in the moments following his
leap out the window. She wasn't sure why she had kept it to
herself, just an instinct, she thought. She would find the right moment to reveal her incendiary secret. The right time would come,
she thought. Nevertheless, she wanted to tease him, to watch his
reaction as she dangled something in front of him but held it out,
obscured in a cloud of uncertainty. She wanted to watch him grope
in the dark, for something, something she was still unsure of.

"There was something strange about Rosen's apartment when I
was there that day."

Obviously surprised, Michael clicked off the suite's television.
He watched her as he answered. "What do you mean, strange?"

"I don't know. Like someone else was there." She looked away,
not allowing her eyes to meet his but intensely curious as to what
he was thinking.

"Did you see someone else?" he asked.

"No, I guess not." "It was just a feeling, that's all."

"Well, could anyone else have possibly been in the apartment?" he asked.

She could tell he was worried about witnesses, not mistresses. She watched him as she spoke. She was now sure that he had no clue about Samantha or any reason to even imagine that she'd been in Rosen's apartment, let alone that she entered with her own key. So she would play with him a little. That information was more valuable as a secret, still hers alone, until she figured out how best to use it. Or with whom. She understood, deep down, that this was a destructive part of her personality, something she couldn't understand—or control. It had become who she was.

"I doubt it, but I guess anything's possible. I should have never mentioned it. As I said, it was just a feeling. I didn't care for him at all. I was surprised when you decided to do business with him."

"I can't like everyone I do business with. Neither at Gibraltar nor at Tartarus. It's funny, neither Catherine nor Jessica trusted him either. They kind of warned me. I should have listened"

"Jesus, Michael. One's just a washed-up, old actress and the other one's a hairdresser. She blows out hair for Chrissakes. What could they know?"

Michael laughed, but then she could see him checking himself quickly as he watched her expression harden. "Well, they were right. They knew more than the SEC, the French regulators and some of the most successful wealth managers in the world."

"Michael, now you know why he jumped. The money he owed us pushed him over the edge. I know you didn't believe me when I told you I didn't push him."

"I wasn't sure." Michael said, softly.

"You thought I pushed him," she said.

"You're right. I did. And I still may."

She tilted her head slightly, trying to recall precisely her thoughts and the sequence of movements on that day in Rosen's apartment. Odd as it was, she knew Michael might have a point. "I thought about it but, the truth is, he just jumped when I threatened him." And to herself she said, I think so, anyway.

"The French police are calling it a simple suicide. Once Rosen's fraud was exposed, it was a very plausible motivation."

"He screwed a lot of people, Michael. I *might have pushed him* if he hadn't jumped. I just don't know. Maybe I even made a move in his direction, which caused him to jump. It started out with everything happening kind of normally, whatever that means. But, then, all of a sudden, it all seemed to move so quickly. You know, I've tried to re-enact the whole thing in my mind so many times that I'm no longer sure what really happened. Maybe I've just imagined it so intensely that it's become reality, but only in my head. Things have gotten so grey."

"I always thought you were a black and white type. Didn't you have a plan before you went in there?"

"Of course I did. I don't do anything without a plan. You know that now, don't you?"

"I'm afraid I do. Well, what was the plan?"

It was as frightening to her as she knew it would be to Michael but—she couldn't remember. "My plan was to threaten him until he wrote a check."

"And if he didn't?"

She had no plan, or at least none that she could remember. "They always do, Michael. They always do ... Except this time."

She thought he bought it since she could see his attention shifting, as though something had just entered his mind. "I just remembered, at our dinner, Rosen gave me the name of a Swiss banker, a Hans Ulricht. He told me this guy could invest my money through his bank."

"Invest it?" she asked.

" 'Launder' is probably more accurate. But, basically, Rosen said this guy would set up a Swiss account for me. It would be a place to send the Tartarus profits where they would earn interest or be invested and the IRS would never know about it so there'd be no tax liability. I think his bank actually invested with Rosen. So Ulricht and Rosen scratched each other's backs."

"I think they scratched each other's something else." she said. "And, speaking of itches, what's going on with Samantha?"

Michael stared again into Sindy's eyes; he was clearly trying to read her. "What do you mean, 'What's going on with Samantha?' What would be going on? She's in shock still, of course, after the whole thing with Rizzo. Is that what you mean?" He sounded defensive—or worse, protective—of Samantha.

"Oh, I don't know, Michael. I would think nearly being drowned and stabbed in your backyard by one of your so-called clients would at least necessitate a heart-to-heart conversation. The type, you know, that sometimes brings couples back together, so to speak. Don't you think she knows about us?" There was a sharp edge to her words. Yet she felt relatively unruffled. She knew it drove him crazy.

He looked away. Not a good sign, she thought. "I don't know if she suspects you," he said, "although that's possible. I'm not even sure what she's thinking at this point. But I do think she knows things have gone terribly wrong."

She knew he was lying.

"And is that what *you* think, Michael? That things have gone terribly wrong?"

"I don't know what I think," he said. *Not a good answer, Michael,* she thought. *Not a good answer at all.*

Chapter 56

E verything had changed but the sex. Michael knew he had to find a way to cut Sindy Steele out of his world. Yet he still needed her—and now he'd come to fear her.

The bedroom was a disaster. Two empty bottles of wine, dishes with the remains of filet mignon and baked cod were scattered on the plush hotel carpet along with Michael's navy blue pin-striped trousers and suit coat and Sindy's torn pair of Agent Provocateur stockings and sheer black bra. Sindy, naked except for the pink furry handcuffs hanging off her right wrist, which, for an agonizing but lovely half an hour, had secured her to the bed, slowly made her way from the master bath to the red club chair where she collapsed. Michael, still in bed, watched her, wishing he had a camera to record the long, lean, white figure, the jet-black hair, the baby pink "bracelets"—all exquisitely framed by the lush red velvet chair. He knew these scenes would need to end, soon. They should have ended already. They should have never begun. But Michael had no idea how to bring the curtain down safely. His cherished ability to compartmentalize was failing him; the walls were no longer secure.

"It's too bad that photographer, Herbert Stein, was killed last week. He would have loved to photograph you. You look like one of his models, the nude ones."

"Really? Tell me, what did Stein's models look like?"

"They were strong, tall, powerful yet slim women. They all had great, long legs. Some were a bit edgy. His pictures of them certainly were."

"So," she hesitated, "What am I? Strong? Tall? Powerful but slim? Or edgy? Am I edgy, Michael?

"Oh, you're all of them. Definitely edgy—with great legs." He watched her, scrutinizing her face, searching for what might be going on underneath. Usually, complimenting her legs would at least bring a smile. This time she just looked away.

He knew something had changed. But worse—much worse—she knew it too.

Chapter 57

Sindy Steele was asleep.

Wide awake, Michael put on a plush, white terry cloth robe, left the bedroom, silently closed the door behind him and settled into the chair by the desk in the suite's living room. He took a deep breath, opened up his Apple laptop and clicked on his portal to Alex's world.

Seeing Alex come to life on the screen always jolted him.

"I need your help. Now that Bishop McCarthy's dead, I'm not going to be able to get a meeting inside the Vatican anytime soon. I need you to tap everything you can of Petrucceli and Lovallo's— their cells, landlines, internal Vatican recording devices, hidden bugs. I need for you to step up what you've been doing. I need everything."

"It's strange," Alex said, "you know, to eavesdrop on these guys—they're all guys—through cyberspace. It's like I've tapped into their magic formula—the spirit or whatever it is, something none of us can see."

"You mean—as though you're on their turf?"

"*Death* is their turf. People think these bishops and priests and popes really know what happens when you die—or that they can get you a reservation or a better room in hotel heaven—you know? It's what they sell, why they're in business. It's all bullshit."

"And now we're competing with them—*we* have an alternative theory."

"It's more than a theory, Michael, or you and I wouldn't be talking right now. The problem *they've* got is no one is really sure whether it's true."

"*And we can* prove ours—or we will—once we're ready to expose you."

"Yeah, but that's not going to happen for a long time. We've got to be prepared before we let this genie out of the bottle. I've been researching artificial intelligence and there's still so much to my existence that I don't know."

The thought had Michael's mind spinning. "You're *researching* artificial intelligence? You *are* artificial intelligence, Alex … aren't you?"

"Yeah, I really wouldn't know. I've kind of told you that. Just like you don't really know what's going on with your own brain, do you?"

Michael tried to think it through. Alex's *thinking* was confounding him. "No, not really. You're right."

"So, in my research, I've read that the Silicon Valley people think that computers will match human intelligence by 2029."

"Well, for the first time in your life, you're ahead of your time."

"It gets better—they think computers will overtake the human mind by 2045." Now Alex was laughing.

"What do you think?" Michael suddenly felt he was touching Alex's core. Maybe it was just the incredible software, but he'd been able to get deeper into Alex's thinking than he'd ever been able to do when Alex was actually with him, say, in Queens.

Alex had frozen again, as he tended to do when the issue appeared to be extremely complicated.

"I think … that Silicon Valley has its *own* limitations. All they can see is what is on the surface. The way everything has been connected on the Internet and in cyberspace—all this information that's flowing, computers are digesting it all a lot faster than humans. Even the best computer geeks can't see what's happening inside all these black boxes. Just like, I said, you can't see what's happening inside your brain."

Michael stared into his brother's eyes for what seemed like a very long time. Then Alex froze up again. "I think we're both exhausted," Michael finally said.

Seconds later, Alex returned. "Computers will overtake the human mind long before 2045."

From the way Alex emphasized each word, he sensed it wasn't just an expression but a carefully crafted prediction based upon more than Michael could comprehend.

"OK, back to today," Alex said. "We have to do something about Sharkey."

"We have one big advantage over him."

"What's that?"

"You—you and your technology."

Michael closed his laptop.

Chapter 58

Michael could see Samantha watching him closely.
"This is the table that Richard Burton and Elizabeth Taylor preferred," he said. "It was also Richard Nixon's regular table."

"Maybe we should change tables. None of those stories ended well." Samantha was serious.

Michael tensed, "We have a lot to talk about", he said awkwardly. He dreaded these conversations; he knew he'd screwed up badly. Worse, he didn't have a way out.

It was a subdued yet spirited crowd at Le Perigord; well-dressed and, looking from a distance, it appeared that life had been good to them. The noise level was just right, enough to preserve the privacy of intimate conversations within the boundaries of the table, but not so quiet that you felt isolated.

"A long time ago, I married a good guy, a loving man, someone so different than your brother. You even kept your distance from him. Now, you've *become* him—and our relationship is looking like the ones he had with all three of his wives." Samantha's tone was stern, yet her eyes were moist.

He felt resigned. Resigned to something that even he couldn't put his finger on.

"I didn't even know it was happening. It's like a midlife crisis, I was bored in my corporate world, and then Alex's murder, and that whole life opening up. It all came together so fast."

"I know, Michael. But, it's turned *our* world upside down. We've both been nearly killed. Thank God, Sofia is far away at school or, Lord knows. In just a year—we've had enemies, real ones, people that want us dead—Sharkey, Greta Garbone, Rizzo, the Vatican for Christ's sake, and those guys with all these names, Gump—"

"Lump," Michael corrected. "He's dead."

"Don't correct me." Samantha said, now verging on anger. "Of course, he's dead, Michael, and so are Greta and Rizzo for that matter. Until all this happened, the only people we knew who died were old people who lived their lives in peace, got sick and then, sadly, passed away. Now, it's like we're in a shooting gallery." She paused, looked at Michael, waiting for his reaction, for him to show his feelings.

But Michael was still trying to absorb her words and the ramifications of the new life he had brought to them both. He always felt his reactions—both inside and out—were on a five-second—or five-hour—time delay. That wasn't always a good thing.

Samantha continued. "The thing is that's only part of it, and you know it."

"What do you mean?" Michael asked, although he knew. He was just trying to buy time, time to think.

"Do you seriously believe that I don't know what you've been doing?"

Michael began to speak, although as he opened his mouth, he was still unsure what words he would utter. After all, Samantha knowing what he was doing could mean many things, beginning with the computer-enhanced Alex, and ending with Sindy Steele. He was saved from the decision as Samantha continued.

"I know affairs when I see them. You were never good at lying. You don't have the personality or, for that matter, even the short-term memory for it."

"You're right. I know. There's a lot of ground we need to cover or, I guess, recapture. But, I love you. I've always loved you and I'll do whatever it takes to get us back on track."

Samantha's face softened somewhat. He was relieved that his words appeared to be the ones she wanted to hear. "Michael, I've never stopped loving you. It's just that things—and maybe *you*— have changed. Changed a lot. It's going to take a lot of effort—for both of us—to make this work."

"I'm going to make those changes." Michael answered, before Samantha had even finished. But I—we—have some short-term problems that I don't have easy solutions for. More important than anything, I have to get us safe again. Otherwise, the rest is meaningless."

"How are you going to do that?"

"I have a plan. I'm going to put an end to all of this. I need a little more time to work out all the details. You have to trust me. I'll tell you everything very soon."

But ... how? You have to tell me more than that."

He wanted to tell her, he ached to tell her—but the plan in-volved the one person Samantha did not want to hear more about. "Someone's an integral part of this—and I know you don't want to hear—"

"Not Sindy Steele—"

"No, let me rephrase it—it involves some very advanced tech-nology that—"

"Oh, God, Michael—"

"OK, how about if you just give me a few weeks and trust that I will get this taken care of. For now, why don't you go ahead and say what's on your mind, what's important to you as we put our lives back together?"

He could read her and he knew he'd gotten a temporary pass.

"First of all, you and I have a partnership. We will be in this together. I am not only your wife but your business partner. I was always an asset to you in your career, in your legitimate, corporate career, at least. I can do the same—and maybe more—for you in Tartarus."

He was surprised. He'd anticipated that Samantha would want him to give up the business and go back to just running Gibraltar, living the life they lived before Alex was shot.

"Agreed. I could use your help, as long as you can take the pressure, the craziness."

"Pressure? Craziness? Michael, I was within seconds of drowning at the hands of that madman yesterday. I grabbed his balls for God's sake. I've watched you get kidnapped and then nearly shot by your brother's nutcase ex-wife. I think I can handle the pressure."

"You're right."

"Next," Samantha said, "I need a sign-on bonus to commemorate our new partnership."

"A sign-on bonus?" He looked perplexed.

"Yes, you and I are going to visit Harry Winston and look at a six-figure token of your appreciation." Samantha had that look that said, 'don't even think of changing a comma in the agreement.' Michael understood. He was happy to be on familiar territory with Samantha again.

"Done. We'll go tomorrow."

She smiled. "There's one more little thing. I wasn't born yesterday."

"Oh?"

"Sindy Steele has to go." As she waited for the impact of her words to sink in, her cell phone rang. She looked at the display, the caller ID read "Sindy Steele."

Chapter 59

New York City

He'd been asked to meet with Richard Perkins at noon at Gibraltar Financial's Fifth Avenue headquarters but he'd arrived early. Michael rarely visited the building, preferring to meet as much as possible on his own turf, several blocks further downtown.

Looking to kill a few minutes, he went into John Hightower's office to see if the new budget projections were ready yet. The door was open, but not seeing Hightower, Michael entered anyway and took a seat on the visitor's side of the desk. It was obvious that Hightower was here, so he decided to wait for a few minutes and make a quick call to Karen.

As he reached across the desk and gripped the telephone, he noticed a typed document nearby. It was his own name on the paper that caught his attention. He looked out through the open door and into the hall, neither Hightower nor his secretary were in sight. He read the document:

> We want to thank Michael Nicholas for his years of hard work here at Gibraltar. But, there comes a time for all of us

to turn the page. A time for new, fresh leadership. Leadership that looks ahead at our opportunities and not back at our challenges. Perhaps, also, a more worldly view—yet one that is fiscally responsible. And while I will bring a new leadership style to the office, I can assure you that nothing will change. It will be business as usual. Except now, we will have access to more capital and greater resources to generate growth for the organization. So, let us move on and upward. I want to assure you, this has not been a takeover by Cartan—but a merger, a merger of equals. We will retain our independence, our way of operating. We will retain the culture that has made us so successful. But, make no mistake, as we move forward, I will be looking at the best practices of other organizations and, as any prudent business manager would, will be seeking to find ways for us to do more with less, to work smarter as an organization.

Losing track of time, Michael was still staring at the document when he heard Hightower's voice.

"So now you know. I'm addressing all Gibraltar employees tomorrow morning—right after Richard's announcement that I'll be replacing you as CEO."

"I see you touched all the bases: no changes, merger not takeover, retain our independence. Blah blah blah."

"Yes, the big lies that employees need—actually *want*—to hear at such times," Hightower said.

"And that we've always been so willing to tell them."

"You know as well as anyone, they'll forget them by the time the facts of life became apparent."

"I'm no saint in this area, but at least I understand when I'm saying something that may be wishful thinking."

"Yes, and it's amazing that these people never figure it out, isn't it? But, that's the reason Perkins wanted *me* in charge instead of you. You're too unpredictable. All that corporate culture, values and vision stuff is a waste of time. That's why you'll be gone when I give *my* speech ... And you thought I could only run spreadsheets."

"I still do."

"Perhaps I'd better call Richard now that you've seen this." Hightower dialed his boss' internal phone extension, but Michael could see there was no answer. This was unusual. Someone would always answer Perkins' phone, he thought. Yet the phone just kept ringing. Richard's office was just fifty feet away. Both he and his secretary were in. Odd, he thought, for the phone to just ring off the hook. Unheard of, actually, in the Gibraltar culture.

Hightower then pressed the button on his phone console for his own secretary. Again, the phone just rang. "Come on, Georgia. Answer the damned phone. What's going on out there?" Hightower turned around and looked out the glass wall of his office and through the white horizontal shades that only partially obstructed the view directly outside his office. Michael turned around in his seat to look out too. No one was there.

"What the hell's going on? Where is everyone?" Hightower said, appearing almost hysterical.

Michael figured that Hightower was afraid to be alone with him. A thought he relished.

It was then that Michael heard a shuffling noise and the loud voices of men, an indistinct but unfamiliar sound for the hushed halls and offices of Gibraltar Financial's headquarters. He looked up to find a startling scene: five men, three in suits and two uniformed NYPD officers, entered the office.

Michael's stomach dropped. What had happened? Was he being busted? Had the feds tapped his phones? Was it something to do with Sindy? ... His mind raced through any number of possibilities. All of them bad. Very bad. He'd been set up. That's why Perkins was nowhere to be found. They had arranged to arrest him here, in front of everyone. And a perfect set up for employees to accept a new CEO.

As they approached him, he stood up from his chair, ready to listen to what he knew was about to destroy his life. He thought of Samantha and Sofia.

But as he did, the men walked right past him—and approached Hightower.

"What is this?" Hightower said, but his voice lacked the tone of offended British snobbery that characterized his earlier remarks. "What are you men doing here?"

The lead agent, a tall, powerful figure with an ill-fitting suit and a collar a half-size too large, came around the desk and stood face to face with Hightower.

"John Hightower, I'm with the FBI, these gentlemen are NYPD. You are under arrest for conspiracy to commit securities fraud and for violation of the Securities and Exchange and Insider Trading Sanctions Act. We're going to need to put these cuffs on you. Please turn around. You have the right to remain silent, the right to an attorney. Anything you say may be used against you."

Hightower turned around, placing his arms behind him. The officer quickly clicked the steel handcuffs around his wrists. Michael watched as Hightower looked straight ahead through the glass wall of his office, and saw the peering eyes of all the secretaries as they looked right back at him.

Chapter 60

New York City

Samantha knew who was calling her.

The ring tone disrupted her study of the glittering selection of earrings as she leaned over the glass display case. Tempted to let the call go, she reluctantly dug her cell phone out of her Chanel bag.

She quickly exited Mariko, the upscale costume jewelry boutique on Madison Avenue, and stood outside the shop's door, half-watching the passing pedestrians as she listened to voice she least wanted to hear.

"Samantha, this is Sindy Steele. You've been ignoring my calls. I understand, and know this is awkward for you, but we need to speak. Don't ask any questions now. Please, just trust me. How close are you to the Surrey Hotel?"

Samantha's mind raced as she thought of the possible scenarios behind Steele's plea. None of them were good. "What do you mean? What's this about?" she asked.

"I can't tell you over the phone. You need to meet me. Now. Please. There's a bar in the Surrey, Bar Pleiades."

Further annoyed that Steele would be familiar with a place that she and Michael had often visited, she nevertheless continued, "I know it well, of course. I'm just a few blocks away, but it's late and I plan on heading home." Her voice turned stern, "What is this about? And where is Michael? Why are *you* calling *me*?"

"Samantha, I'm calling you because I know something very personal about you that you don't want Michael to know. That's all I'm going to tell you. Meet me in ten minutes in the bar. Good-bye." Steele didn't wait for an answer. The call had ended.

Although curious as to why Steele would try to reach her, Samantha had ignored her earlier call. There was no reason she would ever need to speak with her husband's mistress, especially now that she was sure Michael was about to eliminate her from their lives. So why, she wondered, did she take this call today? Was she unsure of Michael's resolve—or was she just curious?

And what could Steele possibly know about her that she wouldn't want Michael to know? There was only one secret she had kept from Michael—and other than Angie, the only other person who knew about it had jumped to his death in Paris.

Regardless, she headed to the Surrey Hotel.

Chapter 61

Sindy Steele could feel the Zen-like calm that was the Bar Pleiades.

The room had a sophisticated Coco-Chanel-inspired décor: subdued colors, smooth black lacquered cocktail tables, red velvet upholstered chairs, and vintage black and white fashion photographs on tan quilted fabric-covered walls. It was, she thought, an elegant setting for the opening scene of a murder.

They sat at their banquette facing each other, the wife and the mistress. She wondered if Samantha was thinking the same thing.

"Thanks so much for meeting me. I'm sure you're wondering why I asked to see you."

Samantha took a large sip of her drink, "Yes, I must admit, I didn't expect you to call me."

"Well. I apologize for the intrigue. But I have a surprise for you." She thought—fleetingly—of the Glock in her purse.

"Well, you got me here and, despite my better judgment, I'm listening. This week has already been horrendous. How much worse can it get?"

"Yes, Michael told me about the whole thing with that man, Rizzo. I guess if there's one consolation, it's that he won't bother you or anyone else ever again."

Samantha took a long sip of her drink, stared straight back at her and said, "I know you're sleeping with Michael."

That didn't take long, she thought. Sindy tried to anticipate the direction of their conversation as a chess player thinks through the likely sequence of moves. Samantha's quick move surprised her. Nevertheless, she was sticking to her plan. She had to wait for the opportune moment, when Samantha's attention would be sufficiently diverted, to drop the capsule in her drink, the first but irreversible step. Their conversation had turned combative quickly; she knew she'd have to make her move soon or risk having Samantha leaving abruptly.

She wasn't used to losing the initiative. This was her meeting, she thought, not Samantha's. To slow down the pace, she'd agree with her.

"You're right about that."

Samantha began to speak but, Steele cut her off. "Before you get all offended or hurt or moralistic on me, you need to know something."

"I don't need to know *anything*." Samantha shot back. "Your 'affair,' or whatever you want to call it, is over."

"Really? I guess you know something that I don't since I just left him last night." She noticed a well-concealed expression of surprise. "But, let me ask you something." She paused. "Aren't you curious what it is that I know about you? After all, that's why you came, isn't it?"

It stopped Samantha in her tracks. Her head, no longer leaning in, tilted back.

"What secret could you possibly know about me?

Sindy paused, then paused even longer until even she was uncomfortable.

"Tell me, do you miss Bertrand Rosen?"

She knew she struck gold. It was clear Samantha was rattled.

Samantha took a deep breath, "I beg your pardon?"

"I saw you there."

Samantha looked like a deer in the headlights. She reached again for her drink, her hand shaking, the huge diamond on her finger reflecting the candlelight from the table.

"My life's none of your business. It isn't now and it never will be. And, as long as I choose to be married to Michael, I'll control a good deal of his life. Don't let the last few months fool you. If you think Michael will turn his back on me, you don't know him. Sometimes, frankly, he just thinks too much, but when push comes to shove, you won't stand a chance."

Samantha's eyes were wandering, glancing around the intimate room at the other patrons. She was avoiding Sindy's glare.

Sindy knew that it was time. She slowly placed her hand under the table and found the soft brown leather of her Coach bag that was resting between her thighs. She reached inside and gripped the sticky, gelatin capsules in her fingers.

Samantha's face suddenly relaxed, as she rose up to greet a young couple who had just entered the bar from the lobby.

In one swift motion, Sindy rose slightly, moved the table out for Samantha—and dropped the capsules in her drink. A slight fizz briefly appeared before the head of the pale pink drink resumed its normal appearance. It was done.

It would take the pill ten minutes to bring Samantha to her knees. First, she'd feel light, followed by dizziness, then the room would begin spinning. She'd realize something was terribly wrong but would be unable to gain control over herself. Sindy would then offer to help her, while Samantha would wonder whether Sindy had drugged her. By that time, she'd be conscious but helpless. Sindy would help her out of the bar and into her car.

Samantha sat down and immediately finished her drink.

But Sindy's eye caught a glimpse of a man entering the bar. She didn't know him but she recognized him. Her mind quickly shuffled through a file of images, faces she had seen before and places she might have seen them. She realized that she had gone through this same rewind of people and places once before. It was the same face—and something about the eyes. A flash of recognition swept through her. She remembered where she'd seen him, twice before. She looked back at a tiring Samantha Nicholas and felt a sudden heaviness in the pit of her stomach. This man would change everything tonight.

Chapter 62

New York City

With his distinguished profile, white hair, tailored three-piece suits, and a gold pocket watch, Hans Ulricht looked every inch the Swiss banker that he was. Born in Berlin, just before the Second World War, to an infamous Nazi, dark rumors swirled around him every step of his career.

His father, Friedrich, served as a Nazi leader and Minister of Armaments and Munitions in Hitler's cabinet. Upon his arrest near the conclusion of the war, Friedrich Ulricht's cooperated with the Allies and claimed to have been surprised that he was arrested. At the Nuremburg trials, he acknowledged the scope of the Nazi atrocities, while denying he had any knowledge of them until after the war. However, the charismatic Ulricht took responsibility as a senior officer of the Third Reich for the horrors. That slender ethical thread—taking responsibility while denying prior awareness of the crimes—spared him the fate of ten of his contemporaries—execution by hanging.

Hans remembered the constant whispers that followed him, with his mother in the local shops or entering a new school. At first, when he understood that his father was in Spandau prison, he was ashamed. But, as he entered his late teens, his feelings changed. The constant flow of letters from his father instilled in him a deep sense of German patriotism and pride. Those who considered Frederick Ulricht a war criminal were misinformed.

He remembered greeting him on the day he was released from Spandau in 1966, after serving his twenty-year sentence. Hans was then twenty-six, his father, sixty-three. In the years that followed, Hans grew close to his father and eventually learned the truth about his knowledge and complicity in the Nazi atrocities. Yet Hans still considered him to be a war hero.

Hans himself was in the twilight of his career at the International Bank of Switzerland, a senior director and managing partner of the firm. His father had died in 1981; despite his notoriety, his connections within the elite of post-war Germany had assured Hans of entry into the inner sanctums of the richest circles. Now seventy, Ulricht brought billions of euros annually into the treasury of IBS, most of it well hidden behind walls of discretion and secrecy that has defined Swiss banking for centuries.

As he sat in Jonathan Goldstein's office at Cartan headquarters, Ulricht wondered how Goldstein would have fared at the hands of his father's Nazi machine. Not very well, he suspected. But this was a new world and a different time. The Goldsteins of this world once again controlled money. The Nazis' work went unfinished. It was Hans Ulricht's fate to have to cater to the likes of Jonathan Goldstein, just as he had accommodated the peculiar personality of Bertrand Rosen. Sitting with his father forty years ago, he didn't imagine that Jews would again exert such dominance over financial matters. But his father also taught him about the need for discretion in his utterances and the necessity of keeping his ethnic prejudices to himself. Hans Ulricht was always, despite his inherited, deep-seated arrogance, polite and politically proper.

Just as he knew that those attributes had served him well, he also knew that discretion and good manners were not the virtues anyone would attribute to his client, Jonathan Goldstein.

"The fact that you chose to invest my money in Rosen's funds is your fucking problem, Hans." Ulricht watched as Goldstein bellowed from his desk, his eyes flaring. "I expect to be made whole."

"But, Jonathan, you know as well as I do that IBS does not guarantee the risk, particularly when you have us invest in outside funds, such as Mr. Rosen's. We are separate entities. This was your choice. IBS can't be held responsible for the problems with an outside manager."

Goldstein's face turned red, his eyes narrowed their glare onto Ulrich. "Fuck you. I don't get screwed. I do the screwing. I don't let anyone walk over me. Least of all some old Nazi."

It was at this point that Ulricht exercised the ultimate self-restraint, remembering his father's advice to keep certain areas of his life out of the realm of any discussion, acknowledgement or, worse, outward anger. But Goldstein continued his rant. "And I don't give a shit about your fucking Swiss discretion. You and Rosen were in bed together. You know it. You introduced me to him. You and your bank made millions in fees off my investments with him. You had a fucking fiduciary obligation to vet his funds and his operations. You didn't do your job. IBS screwed up. Now you go back to your fucking neutral little country and figure out how you're going to replenish my money."

Ulricht planned on quietly holding his ground, if he could, without further enflaming his client. "Jonathan, I'm not sure there is anything I can do. This is most unfortunate, I agree and I understand your displeasure—"

"Displeasure?' This is more than displeasure. Cut the diplomatic shit, Hans. You need to think real hard. I'll bury you and your fucking bank before I'm going to lose four-hundred million dollars. Do you understand? You and IBS have a lot at stake. The regulators and federal investigators will be all over this. They'll be analyzing and questioning every trade. They'll be looking for where you got your information. And not just regarding Rosen. They'll be looking at every deal, every trade you've ever done, even investments that have nothing to do with Rosen. They'll analyze your relationship with everyone you've ever spoken to—" Goldstein paused, as though he wondered whether to continue.

Ulricht watched him, surprised by his hesitation. But, either satisfied it was safe to continue or unable to suppress his impulse, Goldstein dropped his nuclear nugget, "and that includes your British friend, John Hightower."

Ulricht was stunned to hear Goldstein mention Hightower. He didn't think that Goldstein was even aware of their relationship. Hightower had just been arrested and was sitting in a downtown jail frantically trying to raise bail after his assets were frozen by the authorities. Hightower was a tidal wave of vulnerability for Ulricht and IBS. His late-night phone calls and "inside" information on the Cartan-Gibraltar merger made IBS and several of its clients three million euros in just a few days. As a result, Hans Ulricht feared he was already a doomed man. It was just a matter of time before Hightower would talk. If the wiretaps and trading pattern analyses hadn't already implicated Ulricht and IBS, Hightower would. He was only surprised that Goldstein knew about it.

"Jonathan, I can assure you, whatever trouble Mr. Hightower has gotten himself into has nothing to do with IBS—"

"Not just IBS, Hans. Not just IBS. *You. You*, Hans. Don't look at me like I'm some kind of money whore because I'm willing to bet that next year this time, you'll be clinging to whatever little money you've got left that your attorneys haven't taken—or the government hasn't found yet—and praying to your god that you don't have to finish your fucking life in some prison cell serving wiener schnitzel to a bunch of ungrateful rapists who'll own you like you've never been owned before."

Ulrich despised Jonathan Goldstein and wondered how this man, so different from himself, could know precisely what woke him up in the middle of the night in a cold sweat.

Chapter 63

Yes, Sindy thought, she had seen him twice before.

The scenes flashed before her as she watched Samantha—who was no longer speaking, her mouth half-open, her eyes glazed and half-shut, her head lowered halfway toward the table.

She remembered him. She had been dining with Michael in L.A. at La Dolce Vita, twirling her spaghetti. He had passed not too far from their table, on his way from the men's room. It was the same night that photographer was killed outside their hotel. Even then, at that dinner, she remembered thinking she recognized him, but she had not been able to get a good look at him. She watched now as he leaned close to the bartender and, in a voice she could just barely hear but knew she had heard before, ordered a Campari and soda. He then turned slightly toward her, just enough for her to see his face more clearly, to see his eyes, the piercing eyes that were different colors. Astoria. Piccola Venezia, the night she sat at the bar while Michael and the bishop had their dinner. She remembered his eyes.

Samantha's head was only inches off the table. Her delicate

fingers still grasped the empty martini glass. Sindy checked the bottom of the glass to be sure there were no obvious signs of the capsule. The pill had done its job, but tonight's plan would have to wait, at least until she could identify the stranger who had turned up three times—in Astoria, then L.A.—and now, here.

Leaving Samantha passed out at the table, she rose up and walked out the door.

Outside, she looked up and down Seventy-Sixth Street and, convinced no one was following, turned left toward Fifth Avenue and her car. She knew that when Samantha awoke, whenever and wherever that was, she would be unable to recall the details of the final minutes of her evening.

If anyone asked, Sindy would simply say that Samantha had become intoxicated and unpleasant, so she left her there. She laughed wildly and said, loud enough for anyone to hear, "Maybe she was on drugs."

Chapter 64

While Puccini's opera played softly in the background, Frank Cortese sat watching Samantha as she lay sound asleep on the large king bed under the fluffy, white, down comforter, her head nestled on the oversized, soft, feather pillows.

Still attired in his silver-grey suit, white shirt and red tie, he stroked the sleek, sharpened, silver stiletto that he held in his lap.

He pressed the release button on the stiletto. The seven-inch blade silently snapped out of its case. He turned it over, inspecting it, admiring the Italian design and the polished silver. He took his handkerchief and meticulously rubbed it clean. He knew he hadn't used this particular tool in months but handling it made him feel calm when he found himself agitated.

The warm lighting, stylish decor and subdued color tones of the Surrey's junior suite further eased his nerves. He'd been watching Michael Nicholas for weeks and had silently gotten to know him— and Steele—quite well. But in the course of his surveillance, he had become *obsessed* with the beautiful woman asleep on the bed.

While in the bar watching Steele, it was clear that Samantha was in grave danger. He observed that even though Samantha was fading away in front of her, Steele's attention was elsewhere. her eyes darting around the room, checking to see who was watching. He had learned to read the nuances; he knew well the subtle foundation work that goes into each assignment. He was sure that Steele was going to murder Samantha.

The irony of his situation wasn't lost on him as he held his cell phone to his ear with his free hand and waited for Monsignor Petrucceli to answer.

"Monsignor, I know the hour is late." It was three in the morning in Rome. "I would not call except for the urgency of the situation, my friend."

"What's wrong, Frank? Are you alright?"

He opened the knife again.

"Frank, are you there?"

Cortese carefully closed the instrument and placed it back in his coat pocket before turning his attention back to his call.

"Oh, yes, yes, of course, Dominick. But I am in an unusual situation, you see. I was following our friend in the bar of this hotel this evening while the lady assassin was sharing drinks with Mrs. Nicholas. I think perhaps this Signora Steele, is perhaps, as the Americans say, a loose cannon. Dangerous, you understand? I believe, Dominick, that she is also jealous of this Samantha. Anytime two women share one man, it is not good, *si*? But then, at the bar, you see, she may have recognized me from an earlier rendezvous. I believe she either got Mrs. Nicholas here very drunk or may have drugged her."

"Frank, when you say, 'Mrs. Nicholas *here*,' what exactly do you mean? Are you *with* her?"

"Yes, precisely. Steele left Mrs. Nicholas passed out in the bar at this hotel. I could not leave her and walk out myself. I took a special room here and helped her up. I have carefully placed her in the bed and called for the hotel doctor. He says she is good, she will recover, she needs rest. So, now she is resting. All is well."

"Frank, am I missing something? What are you doing there, *with her*? Why did you get involved with this?"

"She would have been harmed. The authorities would have been called. It would have brought attention to all of these people. It would then have complicated our own plans. Do you understand?" Cortese knew this was only his own rationalization, but he also knew it actually made sense.

"Yes, Frank. I think I understand but, you know what you have to do this weekend, don't you? Your assignment has nothing to do with her—"

Cortese grimaced as he looked at Samantha Nicholas. He whispered into the phone, "Yes, Dominick. I know. Of course. There is no problem. I have watched her. She is a good woman."

"Frank, think about this before you answer, but are you possibly attracted to this woman?"

He looked again at her as she slept. She was the most beautiful woman he had ever seen. But he knew Petrucceli was now nervous, waiting for his answer.

"Tonight I save her life so that on Sunday she can be a widow. She is too good for this Michael Nicholas. But, a woman such as this, they are not drawn to men who live the life I do. I understand I cannot afford the luxury of such attractions except, of course, from a distance. I love many such things, my friend, but always from a distance. It is where I am, unfortunately, most comfortable."

"Frank, it is late and you are lonely. This is the time to listen to the voice in your head, not the one speaking to you from your heart." Cortese could hear Petrucceli's deep sigh, "Frank, you must leave. The morning light will bring clarity to what the night conceals."

Cortese closed his eyes. "Very well, life is complicated and delicate."

Chapter 65

Samantha Nicholas woke up to a splitting headache and the persistent ring of the telephone near her bed. She was still half-asleep but as she listened, the words gave her a fright.

"A visitor is on his way up, Mrs. Nicholas."

Before she could ask who it was, they had hung up. Who is coming? How do they know my name? She recognized the room; she and Michael had stayed at the Surrey many times over the years. But how did she wind up here? She remembered sitting in the bar with Sindy Steele, the terrible conversation, and then ... the drowsiness. Yes, she remembered feeling drugged. The rest was a blur.

She heard the click of the electronic lock on her door. She recognized his voice immediately, "Samantha, it's me. Are you OK?"

She picked up the first object she could get her hands on. The heavy Baccarat crystal vase flew by, narrowly missing Michael's head, and smashed into the wall behind him, shattering the formerly fine French crystal into a hundred pieces.

Her thick blonde hair matted, still in her clothes from last evening, she knew she looked crazed but with the effects of the drugs wearing off and seeing Michael in front of her, she felt energized with adrenalin—and anger.

"How could you let that nutcase woman come near me? How could you?" she screamed.

"I had no idea you were seeing her. I've been crazy since last night when I couldn't reach you. I've been searching and calling all over. Fletcher had the NYPD helping. Finally, Sindy told me she had met you for a drink last night."

"Met me for a drink? Is cyanide a drink? Leaving aside everything else that we have discussed—and I don't mean to minimize your relationship with her, I'll deal with *that* again later—even *you* must realize this woman is dangerous. Do you understand this? She *drugged* me, Michael. She called my cell and said we had to meet, so I met her downstairs, we had a drink and then, all of a sudden, I was passing out. The next thing I know, I'm waking up alone in this hotel room. What's going on?"

"I don't know where to begin, Samantha. Everything's just gotten crazy, it's all out of control. I know that. I had no idea she'd contacted you or I would have stopped you."

"You haven't slept with her again have you?"

Michael didn't answer.

"Oh my God. I must be crazy. You had *sex* with her after our discussion, our agreement, just a few days ago?"

"Samantha, I'm so sorry. I know it was ridiculously wrong but—"

Samantha stopped him. "But what? *But what, Michael?* What could you *possibly* say after 'but'?"

"She's a cold-blooded killer. I'm afraid of what she might have done if I broke everything off with her." He watched for her reaction, "Samantha, she could kill either one—or both of us."

Samantha put her face in her hands, "Oh my God. Oh my God. Was she trying to kill me?"

"I don't know. I'm honestly not sure what she was up to. She said she was sitting with you—and someone came in and then she had to leave. She said you were upset and drunk—and maybe on drugs—and so she was going to leave anyway but then someone entered the bar. This guy she said had been following us—her—and she had to take off."

"Is that how you found out where I was?"

"Actually, no. I called her *after* I found out, to see what she knew. Until then, I had no idea you'd met with her."

"How *did you* find out then?"

Michael hesitated. She had a feeling he was going to say something crazy—and he did.

"Alex—"

"Oh, no. No. You can't be serious. No, Michael, Alex is dead. You've been talking to a computer. Don't you understand that? Please, tell me that you do."

"I asked Alex to help me find you."

Ignoring her, he said, "He told me where you were and to get to Sindy and so I called her right away. She then told me what had happened and where she left you. I then called the hotel, and some of our friends at the front desk here told me that they knew you were here. They were very nervous about disclosing it. They probably thought you were having an affair with this guy or something."

"*What* guy? If I knew who it was, *I would.*"

"They finally said that a stranger, a man, checked you in, paid cash for the room and left shortly after he brought you up. They said you were passed out."

"Oh my God. Some guy we don't know got me the room and put me to bed? Who could it have been?"

"I don't know. Maybe it was the guy Sindy saw at the bar and was worried about enough to cause her to leave."

"Michael, what do you mean, you don't know? How can you not know? How can you know part of the story but not the rest of it? Didn't you ask her?"

"She's not a normal person, Samantha. She doesn't explain things. There's always a lot of mystery surrounding her."

"Michael, I thought we had already talked this through. I believed you when you said you were going to end this with her. Not having sex would have been a goddamned logical place to start, don't you think?"

Chapter 66

New York City

Michael watched as both Lesters eagerly indulged in I Sodi's thinly layered cheese-and-meat lasagna while he savored the homemade linguine prepared with butter, grated pecorino cheese and pepper. The intimate, dark and cozy West Village restaurant was one of his favorites.

He marveled how, roughly a year since Alex's death, the conversation amongst the three of them seemed to flow so easily. And he wondered if Skinny and Fat Lester were now as much at ease with him as they had been for so many years with Alex.

"Did Alex ever involve Donna in the business?" Michael already knew the answer but his plan was to lay the groundwork for Samantha's involvement in the business.

"No, Donna was Alex's *wife*."

"Lester," Skinny Lester interjected, "I think Michael's aware of that." Then, turning to Michael, he said, "You've got to remember, Michael, Alex never married the types of women you'd bring into a business, unless it was a strip club. All three of them, they were great-looking, and if there was anything missing, he had that plastic surgeon on Park Avenue take care of it."

"The reason I'm asking is that I might have Samantha get more involved with us. You know, to help entertain some of our clients, maybe hang around the offices sometimes during the day when I'm not around. She's a good business person and she's smart."

Fat and Skinny Lester exchanged a quick glance. Skinny Lester, raising one eyebrow slightly, leaned in closer to Michael. "Michael," he was nearly whispering, "How's this going to work with The Terminator?"

Michael couldn't help but smile at the endearment, "You mean Sindy?"

"Yeah, we mean it as a compliment. You know, for pushing the French guy out the window." Fat Lester offered. "Guys she doesn't like seem to die."

"We've known you almost since the day you were born, so I'm going to tell it to you the way I see it," Skinny Lester said.

"I wouldn't want to cross her, I'll tell you that." Fat Lester added, looking at his cousin to be sure everything was OK.

"Well, listen guys. I trust you, and I trust your judgment on people. There's going to be a lot happening over the next few weeks. I need for you to keep an eye out for Samantha for me. I want you guys to stay as close to her as you can when I'm not around. At some point—probably right after Labor Day—I'll be out of the country."

"Going to our Paris office or with your suits?" which was how Fat Lester referred to Michael's corporate world.

"A little of everything, including vacation. Samantha will join me in the South of France. But first, I may do some Sharkey fishing …"

Despite the personal turmoil, Michael felt good about Tartarus and now had no doubts about his ability to take his brother's business to new heights.

"Well, it looks like we're all making some money. I think we just had a great quarter," Michael said, adding for Fat Lester's benefit, "A great three months."

"Yeah, man," Skinny Lester said. "I've never seen anything like the last several months. And the receipts coming in from Paris are damned good, too. Even with Rosen not paying,"

Fat Lester finally put his fork down and said, "I've gotta tell you, I never thought we could make money off the Frenchies. I thought they just read books, drank wine and chased women. The last part's OK."

"They're all so serious." Skinny Lester added. "I mean they're snobs. They go to the opera and the theater. That's all good but they take everything so seriously. I don't think they have a sense of humor. They don't ever laugh."

"I hear they read a lot of those foreign-language books," Fat Lester chimed in before wiping his dish clean with a piece of bread. "They also watch those foreign films with the subtitles."

With a perfectly straight face, Skinny Lester said, "Lester, the films with the subtitles are probably American films in English, they're not really foreign."

"Yeah, I know. They don't understand English, other than croissant, which is really just a roll; French fries, which was invented by McDonald's; and déjà vu, which Yogi Berra made famous."

Michael and Skinny Lester exchanged a quick, knowing glance. Michael hoped that Fat Lester was indeed smarter than he appeared but feared he wasn't.

"I saw that look," Fat Lester said, laughing. It gave Michael hope.

Chapter 67

New York City

Michael heard the all-too-familiar ring of his cell phone. As he reached into his sport coat, he thought of all the life-altering phone calls over the past year that he received while he was dining out, beginning with the one he had with Alex at the exact moment he was shot.

"You know," he said to the Lesters, "I'm beginning to think I should let some of these calls go. It's never good news."

"Michael, some strange things have happened." Donna hadn't called Michael in weeks but he could tell by the halting tone, that it was unlikely he would be finishing his linguine.

"What's wrong? What happened?"

"I can't go into it over the phone. It's has to do with Alex."

"Donna, what do you mean with Alex? Alex's gone." He recognized the irony of that remark coming from him and wondered whether it was the most sensitive thing to say, but Donna wasn't exactly the most sensitive woman in the world, either. She and Alex actually were a good fit for each other.

"That's just it. This thing with Alex, you know, we've talked about it before, it just doesn't seem to go away. Father Papadopoulos called. He said he had to tell me something before it was too late."

"Before it was too late? What does that mean?" Michael asked.

"I don't know what he meant by that. I wish I did." Donna said. "You know these priests, they talk in riddles. Everything's a goddamned mystery."

"Well, what did he have to say?" Michael said softly, trying to keep Donna from getting too excited.

She continued, "Remember at the cemetery the other day, you must have said to him that, of course, Alex was dead because he, Father Papadopoulos, had seen Alex's body in the casket before he closed it? And he told you that yes he did?"

"Yes, of course I remember. I was mostly just being sarcastic although I don't think he realized that. So?" Michael was rolling his eyes.

"*So*, I'll tell you *so*. *So*, now he tells me that he lied to you."

"What do you mean, he lied to me?" Michael wondered whether Donna had been drinking.

"Michael, I mean he never saw Alex's body in the casket. The casket was closed and sealed from the moment it reached the funeral parlor. For all he knew, Jimmy Hoffa was in there. It was highly unusual. He never even saw Alex's body at the funeral home when he did the blessing those nights. The casket was always closed—and locked."

"But, wasn't it *your* decision that Alex's casket be closed?" Michael asked while quickly trying to think through the situation.

"Yes, I did request a closed casket. I think that's what Alex would have wanted, not to have all those people staring at him while he was dead, you know? Your brother was vain—I think he was worried that if some of those young girls he was always chasing after saw him dead, they wouldn't go out with him anymore. But anyway, Father Papadopoulos told me that he'd been told that even *he* wasn't allowed to bless the body with the casket open, you know, in private like they do before the public is allowed in. That they were instructed to not only keep it closed for public viewing but that it was to be permanently sealed once Alex was laid out in it. That, Papadopoulos said, he had never heard of before."

"And who is *they*, the ones who ordered this? Whose instructions were they?"

"I don't know and Father Papadopoulos didn't seem to know. It must have been someone at the funeral home."

"And he just called you up out of the blue to tell you this?"

"Yes, that's when he said he had more to tell me before it was too late." Donna was now screaming into the phone. "I don't know what that's supposed to mean. He said one of us needed to come to the cathedral right away. Michael, this is all too much for me. I hate those churches. I was Jewish until I married your brother. You've got to call him and go see him. Right away ... please."

Not wanting to alarm the Lesters, Michael kept his voice low and measured. "OK, don't worry. I'll get to him. But did you ask him what he meant by 'before it's too late'?"

"No, Michael. I missed that particular point. I don't really give a shit about the priest or what he meant by that. I'm still trying to figure out where your son-of-a-bitch brother really is these days."

"I know, I understand, Donna. I was just asking in case he happened to mention it. ... Donna, listen to me. *Alex is dead.*"

As he said it, Michael wondered exactly *why* he was so sure that his brother was dead. As real as Alex appeared on the laptop, Michael realized that he was no longer the Alex Michael had known, he'd grown, he was more aware of others, more sensitive, his memory was nearly photographic. And wasn't that the way the artificial intelligence software was designed to work?—or was it simply Alex without booze—an Alex on detox and plenty of sleep. Either way, it was a healthy Alex.

After a silence, Donna, repeated her point, "He never saw Alex's body. He never saw him dead at all. And, by the way, I keep getting these obscene emails ..."

Chapter 68

Rikers Island, New York

As he stood at the prison's bank of telephones, Hightower was nervous; he had never felt so vulnerable, nor had he ever dressed in orange. Always cocky and sure of himself, he now silently prayed that Richard Perkins would answer the phone. When he heard his boss' voice, he hoped that his fortunes would soon change.

"Richard, thank you so much for taking my call. I was worried that you wouldn't."

"Well, John, I must be honest with you. I just picked up the phone. I didn't know it was you. In view of the situation, it's not appropriate that we be speaking to each other."

Perkins' smooth Southern baritone voice was always so soothing, so comforting to Hightower. Now, however, it had an unfamiliar, stern, disconcerting edge. "I can't condone what you've done and I'm deeply disappointed."

"Richard, there's more to this than it appears. It's not what you think. You have to hear me out. Please, give me a chance to explain."

"John, I really don't want to know any more. I shouldn't even be speaking with you, under the circumstances."

"Richard, they've frozen all my assets, I can't even write a check to get out of here."

"You have an attorney, don't you?" Perkins was speaking to him as though he was an errant schoolboy.

"Yes, I have an attorney but even he's waiting until they've put a lien on my home, for God's sake. This is crazy. All of a sudden, I'm broke. I'm powerless. The pimps here have more pull. They've got cash and people outside helping them. No one will even talk to me."

Perkins' voice turned cold. "John, I can't help you."

Hightower, desperate, needed to keep Perkins on the phone. "Richard, do you know a man by the name of Hans Ulricht?"

First, there was just silence. Then, "Good-bye, John."

He knew Perkins would never again take his call.

Chapter 69

New York City

As Michael approached the cathedral, he knew something bad had happened.

The drive from I Sodi on Christopher Street to the Greek Orthodox Cathedral uptown took nearly half an hour. Traffic was a standstill on Seventy-Fourth Street, so Michael paid the taxi driver and walked the last two blocks. An ambulance, its red lights flashing and sirens screaming, was burning rubber as it drove past him. Two NYPD police cars were sitting in the middle of the one-way street, blocking off all traffic behind them. An officer was leaving the church, taking his time while the horns from at least four blocks of stranded cars blasted away. Michael considered asking him what had happened but decided to proceed into the church and find out himself from Father Papadopoulos.

He passed through the tall, heavy wooden doors and into the Byzantine Empire, as he often referred to Greek churches. Despite being dressed in a dark blue suit, he felt underdressed for the formality typical of the ancient church. Seeing a priest in his full regalia of robes and vestments, passing quickly from the vestibule of the church, Michael called out, "Father Papadopoulos."

The priest stopped in his tracks and turned around, at which point Michael immediately realized his mistake.

"I'm sorry, Father, I thought you were Father Papadopoulos."

"I'm afraid, my friend, that Father Papadopoulos is not here. Did you have an appointment to see him?"

"Yes, I just spoke with him, less than an hour ago. He asked me to come over and meet with him. I'm Michael Nicholas."

"Ah yes, Mr. Nicholas." The priest's expression indicated that Michael's visit was not a surprise to him. "Yes, yes, of course. I was expecting you. Father Papadopoulos told me he was to meet with you. Let me introduce myself, I am Father John Papageorge. I have assisted Father Papadopoulos for the last several months." He moved quickly to look into the nave of the church. Seeing it was empty, he motioned Michael to follow him. "Please, let's get out of the vestibule. We will have privacy in the pews."

As they walked, Michael remembered how one of his close friends in college used to tease him that all Greeks had last names beginning with "Papa." And now, here he was dealing with Papadopoulos and Papageorge.

Father John Papageorge's cream and deep red, gold-embroidered robes gently flowed as he walked, leading Michael further inside to the main body of the cathedral. Michael glanced at the Corinthian marble arches, dark wooden pews, deep red carpeting and ornately painted portraits of the Apostles. The religious icons on the walls, the gold crosses, the white candles, the strong, pungent scent of burning incense—all brought back powerful, almost haunting memories of his childhood Sunday mornings. Even then, he viewed the cathedral as a passage into another time, a place somewhere between life here on earth—and the afterlife. He still did.

They sat down at the end of a long pew and, as though the priest could read Michael's thoughts, he placed his hand on Michael's shoulder and whispered, "You know the nave of the church, where we now sit, represents the entrance of the Christian to God's kingdom. It is the first step to the next world."

Michael remembered how Father Papadopoulos, at Alex's funeral, described Greek churches as "God's waiting room."

But Michael wasn't convinced about the direct progression into God's kingdom from where he was now sitting. "Father, has something happened? I saw the ambulance leaving and police cars as I arrived."

Solemnly, Father Papageorge spoke. "Michael, Father Papadopoulos had a massive heart attack. It was right after he spoke with you. He was gone before the ambulance even arrived."

"He's dead?"

"Yes, I'm afraid so. I'm sorry to tell you this." He paused to allow Michael to absorb the news. "How well did you know Father Papadopoulos?"

Michael had to think. He wasn't sure how to characterize their relationship. "I've known him for probably twenty years. He baptized, married and buried a lot of my family. I can't say, though, that I knew him well. We were never disciplined in our approach to the church, I'm sorry to say."

"Michael, I hope you will excuse my directness at this difficult time, but I want you to know, I am familiar with the circumstances that led to your presence here today."

"Well, I must confess, I'm a bit baffled as to why I'm here. My sister-in-law, Donna Nicholas, called me earlier to say that she had spoken with Father Papadopoulos, who had told her he needed to explain something, something regarding my brother Alex's death. And he said he needed to do it, 'before it was too late.' "

"Is that all you know?"

Michael had an uneasy feeling from the question. "The only other thing he told her was that, even though he had blessed my brother's body at the funeral home and presided over his funeral in Queens, he had never seen the body. He told her that the casket was permanently sealed right from the beginning."

Father Papageorge listened intently, "Yes, as you know, Michael, this was very unusual, although not unprecedented. There is no dictate that we have to actually see the body in order to bless the soul and facilitate its passage into the kingdom of heaven."

"But when we were at the cemetery the other day and I asked Father Papadopoulos whether he had actually seen my brother's body, he implied that he did. Why would he have said that if, in fact, he knew he hadn't ever seen the body throughout the whole process? And what was it then that he wanted to tell us 'before it was too late'?" Michael said.

The priest's eyes darted slightly to the right. "Father Papadopoulos knew, most specifically, of the rumors and questions as to whether, somehow, your brother was still alive. I believe he simply wanted to explain to you that, even though he had not actually *seen* your brother's body, that he, nevertheless, was convinced your brother was dead. He wanted to put your mind at ease."

Michael's face was tense. "But, it just doesn't make sense. Why would he call Alex's widow out of the blue to tell her this? Something just doesn't fit. And when I called him—less than an hour ago—right after I spoke with Donna, he urged me to meet with him immediately."

Father Papageorge's tone became almost dismissive. "Michael, we all try to find more meaning in everything, particularly where death is concerned. I think you may be reading too much into Father Papadopoulos' selection of words. I did discuss this situation with him. He simply wanted to put your mind—and your sister-in-law's—at ease. So you could both sleep soundly knowing, for certain, that our dear Alex is with the Lord."

"But," Michael persisted, " what was the urgency? What did he mean by *before it is too late?*

This time, Father Papageorge looked directly at Michael. "Perhaps he had a divine premonition that his time here on earth was nearing its end."

Chapter 70

Greenwich, Connecticut

Hightower was finally home. After one night in Rikers Island, he was dirty, unshaven and could smell his own body odor. Despite the plastic bracelet securely attached to his right ankle, a condition of his release on bail, he was free.

Although relieved to be in the comfort of his own bedroom, he was disoriented. He began to undress, ripping off his suit jacket, pulling off his trousers. In his haste, he lost his balance but steadied himself on the side of his bed. He took off his underwear and socks, throwing them all in a big pile on top of the suit on the blue carpet. On his way to the shower, he picked up every item of clothing that he had worn to his office and then prison and stuffed them in the leather trash basket.

Hightower referred to his master bathroom as his "Roman Spa." Dark green marble counters, oversized Jacuzzi bathtub, all-glass surround steam shower, polished brass accessories, walnut wood cabinets, a white porcelain toilet and even a bidet.

But this evening as he entered his shower, Hightower felt more like a felon out on bail than a Roman emperor. Even the brief, cursory discussion at the jail with his new attorney left him feeling that his freedom was temporary. His attorney's words echoed in his ears and reverberated right to the pit of his stomach, "I have to tell you, John, this will be difficult. The feds don't usually bring these types of charges unless they're confident that they can go all the way. Assuming the wiretaps were legal, and I can only assume, at this point at least, that they were, we have an uphill fight." His final words as they shook hands seemed to Hightower even more ominous, "*For now*, John, just enjoy your freedom."

But he recalled there was one other statement from his lawyer that caught his attention: "Unless, of course, you have information, *testimony*, John, that could deliver a bigger fish to the feds."

"Like who—whom—do you mean?" he had asked.

His attorney had looked both ways then leaned in close and whispered so that even the guard standing nearby couldn't hear, "A Swiss banker would do for a start."

Now as he closed the shower door, turned on the water and then switched on the steam function, he felt a rush of soothing relief. The jets of hot water spraying from the oversize rain faucets ran through his hair and over his body, along with the hot steam pouring through the eight nozzles built into the marble wall. It was helping him to ease the humiliation of his arrest and the hell of his overnight incarceration. He closed his eyes and took a deep breath, inhaling the hot steam deep into his lungs.

He noticed a rapid accumulation of water on the floor of the shower. Just my luck, he thought, the damned drain is clogged, tonight of all nights. I just want to enjoy my shower. He looked down, through the rising water, already two inches deep, at the brass drain cover below.

Determined to complete his shower, he grabbed the large bar of his treasured Fortnum and Mason champagne-scented soap, and began to vigorously scrub himself all over. The water continued to rise, reaching now above his ankles. It would soon rise above the marble ledge at the foot of the glass door. He stepped up his pace, determined to finish his bathing before having to turn off the water to avoid flooding his bathroom floor. The water pressure, he thought, seemed unusually strong. The glass walls, reaching up to the ceiling, securely enclosing the shower, were covered in a steamed fog. He reached out to the faucet controls to decrease the water volume. As he did, he thought he saw a shadow pass by outside the shower door. He gripped the main water control knob, but as he turned it counter-clockwise, the handle twirled freely. The water continued to shoot out of the multiple nozzles in the square showerheads embedded flush into the shower's ceiling. He thought about opening the shower door but wanted to avoid a flood of water rushing out onto his bathroom floor. Then, as he looked at the door's handle, he saw a strange object. He wiped the fog off from a small portion of the door to get a better view. It was a steel rod, placed through the handles of the shower door and adjoining panel of glass. He tried to open the door. It wouldn't move, the rod had anchored the door in place.

Panic surged through him, heightening his senses but weakening his legs. Through the fogged glass, he thought he saw the shadow again. But this time, instead of disappearing, it became larger and grew as it seemingly came closer to the shower's glass walls until it looked like a large, dark cloud passing through the bathroom; a form, at first indistinguishable but real. With the water rising rapidly around him, now above his knees, Hightower took his hand and wiped a larger clearing in the fogged-up glass. He stared out through the opening, hoping to recognize the figure behind the shadows.

Over the din of the water rushing out through the powerful showerheads, he spoke, his tone controlled, at first. "Who are you? What are you doing?" But the figure neither answered nor moved.

Hightower screamed, "Help, please help me."

He strained again to look through the glass. It was a man, standing about ten feet outside the shower. He didn't move. His mouth appeared to be open, as though he was sighing, or relieved.

He looked upward, toward the heavens, as though he was in a trance.

Hightower could feel his leverage being diminished as the water rose, enveloping more of his body and making his thrusts more difficult and slower.

"I can pay you. I have money. A lot of money. Just let me out. Please. I'll take care of you. Help me." The stranger still didn't move. "Hightower beat his fists against the door, each time leaving an imprint on the fogged glass. "Who are you? I'll pay you anything."

It was in those precious and clear moments that Hightower reflected on how much extra he'd paid for this hermetically sealed steam shower with extra-thick tempered glass. He quickly speculated in his calculating mind about whether the choices he'd made at some juncture in his life had perhaps led to this moment. But, he thought, which ones? Even if his life was to end, he wanted to know.

The space on the glass that Hightower had cleared fogged over again. Hightower, silent now, looked up to the shower's ceiling, trying to calculate how much time, how many minutes, he had left before it would reach the ceiling, enclosing him in his tomb of water.

Through it all, however, he heard something very strange. It was music, classical music, coming through the built-in stereo system. It was getting louder. He knew the piece well, it was Wagner's opera, *Tristan and Isolde*, part of his music collection. For some bizarre reason, he now recalled that it was Adolph Hitler's favorite opera.

The water reached his chin. Soon it would force him to leave his feet and float up to the top. There was only a foot between the top of the water and the ceiling, where Hightower knew he would swallow water instead of breathing air. He prayed for a miracle. He continued to fight, but his movements were now severely restricted by the pressing water, blunting his thrusts against the unyielding door.

Whether or not it was his imagination or the workings of his brain under stress, he wasn't sure. But the volume of the music had reached an earsplitting level. He could hear it above the rush of the water as he repeatedly pushed himself up with his feet to gain the last few moments of air. He swore he could hear Wagner's piece reaching a crescendo, almost in parallel with the water nearing the ceiling, as he began the process of drowning.

Chapter 71

"This is where you sit and wait for the end." Cardinal Lovallo said softly, delicately holding his cup of cappuccino over the white marble table inside the Caffe Greco. "Or so Georgio de Chirico believed."

He lowered his head and fixed his stare on the young monsignor. "This cafe, Dominick, is 250 years old. Yet today, it seems younger than *you*. What is troubling you, my son?"

Monsignor Petrucceli heard the question but had let his mind drift. He wondered where it all went wrong. How had his life veered from service to God, a holy endeavor, to arranging for murders and babysitting marginally literate criminals?

"I am concerned about Mr. Cortese," he said, finally.

Cardinal Lovallo's head leaned backward. "Concerned, with Frank? How is this possible? What do you mean?"

"He called me early one morning, it's probably nothing, but I just worry; worry that perhaps he may have some fixation or attraction to this Samantha Nicholas, the wife of our soon-to-be-departed Michael."

"Dominick, you can't be serious. Frank is a blood brother. He is a professional, no? Attractions of the heart have no place in his work, nor in his life for that matter, at least as far as I have seen in all the years we have known him."

Monsignor Petrucceli felt that twinge of uncertainty fighting with the need to show absolute confidence in Cortese to the cardinal. Playing it down the middle, he knew, would open up an endless stream of questions that would then lead to doubt. In three days, Cortese would be carrying out the most sensitive assignment on their behalf. There was no room for failure, yet last night's call was disturbing.

"I have no doubt that Frank will carry out our mission as he has always done. I suspect that occasionally, like all of us late at night, he becomes lonely. Nothing more."

"Ah, then, I trust this is settled, Dominick. We are men, yes? We are only human. The attraction of the flesh tempts us all at times. If this were anyone else, I should be concerned. But, Cortese is incorruptible. His eyes—with their different colors—may stray but his aim is correct. He will not fail us."

"There is more." Petrucceli watched the cardinal's eyes narrow, almost imperceptibly. As the cardinal slowly sipped his cappuccino, Petrucceli continued. "Our guest, Mr. Sharkey, has had some involvement in an attempt to harm Samantha Nicholas."

"What kind of involvement? What has happened?"

"The police shot and killed the man just as he was about to drown her in her swimming pool. She was unharmed. This man, a John Rizzo, and Joseph know each other and were in telephone contact moments before he was shot."

The cardinal shook his head back and forth in apparent disgust. "My God, this could have disrupted our whole plan. Is Sharkey insane? There is no reason to involve this woman. She can do us no harm. What was he thinking?"

"It is possible that he is a psychopath. He thinks we are too slow to deal with Michael Nicholas. His anger knows no bounds. Mostly, however, he is simply not in control of his mind, his emotions or his actions. I will meet with him tonight and try to calm him down." Petrucceli paused, ready to tell the cardinal about Sindy Steele's attempt to harm Samantha Nicholas, but decided not to further upset him with yet another incomprehensible sequence of events.

The cardinal appeared firm. "Sharkey is dangerous yet he is nothing more than a street thug. Because of the indiscretions of some of our brothers, *we are* indebted to him, and he knows too much for us to abandon him now. Nevertheless, Dominick, I worry that we are in a deal with Satan's disciple."

"I will take care of the situation." Monsignor Petrucceli said as he looked into his cappuccino.

Chapter 72

Rome, Italy

Monsignor Petrucceli was well known at Ristorante Tullio. As the waiter silently refilled their glasses from the bottle of Amarone, Petrucceli meticulously carved away at his *fritti vegetal*, a Tulio specialty.

"What the hell is that?" Sharkey asked, pointing with his steak knife at his host's dish.

"It's calf's brains, Joseph. You should try it next time."

"How do you eat that stuff?" Sharkey said, still looking at Petrucceli's plate.

"It's a delicacy, Joseph. It's a favorite of the Romans here."

"Excuse me, Dominick, but all I can think of is that Anthony Hopkins movie, *Hannibal*, where he—"

Disgusted, Petrucceli cut him off. "I remember the movie, Joseph, but I would prefer not to remember it at this moment, if you don't mind."

Unfazed, Sharkey continued. "Whatever. It was a great movie. I mean, to serve a guy his own brains for dinner --"

"Joseph, I beg of you. Please, can we change the subject?"

Petrucceli, although seething, calmly placed his knife and fork on the plate. He then sat perfectly still, as though collecting himself, before he spoke again. "Now, Joseph, tell me how you are doing."

Sharkey looked as though a small bomb had gone off inside his head, his face contorted. "How the heck do you think I'm doing? I'm living in a goddamned hotel with a bunch of Italians. I'm like a trapped rat. I'm sitting here with you, watching you eat a plate of brains. How do you think I'm doing? What kind of question is that?"

"Joseph, perhaps you would prefer if we brought you into the Vatican community. We have special guest apartments where you could reside. Maybe living there—until it is safe for you to return to the U.S.—would relieve some of your alienation, yes?"

"Do they have room service?"

Petrucceli wondered how a benevolent God could have created such a man in his own image and then placed him there with him that evening.

"No, but you could dine regularly with others of our holy community. Often the meals are taken at communal tables where you could interact—"

"Are you nuts?"

No sooner had the offer left his lips, Petrucceli realized how ridiculous it was to think Sharkey would consider it. Such a move would, however, have been a perfect way to begin to rein in and control him, he thought. In the event more drastic action ever became necessary, having him inside the Vatican walls would make any such moves easy to accomplish—silently. But clearly Sharkey wasn't about to relocate to any Vatican apartment. At least not yet, not voluntarily.

"Alright, Joseph, let me rephrase the question. Is there anything I can do for you that I'm not already doing? After all, *we* didn't indict you for several murders and attempted murders. Your own country did that. You are our protected guest here, Joseph. You are staying in one of the finest hotels in Rome. You are eating in our best restaurants. You have been provided plenty of spending money. We didn't create your situation or your problem. We are trying to help you and we are doing that, because ten years ago, you did us a big favor."

Sharkey was unfazed. "When are you going to get rid of Michael Nicholas? Until he's dead, I have no chance of going free. Once he's gone, the cops have no one who can testify against me in any of these murders."

"Listen carefully, Joseph." Petrucceli preferred not to share the plan with Sharkey but it might be the only way to keep him from doing anything else. "The day we have spoken about is nearly here. Next Monday, your Labor Day, it will be done. Then, I pray, the charges against you in New York will be dropped due to the lack of substantial evidence and you can then go home and resume your life."

Sharkey perked up. "How will they kill him?"

"It doesn't matter, Joseph. But it will be done."

"No, Monsignor Dominick, *it does matter*. It fucking matters to me. I want to know how he's going to die."

"I don't understand, Joseph. These are not details that I wish to dwell on."

Sharkey leaned across the table, his face now just inches away from Petrucceli's. "Well, you see, Monsignor, that's the difference between you and me. I don't just dwell on it. I savor it. I relish every moment from that first split second when the man knows he's going to die until he takes his last fucking breath. That's the *payoff*, my friend. That's what it's all about. And the longer that is—and the more painful it is—the better. And in those last gasps, as he thinks about his wife and kids and all that shit, I want him to know that he's dying because he crossed Joseph Sharkey. I want to be his last regret. I live for those fucking moments. Do you understand, my friend?"

Chapter 73

Whitestone, New York

From the moment Michael attended his first funeral, he was fascinated with funeral homes. Like your first love, you never forget your first open casket, he thought.

It was a strange place to visit on the eve of the long holiday weekend when everyone else seemed to be thinking about the beaches, barbeques and baseball.

As he sat and listened, he wondered about funeral directors. What were they like? What personalities gravitate to, and are comfortable with dealing with the dead every day? Could they be normal? He doubted it.

"Yes, Mr. Nicholas, of course. I can assure you that the body was properly cared for once we received it from Flushing Hospital. As you can imagine, due to the nature and positioning of the wounds, the deceased required extensive work in preparation for any viewing." As he spoke, Nick Leventis, one of the proprietors, was checking the file, which, Michael noticed, was neatly labeled, "Alexander Nicholas." He continued. "We were instructed to immediately seal the casket."

"And who requested that it be sealed immediately?"

Leventis, appeared to be in his late twenties, the youngest member of his family to join the century-old Leventis Funeral Home, scanned the several papers in the folder, then looked carefully again at Michael. "I'm afraid the file doesn't indicate who exactly made the request. The notes are from my uncle." After a long silence, Leventis added, "I'm sure that my uncle assumed the casket was to be closed in order to spare the loved ones any discomfort."

"It was your uncle who received the instructions?" Michael asked.

"Yes, my Uncle Paul personally handled all the initial interviews and then coordinated the arrangements. These are his notes I am looking at."

"Can I speak with your Uncle Paul?"

Nick Leventis looked down and closed the file. "I wish it was possible, but my uncle passed away in January."

Chapter 74

Westport, Connecticut

Michael didn't want Samantha to notice as he quietly left their bedroom to head to the wine cellar. She had taken an Ambien, so tonight he was confident she had fallen into a deep sleep.

As soon as he turned on the computer, signed in and lowered the big screen, he could see Alex appearing to be turning up his nose. "What's wrong, Alex?"

"It smells like oak and cork in here?"

What now? Michael thought to himself. "Where is the smell coming from—where *you* are or where *I* am?"

"What do you think, Michael? It's got to be from your wine cellar."

Michael looked around and even inhaled himself. The room naturally did have a distinct scent of oak and cork, since both were such prominent materials there. Alex had to know that—was he just pulling my leg?

"You can't seriously smell anything—let alone *in here*, can you?"

"I'm a little surprised myself." Alex answered; he appeared to be genuinely puzzled.

"Well, it's the type of complaint you'd have if you were alive—alive in the sense that you were *physically* still here."

"Michael, *I am* here, you can see me. But you can also see that I'm not there with you *physically,* say, sitting in a chair in your cellar. That seems to be a hard concept for you. You only had about ten years of college."

"Yeah, I know you're not sitting here in this room with me." But Michael had never been so unsure about so many things. "Alex, this is just so unreal. So unbelievable. You have to understand how strange and incredible this is. I have to ask you a question—and don't get upset with me."

"What now?"

Michael told Alex about the strange call from Father Papadopoulos, his sudden death, and then his visits with Father Papageorge and Nick Leventis. Alex appeared to listen intently.

"Michael, I don't have the answers; not yet, anyway. But I think you are too fixated on my body—instead of the spirit. Even the priests all tell you that. I'm beginning to see their point. Maybe the body *is* just a vessel for the mind. ... But what was your big question?"

"Alex, where is your body now?"

"What an odd question. I just don't know the answer. It's funny, but I expect I will learn the answer at some point. It would be interesting to meet my old self—unless I am that same person."

Michael took a deep breath. He sensed his brother was losing patience with this discussion. It was all too theoretical and spiritual.

"Alex, you would tell me if you really *were* still alive, wouldn't you? I mean,—is there a chance you never died in that shooting—and you're sitting in Brooklyn somewhere and doing all this on some FaceTime program on a computer?"

"I may have gotten pretty good with all this technology—for

obvious reasons—but I'm not exactly a computer geek. Not yet anyway."

But Alex ignored the rest of the question and changed the subject. It was odd and rather abrupt, Michael thought, but again, not unlike something Alex would have done when he was, yes, alive.

"I'm making room for you here, Michael. It'll be like when we were little kids, you know, sharing a bedroom," he said.

"What do you mean?" Michael asked.

"The people that are after you think you have more protection around you than you do. That and some luck are probably the only reason you're still alive. Also, people think that professional killers are smart. Most guys in the underworld are stupid. But, no matter what, they're closing in."

"What have you found out?"

"I don't have specifics yet. Certain things seem to be coming together. Bad things. It's like when the government says they hear "static" before a terrorist strike. They don't have the details, they just see or hear a lot of activity. That's what this is."

Michael could see that Alex's virtual world was becoming more complex and his powers of perception more sophisticated. But exactly how it was happening was a mystery. Alex and everything surrounding him appeared to be a mysterious black box.

"Alex, how do you learn things? What's feeding in to you that causes you to reach conclusions about what's going on?"

Alex seemed to struggle with the question. "What do you mean, what's feeding in to me? I'm connected to a lot of things now. I don't mean with wires, somehow it just happens. I'm connected to the Internet. And now, even when the computer is "off" or sleeping, these links are transmitting information into me. I use Google, GPS, Facebook, Twitter, and all kinds of apps. I can message people—live people. I can intercept things. It's better than being alive."

"Alex, I don't think anyone really knows how these systems work together—and what it might lead to. Your artificial intelligence software is leading-edge stuff. It could be taking on a life of its own—or, of *your* own."

"Don't ask me how anything works. All I know is I can see things happening." Alex said. "Like I said before—you don't know how your mind works either."

"Can you see the future?"

"No, if I could see the future, I'd have you placing big bets on the games and the horses. I'd open a fucking day trader account at Schwab, for Christ's sake. But I can put a lot of things together and kind of predict some things that look logical." Alex stopped abruptly as though something new entered his mind.

"What's wrong?" Michael asked. "Did we lose the connection?"

Alex looked frozen. He stayed motionless another few seconds then, as though the camera moved in for a close-up, his face became animated again, he looked straight at Michael. "They're going to kill you. Very soon."

Chapter 75

Karen DiNardo knew about Michael's second life running Tartarus—but she didn't know his bigger secret, that his brother was at least *virtually* alive and smarter than ever. He had asked Karen to update her research on artificial intelligence. Alex's evolution over the past several months had Michael wondering whether he was imagining things—or had Alex's learning and informational powers rapidly accelerated. As with their discussion the first time he'd asked her to compile the latest information on the topic, he suspected it would become a dance as he withheld his secret—and she knew he was doing so.

"Michael, listen to this." Karen was reading from her report.

In an interview published on Saturday by the German magazine Focus, Stephen Hawking argues that the increasing sophistication of computer technology is likely to outstrip human intelligence. He believes that the scientific modification of human genes could increase the complexity of DNA and "improve" human beings.

In contrast with our intellect, computers double their performance every 18 months," says Hawking. "So the danger is real that they could develop intelligence and take over the world."

"It's been over a year. No wonder he's getting smarter." Michael said to himself, louder than he thought. Karen, as usual, didn't miss a thing

"*Who's* getting smarter?" she said, her eyes piercingly curious.

"My computer," he said, nonchalantly.

"No, you said, *he*. You don't refer to your computer as a *he*, do you? You know, you originally asked me to research this about a year ago. I remember, it was right after your brother was—or died. You never did tell me why you were so interested in all this."

"I know, Karen—and I'm still not going to tell you. At least, not yet. But, I promise you, when I'm ready, you'll be one of the first to know."

"Interesting," she said, which Michael knew was simply her way of delaying until she decided it was safe to resume her questioning. Nevertheless, Karen turned her attention back to her dish of homemade tagliatelle in a Tuscan meat sauce. "I've always wanted to come to Da Silvano. This is even better than I'd imagined it would be." She twirled her fork into the dish, took another bite and then abruptly put it down.

"But wait, there's more." She reached for another document. "Listen to this. This is from *National Science Monthly*:

"It has been rumored that recent breakthroughs in the field of artificial intelligence will allow a *simulated* person to achieve greater intelligence than a real human being but will also be capable of acquiring a higher level of emotional intelligence, thereby able to match or exceed the emotional capabilities of many humans. There is speculation that, should advanced artificial intelligence technology be combined with certain computer imaging and emotion-sensing technologies, that the computer—or simulated person could accurately read the mind and emotions of a real human.

"And wait until you hear this one, it's from an obscure journal, called *Geeksville*, it's kind of like the *National Enquirer* of technology, but sometimes, other reporters admit it's uncannily accurate:

"It is only a matter of time until a cocktail of advanced artificial and emotional intelligence software allows scientists to duplicate the human mind—or perhaps, a particular person's mind. Further, since that new artificial or *synthetic* mind would exist *inside* a computer, it is conceivable that this entity could find its way and actually log onto the Internet—on its own—giving it unlimited access to the entire virtual world—from Amazon and Google to the world's most confidential and sophisticated tracking and eavesdropping programs.

"You can't make this stuff up," she said, reaching for her fork and staring back at Michael.

Chapter 76

F rank Cortese stood at the foot of his bed at the Sofitel Hotel. Familiar routines and places, whether they were cities, restaurants or hotel rooms, were important to him. Perhaps, he thought, it helped him compensate for the unpredictability of his travels as he stalked his prey.

He liked being back in New York City. It was the scene of some of his most prominent assignments. His successes had been splashed in black and white photo spreads on the front pages of the New York tabloids, the *Post* and the *Daily News*: a Mafia don's legs, unnaturally sprawled on the sidewalk in front of a prominent Manhattan steakhouse, partially hidden by the open passenger-side door of his limousine, still immaculately dressed in well-tailored trousers, black Ferragamo laced-up shoes and designer socks; an investment banker, the white, bloodstained, barber's cape, still fastened around his bullet-ridden body, lying on the marble floor of an exclusive Wall Street barbershop.

A trademark of Cortese's expertise was that his executions always remained unsolved. They were most times assumed to be

Mafia hits, not the work of a missionary from the dark world of the Vatican.

The door was double-locked, the chain mechanism in place and the curtains drawn, as Cortese, still in his Italian silk pajamas and white terry cloth hotel robe, surveyed the weapons and accompanying paraphernalia neatly displayed on the bed. The black, Russian-made, semi-automatic Makarov pistol, a screw-in silencer, ammunition cartridges, a nine-inch Italian stiletto; he was as familiar with these instruments as he was with his razor and toothbrush.

His concentration was interrupted by the ring of the telephone. He stared at the black phone on the table near his bed; only one person knew to reach him at the hotel. He finally picked up the receiver and waited for the caller to speak.

"Listen carefully, my friend. There is a change in our plans." Cortese wasn't surprised. The monsignor had already hinted at his concerns. "This Sindy Steele, your American assassin, will be with Mr. Nicholas at the baseball game. Assuming you will be successful in killing him, you will be at risk from this woman. We must assume she will be armed. It will make your escape very difficult. We cannot risk this, Frank."

Cortese listened while Monsignor Petrucceli described the new plan for the murder of Michael Nicholas the next day at Yankee Stadium. When they finished discussing the details of the revised plot, Cortese, satisfied if not pleased with the changes, hung up the phone and returned to his review of the weaponry on the bed.

Then, after carefully placing each item in its designated pocket inside the unique, intrecciato-woven, black leather Bottega Veneta shoulder bag, he poured Campari and club soda into his cocktail glass, grabbed the television clicker and sat down in the comfortable chair near the bed and began his nightly ritual of surfing the hotel's endless choices of cable stations. He suddenly stopped his searching when, quite unexpectedly, he came upon a scene from his favorite movie, one he had seen more times than he could count. As he watched Julie Andrews singing from the top of a mountain, he settled deeply into his chair, happy that *The Sound of Music* would, for the next two hours, take him to another, gentler world.

Chapter 77

Sindy Steele, naked underneath her hotel bathrobe, surveyed the weapons arrayed on the king-sized bed in the master suite she had come to believe would be her home: a standard Glock 17 pistol, a subcompact Glock 26, a screw-in cylinder silencer, two seventeen-round magazines, a sleek, black stiletto knife, and a clear plastic envelope containing two cyanide pills.

She sat down on the upholstered club chair, put her long legs up on the matching ottoman, sipped her vodka and cranberry juice cocktail, reached for her BlackBerry on the coffee table, and replayed the crystal-clear recording of the conversation between Michael and Samantha Nicholas, picked up from the bugging device she had concealed in Michael's cell phone:

"How could you let that nutcase woman come near me? How could you?

I had no idea you were seeing her. I've been crazy since last night when I couldn't reach you. ...

You haven't slept with her again have you? Oh my God. I must be crazy. You had sex with her after our discussion, our agreement, just a few days ago?

Samantha, I'm so sorry. I know it was ridiculously wrong but … she's a cold-blooded killer. I'm afraid of what she might have done if I broke everything off with her. … She could kill either one—or both of us. … She's not a normal person, Samantha."

She switched off the device, stood up, returned to her display of weapons and, with the expert precision of a surgeon, she screwed the silencer cylinder into the barrel of the subcompact Glock.

Chapter 78

Jonathan Goldstein appeared gaunt in his eight-thousand-dollar Brioni suit. This added to his unhappiness. He glanced around the conference table, his deep-set dark eyes assessing the nervous Gibraltar executive team. Then, directing his attention to Richard Perkins, he asked sharply, "Where's Michael Nicholas? *He runs this company, doesn't he?*"

"He's back in New York. We've decided to deal with some things here in this office without him. He had a schedule conflict, so I told him it wasn't critical for him to be here this week and that I could cover for him."

Goldstein didn't waste any time establishing his dominance over his new underling. "Richard, when I call a meeting, I expect the people that work for me to be there. All of them. Nicholas reports to you, it was your job to see that he was here today. There are no 'conflicts' when it's my company. Do I make myself clear? Don't let this happen again."

Perkins answered simply, "Yes, sir. I can assure you, this won't happen again."

Goldstein liked what he'd heard, he knew Perkins was a tough Southern Baptist; a guy's guy—everything he wasn't. Seeing Perkins nearly castrate himself in apologies, made Goldstein feel good, on top of the world. He'd deal with Michael Nicholas later, when he was more confident of the situation. He wondered, however, about this elusive character whose unusual reputation he had learned more about during the last several weeks. For now, as he surveyed the rest of the Gibraltar European management team, all of whom, except for Perkins, reported directly to Nicholas, he needed simply to welcome them into their new reality: the world according to Jonathan Goldstein.

Goldstein wasted no time with introductions or small talk. "I know you are all busy so I will get right to the point and then we can leave this room and go back to our business. Just some things you need to know about me. I don't like meetings, I don't like presentations, I don't like PowerPoint. I don't care how good you sound. I don't even want to hear you. What I *do want* is money. I want to make money and I expect that this company will be more profitable immediately. Right now, you are a mediocre company in terms of profitability. I could make more money with no risk if I had simply bought T-bills. That will change—or you won't be here. And I don't mean you won't be here a year from now. I mean you won't be here in *ninety days*. It's all about the money. From this day forward, as they say, 'show me the money.' " He looked around the room, sipped from his glass of water, and resumed speaking. "Before I move on to some pressing issues, are there any questions?"

The room was silent. Not an executive was stirring. "Sounds like you know a rhetorical question when you hear one," he said.

"So let me continue. After today you'll take your instructions from Richard." He looked to Perkins, seated directly next to him and realized he had forgotten to mention one name. "And, of course, Michael Nicholas, who will be your day-to-day head, as he was prior to the acquisition. But in his absence, let me make some announcements that can't wait until Michael decides he can join us."

He noticed a few of the executives exchanged glances.

"Anyone who tells you that things will not change is a liar. First, we can't make more money unless we have fewer employees. You'll leave here with a list of all the employees who report to you. By next Monday, you will return that list to us with a twenty percent reduction in staff. Figure it out—*or add your own name* to the termination list. If this sounds harsh, it is. We're not running a charity here." Goldstein paused again, took another sip of water, adjusted the gold cufflinks on his French-cuffed shirt, and with a look of complete seriousness said, "I will tell you, though, if you follow me, you'll each make more money than you ever dreamed of. I will make you rich. You decide."

Finished, Goldstein sat down and nodded to Perkins. He watched as Perkins surveyed the room, locking eyes individually with each silent, shell-shocked executive seated around the conference table. He could see they weren't going to challenge Perkins. This was what he liked about him.

Perkins proceeded to speak in his deep but low Southern drawl.

"Just some final housekeeping items folks. First, *I* am your boss. Michael Nicholas is the CEO of this organization, but make no mistake, *I* am your boss. Second, Mr. Goldstein is *my* boss. I'm glad you've had an opportunity to meet him. I know that under Michael Nicholas, you've had a rather free-wheeling, open-door culture. That ends today. Do not believe that because you have met Mr. Goldstein, you may call him. If any of you should ever find it necessary to call Mr. Goldstein, it will be the last call you will make as an employee of Gibraltar."

Chapter 79

Hans Ulricht sat in the Connaught Hotel's bar, swirling his snifter of Armagnac, wondering whether his father enjoyed the same view when he frequented the hotel in the years leading up to WWII. Certainly, he thought, his drinking companion this evening, Claus Dietrich, a nephew of the notorious Nazi, Joseph Goebbels, would have had his father's approval. For tonight, he thought, it was a meeting of two members of the generation that once expected to live a life of power and dominance.

Ulricht breathed in the strong aromatic fumes from his large glass and took a sip of the Armagnac. It burned his throat as it made its way down into his chest, leaving him with a calm, contented feeling. As he spoke, he feared that Dietrich would notice that his eyes were glassy; he'd brought himself back to a lost but happier time in his life.

"I have a clear recollection of driving with my father and Herr Hitler in his big, black, open Mercedes. I was just a little boy, of course, but I can visualize it now as though it happened just yesterday, the crowds waving and saluting as we went by, the other children staring at me, wondering who I was and how I was chosen to ride in the Fürher's limousine. It was such a grand automobile, its heavy black body spotless, the chrome shining in the bright sunlight, the windows were bulletproof, so thick. The flags on the fenders, with our glorious swastikas, were waving rapidly in the wind as we sped through the streets. The Fürher stood up, perfectly erect, in the front seat, next to the driver, his arm outstretched, saluting the crowd. He was like an uncle to me—yet I, like the crowd outside the car, was in awe of him."

He paused, took another sip of his apertif before he resumed, his eyes swollen, glistening. Dietrich appeared to be fascinated.

"Hitler took us that day up to the Banz monastery. To this day, I don't know why, but I remember my father saying that we were taking a detour from our planned itinerary. The monks were shocked when they saw us drive up. We all went on quite a long tour of the baroque monastery while the Führer disappeared into one of the rooms for a long talk with the abbot. We never found out what they spoke about, but when Hitler rejoined our tour, he said, 'There's a reason this Church has survived for two thousand years.'"

Ulricht sometimes wondered how he could have such a detailed recollection of an event that occurred while he was still a young child. He feared that he supplemented his own memory with the details provided by other, more mature observers, perhaps even historians or reporters. At this stage of his life, he was too often unsure of what he actually remembered. He suspected that, occasionally, details or even events that he could picture were what he had read or been told about. The confusion, when he allowed himself to think about it, was disturbing.

Dietrich smiled, his facial expression seemed to erratically and suddenly alternate between an angry grimace and a forced, self-conscious smirk. His quick smile was broad yet looked strained and artificial. "There is a new regime in the Vatican. The new pope is a complex man, but he is our friend; he is a German after all." As his expression reverted back to a smirk, it appeared that there was no coordination between his words and his facial countenance. He was one of those people who smiled at random, disorienting those around them.

The setting in the Connaught's bar room, designed by jet-set favorite David Collins, inspired by English Cubist and Irish 1920s art, with textured walls shimmering in platinum silver leaf overlaid with dusty pink, pistachio and lilac, was the embodiment of the updated, stylish, modern yet still classic English bar. The classic elements of the room suited the two old Nazis well while the stylish elements made them seem out of place, odd figures from another time.

Dietrich was a slight man, like Ulricht in his seventies and impeccably dressed, but possessing a hyper-active, nervous persona. He sat, smiling again, twitching and endlessly moving or rearranging himself in the plush, rich leather chair.

"What a tragedy for Germany that our Fürher never had children. Germany—and the world—would embrace such a man today," Dietrich said, his attention also seemingly drifting to another time.

Ulricht, sensing the drama going on in his friend's mind, nodded in agreement.

Dietrich continued, "I must say that, spiritually, I always felt a special bond with the Fürher. I believe, in the absence of any natural heirs, he would have eventually wanted me to seize the mantle of his leadership. At the right time, of course."

Ulricht stared at Dietrich, who was twitching once again in his seat, and pondered how the two of them could both feel the same sense of divine destiny propelling them to be the natural successor to his revered Uncle Adolph. In fact, Dietrich's revelation left him momentarily speechless.

But Ulricht knew that this was not the time to argue over succession. After all, it was too late for both of them; right now, he needed Dietrich's help, again.

Dietrich continued. "We must stick together, Hans. It is not the life our fathers envisioned for us but we must make do until our country and our party can re-emerge and we can reassert our natural dominance. We are already witnessing a great resurgence of the party in France and Greece—and, of course, in our homeland. And this time, we have even stronger friends inside the Church."

Ulricht felt relieved by Dietrich's tone but still troubled. "I am in your debt, Claus. This Hightower could have led the U.S. authorities to my door."

Dietrich smiled, once again shifting his short, lean legs. "Your father and my uncle were good friends, both patriots. The reach of the people loyal to my society is vast. As you can see, our steel hand can reach a degenerate and touch them, even while they shower." Dietrich laughed, his face alive with excitement. "I understand the authorities in that town in Connecticut—Greenwich—are still trying to understand an apparent plumbing problem in a certain home there. I marvel at the creativeness and superior intelligence of our followers. Who would have guessed that Nazis make such good plumbers?"

"I may still have a problem, Herr Dietrich. I hesitate to seek your assistance again, however." Ulricht looked sheepishly at his drinking partner.

"No, please, Hans. I would like to help you. You must trust me."

"It may not require such a drastic remedy. Perhaps, initially at least, just a threat will be sufficient. But there is a Jewish financier, an American, who may have knowledge, second-hand, of course, from Hightower, which could be damaging. His name is Jonathan Goldstein."

Dietrich smirked. "Of course it is."

Chapter 80

"This is a big game today," Deacon Dan said.

Deacon Dan had been Michael and Samantha's occasional personal driver for eight years. He was a friend and spiritual adviser to Michael, Samantha and Sofia. Although sixty-seven, he worked more than ever, first as a deacon at the Holy Rosary Church in Westport, as a guidance counselor at the high school, and also as the owner of Dan's Driving Service. He presided over Sofia's baptism and would likely do the same whenever she married. Michael had not utilized Dan very much recently since Sindy Steele was serving as both bodyguard and chauffeur. Michael was happy to be back in Dan's new black Cadillac for the one-hour trip from Connecticut to the Bronx.

"Yeah," Michael said, "It should be great weather too. I just hope the Yanks get out alive. They're not playing that well lately."

"I know, I've got Jeter, Hughes and Posada on my fantasy baseball team roster. They're killing me."

As they pulled up to the entrance to the stadium gate, Michael laughed, "Dan, you've got three jobs and a big family, but you never miss a beat with your fantasy team. And, I've noticed that every year you bitch and moan about your team—and then you wind up winning."

"Well, not this year." Dan said. "Where's Miss Steele meeting you?"

Michael paused, wondering whether Dan's highly developed intuitive powers had figured out the nature of his relationship with her. "She's got her ticket. I'm meeting her at the seats—figure we could leave any time after the seventh inning. I'll call you on your cell when we're ready to go. What are you going to do?"

"I might catch a bite to eat up the road."

Michael knew exactly where Dan was going. "So you're heading up to Aqueduct?"

"You know, Michael, I do these things so I can avoid the *major* vices."

Michael knew that the Deacon was a regular at the racetrack. "Have a great time, Dan. We'll meet you at the entrance to the Hard Rock Cafe when we get out."

Fletcher would be at the game, watching, but had promised to stay out of sight. Michael knew he'd be leaving the stadium alone. Fletcher had taken his own car and would come and go separately. With Samantha and Angie safely away for the long weekend, he knew what he needed to do. His stomach was already in knots.

After today, Sindy would be out of his life forever.

As he walked down the aisle toward the seats, the playing field with its magnificent bright green expanse of perfectly manicured grass came into view. It was as much of a surprise today as it was the very first time he had been to a major league ballpark. He still could recall that first time, as a child, holding his father's hand, leaving the entrance tunnel to the stands at Yankee Stadium and coming upon the field, a green pristine stage, seemingly out of place surrounded by the monumental stadium.

Now, as he approached his seats, Michael remembered being in these same seats with his brother. For as long as Michael could remember, Alex had Yankee season tickets; four front-row seats in right field. They were typical of Alex's tastes. He would never want to be in the "corporate" seats near home plate with all the "suits." Yet, his seats were only 250 feet from home plate and, being in the front row, he felt like he was playing right field.

Today, nearly fifty-thousand people packed the stadium for the big holiday afternoon game with the Yanks' bitter rival, the Boston Red Sox. An additional three million viewers sitting in their recliners in their family rooms and drinking beer and eating nachos at sports bars would be watching the big game on television. It was an exciting and festive atmosphere, Michael thought, as he greeted Sindy Steele, who was already seated on the aisle.

She greeted Michael with a peck on the cheek as she stood up, allowing him to take the inside seat on her left. For a brief instant, he thought it was odd that she didn't simply move over and allow him to take the end seat. Maybe, he hoped, she felt he would be more protected with her on the aisle.

"Aren't you a little hot?" Michael said, noticing her windbreaker, despite the ninety-degree temperature.

"I don't know. It just feels a little breezy to me, I guess." But Michael noticed that her attention seemed to be elsewhere. Her eyes canvassed the surrounding seats.

"Looking for someone?" he said.

She turned her attention back to him, grasping his arm. "Just you, Michael. Just you."

As they rose for the national anthem, a man wearing a burgundy golf jacket and Yankee cap came down the aisle and settled into the seat directly behind him.

Chapter 81

At the end of three innings, the Yankees led the Red Sox 3-0. Sindy Steele scanned the faces of the other spectators. Since she and Michael occupied the first two seats of the front row, she only had to look behind them and on their flanks. As they faced the playing field in front of them, the New York Yankee right fielder stood less than fifty feet away. The stadium crowd, always so diverse, was a difficult one in which to seek out potential problems. The only individual who caught her attention at all was the man seated directly behind Michael.

It was time, Sindy thought, to prepare. She reached into her right windbreaker pocket, felt for the subcompact Glock and gripped it with her index finger on the trigger. It was ready. She then placed her left hand into her left windbreaker pocket and massaged the smooth, surprisingly cool handle of the stiletto. If all went according to her plan, however, she would use neither of them. Then she reached below her windbreaker, into the pocket of her skin-tight jeans until she touched the small plastic wrapper containing the two cyanide capsules. She knew she'd only need one but brought the second in case the first became damaged or accidentally dropped. Using her fingers, just as she had practiced so many times, she slit open the top of the wrapper and pushed one of the capsules out and into her fingers. She glanced to her left at Michael. He was watching the game. She could feel the distance between them.

"Beer here, beer here," the stadium vendor called out in his unmistakable New York accent. "Beer here, beer here." Sindy turned around and could see that he was quickly approaching their aisle. She clutched Michael's arm, tenderly, and said softly, "I'll treat you. What could be better on a hot day than baseball and a cool beer?"

"Sure, thanks," he answered, his attention riveted at the play on the field.

She got up to meet the vendor, who was serving the row of fans just one row behind them. She purchased two beers, and as she turned around to walk back to their seats, swiftly dropped a cyanide capsule in one of them. The natural white foam head on the beer covered up any reaction of the liquid to the lethal capsule.

Chapter 82

Bronx, New York

D espite an underlying tension, Michael settled comfortably into the convenient preoccupation of watching the game. He planned on suggesting to Sindy that they leave their seats around the sixth inning and dine at NY Steak within the stadium where they could talk.

The low roar of over forty-thousand people nearly obscured the ringing of his cell phone. Annoyed at the interruption, Michael nevertheless fumbled through his pockets until he found it. He looked first at the phone's screen; it read "Private." Tempted to ignore the call, his eyes focused on the red and white uniformed batter at home plate and the big Yankee pitcher beginning his windup, he pressed the green button on the cell and placed the phone against his right ear.

"Michael, your killer is with you now." The voice was Alex's.

Michael looked around him. He saw a group of men behind him, what appeared to be couples on his left, and Steele, twenty feet away, approaching with two beers in hand to his right side.

"Alex, Jesus, where are you? How are you doing this? Who is this guy, where's he sitting?"

"Michael, *it's not a guy.*"

"What do you mean, it's not a guy?" Michael whispered, fearing the answer but apparently knowing it as he subtly turned his body to the left, away from Steele, and trying to do so without drawing her attention.

"It's that woman you've been screwing around with—she's there with you, isn't she?" Alex's voice was rising.

"Yeah, and the Yanks are up, three-nothing," he said, trying to sound nonchalant. He could feel her eyes on him.

Michael looked at Sindy approaching with the beers. He wondered whether she had brought her pistol with her to the game. It wouldn't have been unusual since she usually carried it for his protection as part of her job.

She sat down in her seat, still holding the two beers, apparently waiting for him to get off the phone.

"Michael, I need to tell you something."

"Hold on, I'll be off in a second." But just at that moment, Michael heard a strange sound coming through his phone. He looked at the screen; the connection was gone.

Michael looked back at Sindy. She held onto the beers. "Michael, I need to tell you something. In Paris, as I was leaving Rosen's apartment, a woman entered. She had her own key."

Michael was confused. Did he hear her correctly, he wondered? It came out of nowhere.

"What do you mean? What are you talking about?" He reached for one of the beers. Sindy held them both away from him, just out of his reach.

"I didn't tell you everything. I hid in a closet when I heard someone enter his apartment. Rosen had just gone out the window,"

"So? I don't understand?" he said, thoroughly perplexed. The crowd cheered wildly in the background. Michael heard it but it sounded now like just background music to the main event that was happening between him and Sindy.

"It was your wife. She entered Bertrand Rosen's apartment as I was trying to leave. She had a key. He was expecting her, Michael."

As she spoke, he noticed that she held onto to both cups, watching his face, as though she was waiting for his response before allowing him to drink. He sensed the importance of the moment. He knew his words and his body language might have critical consequences. He suspected those consequences were in Sindy's pocket. He looked for her Glock but, deep down, doubted whether even she was crazy enough to shoot him there in front of all these people in such close quarters. He thought about Alex's words. And she was waiting for an answer.

"Sindy, why are you telling me this *now*? Why *here*? What's going on? Are you telling me that Samantha was having an *affair*?"

She stared back in icy silence. "Does it make a *difference* to you? Does it matter that your wife was with Rosen?"

"Jesus, Sindy. Of course it makes a difference. But I need to find out what all this is about?"

"What do you mean, 'find out what it's about?' What the hell do you think it was all about? She was *fucking* him." She said, anger edging into her voice and contorting her face.

"Why didn't you tell me before? I don't understand what's happening here," he said, searching her face for clues. He looked around him for help, from what exactly he wasn't sure, yet.

"I was trying to protect you. I wanted to deal with her first, to try and settle it with her. It didn't work out the way I planned, so I'm telling you now."

"Sindy, it's all too fast. I need to digest this. What do you want from me right now?"

And with that, she smiled, handed him the beer in her left hand, and whispered, "You're right. I'm sorry."

Chapter 83

Bronx, New York

Frank Cortese had a good seat to watch a game he barely understood—and the best seat to observe a murder he thought he could predict.

Watching Michael on his cell phone, Cortese knew something unexpected had occurred. He didn't know who the caller was, or what was said, but he knew it had disturbed Michael. Up to that point, Steele had acted according to plan, but she now appeared to be in an intense discussion with Michael instead of doing her job. Why hadn't she handed Michael his last drink?

He wasn't used to scenes spiraling out of control.

According to Monsignor Petrucceli's last call, Steele had turned on Michael and had agreed to poison him. Petrucceli had secretly instructed Cortese to then shoot her, using his silencer while the crowd was already preoccupied with a dying Michael Nicholas. Cortese would then lose himself in the commotion and slip out through the nearby stadium exit onto the street.

But something was wrong. He watched as Steele repeatedly withheld the poisoned drink. Cortese had to wait until Michael was either dead or in his final moments before shooting her through the back at the precise point where the bullets would be sure to penetrate her heart. His disguise would ensure that even if he were later spotted on surveillance cameras, his identity would not be revealed.

But just as Michael appeared to be finally taking the cup of beer from Steele, a roar erupted from the crowd. Everyone around them, including Michael, suddenly stood up, their eyes following the trajectory of the white baseball heading toward them, their hands reaching up, straining to catch the prized souvenir. As the ball came closer, seemingly headed directly to Cortese, the press of the crowd, reaching over him, jostling for position, nearly knocked him over. As he struggled to stay in his position in his seat, his hat and sunglasses fell to the ground.

Chapter 84

Sindy Steele watched the flight of the ball as Michael pulled his hand back, never taking the beer from her but instead leaping up in an effort to catch the ball heading for the seat directly behind him. She crouched down, protectively holding both cups of beer from the frenetic crowd around her. She watched Michael leap up and saw the ball carom off the straining hands reaching over the man seated behind him, she saw his sunglasses go flying and as he emerged from beneath the tangle of hands and arms, she recognized the man with eyes of different colors.

He was reaching into his pocket for his gun.

She knew now that the situation was not what it appeared to be; she had been deceived. The plot unfolding was different than the one that had been explained to her. They were going to kill *her* as soon as she murdered Michael. She had been set up. She dropped both beers and reached for her Glock.

Not confident she could outdraw or overpower Cortese, she decided her safest move was to jump over the three-foot wall and onto the field. He wouldn't be brazen enough, she hoped, to shoot her once she was in full view of the police and the entire stadium crowd. She had only seconds to leap over the low wall before he would be able to aim and shoot.

She plunged over the concrete divider, landing onto the red clay warning track; she was in a crouch but on her feet when she saw, just a few feet away, the white pinstriped uniform with the blue "33" on the back of the Yankees right fielder, Nick Swisher.

Probably hearing the commotion from the stands behind him, Swisher turned around, at first startled, and then shook his head, smiling, and called out to her, "Oh man, what the heck are you doing out here?" Almost immediately, however, he appeared to focus on something behind her—Cortese—and his expression changed. Swisher began to holler and move away, "Hey lady, that guy's got a gun."

She knew she had no time to waste. She ran quickly, making sudden moves to the left and right as she sprinted toward a gate a hundred feet away along the first-base line. She could see NYPD officers with their guns drawn entering the field from all sides. She glanced back and saw Cortese in the outfield behind her. His gun was out, and he was looking right at her. She turned back around, and, running as fast as she could, she was getting closer to the exit. A blue tide of police officers were entering the field from her left and right sides. It was a race to see which came first: the gate, the police or a bullet in the back from Cortese.

She heard a thundering roar from the crowd cheering her on as she ran for her life. Then she heard loud pops as clumps of grass exploded around her. And then an eerie silence settled over the stadium. The pops continued, raising the grass all around her. She kept running, left, then right; then straight again for the gate.

She was almost there when she heard a series of loud explosions. She knew the NYPD had opened fire and waited for the first sign that she'd been shot.

Chapter 85

Westport, Connecticut

"Is she dead?" Fletcher asked.

Michael had barely sat down, this time in Mario's private back room. He looked around him to see if anyone was within earshot, or worse, gunshot range. "I don't know."

"What do you mean, you don't know? Didn't you see what happened?" Fletcher was either getting excited or he was beginning to panic.

But Michael was calm. "I just slipped out of there along with thousands of others who poured through the exits before the cops could close the gates. I figured it was best if I just left. That's why I called you so we'd both get out and get home before anyone started asking questions."

"Holy shit. What happened to her?" Fletcher's mouth was still open in amazement. "You mean she could still be out there? On the loose?"

"Or dead. Or wounded in a hospital or an alley. I don't know. I've tried her cell and it goes right to voicemail. At least the cops didn't answer. She hasn't tried me." Michael recounted the details, beginning with the decision to meet Steele as they had planned for weeks, not wanting to signal his intentions by canceling their game appearance together, then ending with the frenzied gunfight in the outfield between Steele and the unknown man sitting behind him during the game.

The evening news came on the television monitor above the bar. Michael and Fletcher watched and listened as the news anchor reported the day's event at the ballpark:

"A violent shooting occurred on the field at Yankee Stadium today. As fifty-thousand people watched from the stands and another three million at home, a man seated in the seats in right field reportedly attacked a woman seated nearby, chasing her onto the field while the game was in play. The attacker fired a series of bullets in her direction. The NYPD attempted to shoot the attacker but was hampered by the crowd that, in a near panic, stormed onto the field and out the exits for cover. Unofficial reports claim that at least one person was killed and another seriously injured. There has been no confirmation or official word yet from police spokesmen as to the identity of the victim or victims—or whether they had made any arrests.

"So we know one of them is dead. It's odd that they wouldn't have more details on who was shot or killed," Fletcher said, his eyes narrowing as he struggled to figure out the unusual lack of information. "They must be having trouble sorting everything out with all the chaos that went on—or they want to keep someone they're looking for wondering. And you're sure you didn't recognize the guy who went after her?"

"No, I hardly got a look at him. He was sitting behind me. Then when Ortiz hit the ball into the seats, all hell broke loose. Next thing I know, Sindy's running away, she jumps over the right-field wall and onto the field, Swisher turns around, and this guy from behind me has a gun and he's running after her and firing at her. I think he had a silencer because there was no noise and the gun looked like it had some kind of extension on the end of the barrel."

Fletcher's eyes widened. "He's a pro. Michael, this guy was a professional. That's why the cops are staying quiet. They're probably still trying to figure out what's going down. Plus, we don't know yet who got shot or arrested. The NYPD will probably try and talk to anyone who was seated anywhere near you guys in the stands. They're going over video tapes from all the game cameras now."

But Michael knew he had left out one important detail: his call from Alex.

"Fletcher, I've got something I have to tell you," Michael looked around for the waiter, "but you're going to need a stiff drink first."

"OK, just give me a hint until I get the drink."

Michael's expression turned grave, "While I was watching the game, I received a phone call on my cell."

Fletcher watching Michael closely said, "Yeah, who was it?"

"It was Alex."

With his usual perfect timing, Tiger strolled up to their table. But before he could say a word, Fletcher pleaded, "A double Manhattan, as soon as you can."

Chapter 86

Venice, Italy

Cardinal Lovallo took a sip of one of Harry's Bar's famous peach Bellinis.

"Let us pray he is alive."

"We will know shortly." Monsignor Petrucceli nervously checked his watch and glanced toward the entrance of the bar.

The cardinal, uncharacteristically silent, seemed to be searching Petrucceli's face for a hopeful sign. But Petrucceli had nothing positive to offer yet. He sat, watching the door, waiting, and tried over and over, to analyze what little news they had been given about yesterday's events.

The table was set for three. In a gesture of divine faith, Petrucceli thought, as soon as he sat down, Cardinal Lovallo had ordered three Bellinis. The cardinal finished his, Petrucceli was still nursing his, and the third, which was to be Frank Cortese's, sat undisturbed. Petrucceli sensed that the cardinal wanted to drink that one too but was reluctant to show any lack of faith that Cortese would arrive soon.

With the absence of any official reports on the identities of who was killed, injured or arrested by the New York police, the cardinal and monsignor could not be sure whether Cortese was, as planned, on the Delta flight from Kennedy airport to Venice. The plane should have just landed and the Cipriani's awaiting sleek mahogany speedboat would have Cortese at the restaurant in just minutes.

"Dominick, finish your Bellini, it will calm your nerves," Cardinal Lovallo said as he sat, apparently calm and serene. He looked like a man who had survived many crises.

For Dominick Petrucceli, this was as close as he had ever come to catastrophe. "I'm sorry, my stomach is in turmoil. I won't be able to digest anything until Frank walks through the door."

"God willing, Dominick, he will arrive momentarily."

Finally Petrucceli saw the speedboat in the distance making the turn from the water lanes toward the dock, which was just out of sight. But he couldn't tell whether there was a passenger on board in the cabin below the deck. As the boat disappeared from sight, the low roar of the inboard motors could be heard inside the bar, although only Lovallo and Petrucceli actually heard it.

The next three minutes—roughly the time required for the boat to dock and for the captain and any passengers to disembark and walk the short distance into the bar—seemed like an eternity. Petrucceli nodded to the cardinal, who continued to sit motionless, "Now we will know God's will," he said, not even turning around to glance at the entrance.

Finally, the two narrow wood-and-glass front doors swung open. The boat's captain, dressed in his formal white uniform, held the door open, allowing a tall, athletic woman with long, dark hair to enter before him. He placed her large, wheeled carry-on behind the bar nearby. She nodded to him and tried to discreetly slip him some type of currency as a gratuity, which he appeared to reject, holding up his hands in a defensive type of gesture.

Seeing no one else enter the bar, Monsignor Petrucceli and the cardinal looked at each other, searching for the words to measure the depth of their peril.

The cardinal gave a sigh of resignation. "I will contact Cardinal Sardino," he said, referring to the pope's chief of staff, or consigliere, formally known as the Vatican secretary of state. "He will not be pleased. But whatever has transpired, we must ensure that there are no surprises for the Holy Father." Likely seeing the look of distress on Petrucceli's face, he added, "We will deal with this as we have dealt with many other problems. There is a solution for everything, Dominick. Some are more expensive than others."

But just as they had blocked out the rest of the world, they were startled by the approach of the tall, confident, powerfully built woman who stood over them at their table. It was the woman who entered the bar with the captain. Neither of them had any idea who she could be. One horrible possibility crossed Petrucceli's mind. It's not possible, he thought.

"Gentlemen, I believe you were waiting for Mr. Cortese. Unfortunately, he's dead."

Neither moved nor said a word. They both simply stared at this attractive stranger. Petrucceli wondered whether his worst fear had yet entered Lovallo's mind.

"Perhaps I should introduce myself," she said as she sat herself down in the empty seat. "I believe I spoke with one of you on the phone just the other day. Actually, I have it recorded. I'm Sindy Steele."

Petrucceli was speechless. He looked over at the cardinal, suddenly appearing to age before his eyes, his mouth dropped open. As the stunned, speechless men continued to watch, she took a sip of the untouched Bellini, smiled broadly and proclaimed, "I think from what I've seen so far that we're going to work well together. I just love Bellinis."

Chapter 87

Rome, Italy

Sharkey was awakened by the metallic ring of his bedside tele-phone. As he reached for the receiver, he wondered whether this would be the call letting him know that, finally, Michael was dead.

As he hoped, it was Petrucceli. "Joseph, I have news."

Sharkey caught a grave quality in the monsignor's voice. Priests always get that way when someone dies, no matter how much the guy deserves it, he thought.

"Is he dead?"

"There have been developments. You must—"

Sharkey bolted up from his bed. "Developments? What the hell are we talking about *now*? Just tell me he's dead—and how long it took him to die. That's all I want to know."

"There was a difficulty at the Yankee Stadium. I'm afraid our work is unfinished."

Sharkey couldn't believe his ears. "I should have let Rizzo—"

"Joseph, I don't have much time to speak. You must listen to me."

"Listen? What the—"

"The polizia will be at your door. They will—"

"The *police*? At *my* door? What's going on?"

"You must listen carefully. They will arrest you. This is temporary and cannot be avoided. Trust me. I will have you released very soon—"

"Released? You gotta be kidding me—I'm not going to any damned jail—"

"It is unavoidable. It is for you own protection. I promise you that I will have you out quickly, but you must cooperate and, *most important*, you must keep our secrets to yourself while you are there."

"What's going on? Are you guys screwing me? Is that what's happening here?"

Sharkey didn't wait for an answer. First, he had to get out of that hotel, then he'd figure out where to go. He dropped the phone on the bed and as he began to dress, he could still hear Petrucceli speaking, "trust me, we will ..." his voice trailing off as Sharkey moved around the room.

But before he could even get his pants on, he heard the pounding on his hotel door.

"Polizia—open this door. Mr. Shark, polizia ..."

Chapter 88

Alex Nicholas was online seeing how far he could go. A year ago, that would have meant checking out hundreds of porn sites—now it meant researching what other connections and valuable information he could access in cyberspace. Quickly switching screens, one by one he watched the faces of Michael, Donna, Skinny Lester and Jennifer Walsh as they gazed back into their own computers. He logged into his special directory—a list of every person to whom he had over the past few months sent a special email greeting card. Each recipient, once they had opened their electronic greeting, had unknowingly surrendered their computers to him, providing Alex with a one-way mirror, where he could not only monitor all their email activity and track their precise location but also watch and listen as they gazed into their computer monitor or cellphone.

As he clicked onto "Jennifer Walsh" he watched her, half-naked in a black bra strolling around her bedroom. She must be looking for her blouse, he thought. I wonder where Catherine is?

She came closer, apparently within inches of the screen, she was leaning in, bending down and looking into her laptop screen. Alex watched as she reached behind her, releasing her bra.

"Oh yes," he said, fixated on her breasts now seemingly just inches away. "Jennifer, you still have the best tan lines." And it only got better as she poured a moisturizing cream onto her hand and rubbed it into her now glistening chest and breasts. He paid special attention to the contrast and clear line separating her skin's lush dark tan and the stark white encompassing her breasts. He could feel her skin quiver ... And then she reached lower ...

I think she knows I'm watching her. ... She was, he remembered, one of the few people he had shown the artificial intelligence program to, although at an early stage in its development. She's doing this for me, I know it, he thought. She knows.

But then Alex's attention was suddenly drawn to a notification popup: "Sindy Steele," indicating that she had just opened her computer. Reluctantly, he quickly clicked onto her screen. He checked her location; she was in Rome, apparently in a hotel lobby. Steele had a drink in her hand and was sitting across from a man in a clerical collar; despite his old-fashioned, frameless eyeglasses, he looked to be in his forties or early fifties. Alex recognized the face from some of his earlier surveillance. It was Monsignor Petrucceli.

Neither one of them was smiling. After a minute or so, it appeared that Steele reached over and shut the lid of her laptop. Alex lost the picture except for a narrow sliver at the bottom of the screen. He could still see the table and the lower part of their wine and cocktail glasses. He could also see two pairs of hands, each one either on the table or gripping a glass. When either of them leaned in close across the table, he could again see a face. But he could hear their conversation perfectly.

"I wish we could meet in a more private place," the man said. "We have access to discreet locations, more conducive to discussion."

"I'm sure you do, but after your friend tried to put holes in me at Yankee Stadium, I prefer a hotel lobby. Actually, I used to come here to the Intercontinental with my parents when we visited Rome many years ago."

"You must believe me, Mr. Cortese went rogue. He was to be at the ballpark as a backup, to observe and, if necessary, to help you escape. But he was infatuated with Mrs. Nicholas and when a man gets that way, he becomes like a woman—totally irrational—"

"Excuse me? Did I just step back into the Dark Ages?"

"No, please forgive me. You are correct. I spend my days with eighty-year-old bishops. I misspoke. Often I find that my humor suffers from a lack of fresh air."

"That's OK, how about if we just move on? I'd guess that your perception of women is the least of your problems."

"Perhaps. Nevertheless, Cardinal Lovallo requested that I meet with you today. We need to bring this entire affair—and our relationship—to a satisfactory conclusion, Miss Steele."

Alex noticed movement under the table. Someone's hand was shuffling about. At first he couldn't make out what was happening. Everything on top of the table seemed normal, almost still. He tried to zoom in and enlarge the area on the lower part of his screen. The quick movement and low light level made it difficult for him to figure what was going on. And then the hand stopped still. Alex saw the gun. He was unsure who was gripping it—until he zoomed in further and watched the long slim fingers and manicured nails wrapped around the handle. The elongated barrel indicated a silencer—and it was pointed right at Petrucceli's groin.

"She's going to shoot him in the balls," Alex whispered as though afraid Steele could hear him.

"Miss Steele, I may be able to assist you in rebuilding your life."

"You're going to help *me* rebuild my life?" Steele finished whatever remained of her drink. She was shaking her head. "Maybe you should worry about rebuilding your *church*."

"Believe me, I do worry about that too. But at this moment, I am prepared to make you a very generous offer—one that will permit you to comfortably pursue a life of leisure, without financial worries."

Alex could see the man pushing a document across the table toward Steele. She picked it up and began reading it.

"You must be kidding. This is a fortune. Much more than we agreed upon. What do I need to do? What's the hell is going on here?"

"It's very simple. My superiors want to end this. We need it to go away. Quickly."

She looked up from the paper, "What if I don't accept this—what if I—"

"Please, Miss Steele. I can only present this offer as a token of our goodwill. But remember, there is no one else who can verify any of the truly remarkable conversations or arrangements you will claim to have had with me. But, of course, the decision is yours."

Petrucceli appeared to be checking the time as he strained to read his wristwatch in the darkened room.

"I don't believe this." She was shaking her head.

"Miss Steele, do yourself a favor. Take the money, sign the document, and enjoy the rest of your life in peace. If not, I believe you have a good idea of what we are capable of doing."

"Let me ask you something. Why pay me off? Why not just get rid of me the way everyone else involved in all of this seems to have been *eliminated*?"

"My dear, the Church works in mysterious ways. It was decided that a line had to be drawn somewhere and perhaps a beautiful, intelligent woman was the place where it was deemed that it all had to stop—for now, anyway. Nevertheless, I would not tempt fate any longer. The waters here are cold, even this time of year."

She said nothing at first. Alex tried to guess what she would do. It seemed like she had no choice but, he reasoned, she wasn't the type to fold.

"How do I know that after I sign this you'll actually give me the money?"

After punching something into his phone, Petrucceli placed it close to Steele's face. "I believe you will find that this is your bank account information. Once you sign the document and I press this button indicating 'transfer funds'—half the money will be in your account."

"Half? What about the other half?"

"Ah, there is one other matter requiring your assistance. It's not mentioned in the document, for obvious reasons."

"And what would that be, pray tell?"

Alex could see Petrucceli nervously looking around him.

"We have a final loose end to be eliminated. Mr. Cortese would normally have fixed this for us but since he is no longer—"

Alex couldn't believe his eyes as the screen went dark. He waited impatiently for the transmission to return. ... Seconds later, it did. Sindy was speaking.

"Actually, I'd do him for free."

"We thought you wouldn't be adverse to the assignment."

"No, I look forward to it."

"Not to tell you how to do your job, but we prefer that there be no undue suffering."

"Nothing undue, I assure you."

"So, we have an agreement, yes?"

"Where do I sign?"

"I need to remind you, Miss Steele, that in the event you decide to seek some safe haven, perhaps home in the U.S., and reveal anything of this arrangement, there is the small matter of our esteemed Bishop McCarthy, whom you left hanging in a garage in Connecticut. The local police there were, perhaps, too easily deceived. We were not, however. I believe that some of our followers there can provide enough new information to reopen that investigation and ensure that your role in his *murder* is revealed. Once the investigative files from your unfortunate past in medical school at Stanford are unsealed ... I think you can see the difficulties you will face. I believe that even you, my dear, will recognize the problems that can occur. In short, you will likely spend the rest of your life in prison, although I must say, that with your quite impressive looks, you will be very much in demand there."

"Don't worry about me, I've given you what you want, just transfer the money. In just a few days, I'll complete the last part. "

Alex could hear Steele shuffling the documents that she had apparently signed and was handing back to Petrucceli.

"There," the man said, showing Steele his phone again. "It is done. Congratulations. You are a wise and now wealthy woman."

Alex could see Steele tuck the gun slightly under her thigh as she placed her right hand back on the table. She got up from her chair and the screen went blank.

Alex could only wonder what he missed in those few seconds.

Chapter 89

Paris, France

"Where are you?"

"I'm at Place Vendome, in front of the Ritz. Samantha's shopping nearby."

"Actually, I know where you are. I don't know why I asked. I have news ..."

Alex filled Michael in on what he'd witnessed—and the missing conversation when the connection lapsed."

"So we don't know who Sindy's after?" Michael's heart was racing. He needed to find Samantha. He looked up and down the street looking for her—and fearing he'd see Sindy Steele instead. At least, he thought, she's so tall, she'll stand out.

"It's a guy, we know that. Which means she's going to kill either you or Sharkey."

"Oh well, we have it down to two. Unfortunately, I'm one of them. Is that the best you can do? What happened to computers overtaking the human mind?"

"Who said I was a computer?"

Alex was playing with him.

"Don't you have a help desk or something you can go to?" Michael knew his sarcasm usually covered up his anger or his fear.

"I've just discovered something else too," Alex said.

"It can't get much worse, can it?"

"Maybe."

"Alex—tell me—"

"Sharkey's been released from prison. They let him out."

"What do you mean—how?"

"It looks like the same guys who set him up and put him in jail—just got him out. It's Italy—not New York, you know."

"At least while he was in prison, we knew where he was. Can you track him? Do you know where he is now?"

"No, he doesn't even have a phone ... Listen, this is frustrating for me too."

"Not as much as it is for me. Don't forget, you're *already* dead." As soon as he said it, he wished he could take it back.

"You're the one who keeps saying I'm dead. But how many dead people do you talk to regularly?"

"OK, you know what I meant. What about Sindy?"

"I told you, I had her earlier—but I can't find her now. She may have everything shut down. Or, she's just out of reach of any signals."

"Out of reach—what's even out of reach these days?"

"There's still plenty of places with no signals, especially in Europe where you are. But the most common is—"

"Don't tell me."

"Yes, a plane."

Chapter 90

Florence, Italy

They met in the second-floor private office of DiJulia's Leather Shop on the Via Del Corso, just blocks from the Duomo. DiJulia's, a Florence institution, was owned by a close and trustworthy friend of Cardinal Lovallo. Sindy had been assured that it was secure.

"It's so nice to meet you, Mr. Sharkey. Monsignor Petrucceli spoke very highly of you." She remembered Michael mentioning that Sharkey could be mistaken for an older Christopher Walken. She saw the resemblance, that look of someone capable of sadistic, crazed behavior at any moment, but he looked old and almost frail now. Several days in prison couldn't have helped.

"Yeah, well, it's good to be out of that place."

"Yes, Regina Coeli, it's the most notorious prison in Rome. I can't imagine what you must have gone through—"

"The whole thing was a setup. They planted drugs in my hotel room. I spent a little time—you know, a few days here and there over the years in a New York joint, but nothing like this. No one even spoke English, you know? ... So, my good friend Petrucceli said you'd be able to help me."

"Yes, I'm going to arrange a place for you to stay, at least until we can get you out of Italy—and back home."

"Back to New York? I thought Petrucceli filled you in on—"

"Yes, of course, he did. I'm aware of everything—including Michael Nicholas."

"Well then you know I can't go back to the U.S. as long as he's alive. Petrucceli and his associates were supposed to fix that."

"That's one reason they've hired me. I'm going to take care of everything so you'll be able to return home."

"How are you going to do that? Where is Michael anyway?"

"He's made it very convenient for us; he's in Europe now, Paris. Just an hour's flight away."

"Are you going to handle it, personally? Is this what you do? Professionally, I mean."

"Yes, it is. It's exactly what I do."

"You don't look like the type. I mean, you're a good-looking woman."

"Thank you. I assure you, you'll see that I know what I'm doing."

"You know, I have two big needs now. I think you're the one who can help me with both of them."

She noticed Sharkey eyeing her up and down. He must have had a kind of sick, bad-boy charm, she thought, thirty years ago.

"Well, the monsignor told me to take good care of you. What are the two needs?"

His face erupted in a broad smile and he actually looked ten years younger. "First, one of those Florentine steaks."

"Consider it done," she said, reaching across and placing her hand on his arm. "What's the other one?"

"I haven't gotten laid since I got to Italy."

"Well, I don't want you to think I'm easy. How about if we get you cleaned up and just see how the day goes first?"

"Good. OK. I think you and I are going to get along. Where do we go from here?"

"I'm going to take you to a private home just outside of Rome. It'll be best if you keep a very low profile for the remainder of your stay here. Oh, and the monsignor said to be sure to pick out a leather coat before we leave this shop. The quality here is superb."

"It's hot as hell—what do I need a leather coat for?"

He looked at her as though she was crazy. *He's about to find out,* she thought. Pulling the stiletto out of the narrow pocket of her short skirt, she raised her arm and in one arching powerful stroke, plunged its full seven inches into Sharkey's heart. She stepped back, leaving the knife embedded where it rested. She knew it had done its job. Sharkey hardly moved, his head first tilting downward as he looked at the pearl handle sticking out of his chest, his blood seeping out slowly around it. He opened his mouth, but no sound came out. Breathing heavily, he leaned back, his eyes following her. She stared back as he began to choke on his blood.

"To answer your question, maybe you'll want to be buried in it."

Chapter 91

Paris, France

Michael was staring up at what had been Ernest Hemingway's apartment on the rue Ferou, near the Luxembourg Gardens.

Samantha watched him, with an indulgent yet amused look.

"You must stop and look at that building at least once a year."

"I know, it just fascinates me when you see something like this—so filled with history for a few years—and then it becomes just another building. I wonder how many of the people living there now know Hemingway once did. And can you imagine living in the actual apartment as he did?"

"No, since I'm not sure it's even air-conditioned—which means *you'd* never live in it either."

"Good point."

Samantha moved on ahead while Michael drifted behind, still staring up when his cell rang. It was Alex.

"I can't speak now. Can you text me?"

"Are you *always* with your wife?"

"Yes, when I'm on vacation."

Seconds later, he felt his phone vibrate. He checked the screen.

Steele murdered Sharkey then left Rome. Can't locate her. No signal.

Chapter 92

Paris, France

Michael and Samantha entered the steel-and-glass doors of Pizza Chic, a modern, stylish restaurant on the corner of the rue de Mezieres in the hip Sixth Arrondissement and were immediately greeted by the good-looking, friendly Italian young lady who recognized them from their earlier visits. In addition to the menu, the restaurant was unusual in Paris with its cool minimalist décor, floor-to-ceiling windows, white-and-black-tiled floors, light bulbs dangling from the tin ceiling, and a wood-burning oven spreading a welcoming aroma throughout the room.

For Michael, his life and marriage seemed to be healing. Sharkey was finally gone, forever. There was still one threat—a potential one, at least: Sindy Steele.

It felt great to be back in Paris and even better to return to one of the restaurants that felt like a gentle reminder of simpler times. Even though he had yet to reach his seat, he could taste his favorite pizza, the "Aurora," a thin crust with fresh tomatoes topped by creamy, Italian buratta mozzarella.

Michael and Samantha sat down at their table for six against the restored brick wall near the open kitchen. Angie and Fletcher would be joining them—along with Tiger and his "surprise" date whom he had brought with him to Paris.

"So where do we think she is?" Samantha asked. Like him, she was relieved over Sharkey's timely death but the unpredictability of Sindy Steele remained a dark cloud. Michael intuitively knew that she was referring to Steele, and he could see her searching his face for any clues about his feelings.

"I don't know and I don't want to know."

Michael believed he had no longing for Sindy. In his mind, she was an infatuation, a strong woman who had offered exotic sex freely and provided a sense of physical safety at a time when he felt vulnerable. It was, he thought now, a type of codependency based upon forbidden sex and security, or fear. She—and the events beginning with his brother's murder—provided the perfect storm for what he considered his midlife crisis gone astray.

Michael knew Samantha wanted more from him though. "Michael, she can never enter our lives again. On any level."

Fletcher and Angie entered the restaurant. After the usual greeting, kisses and hugs, they settled into their seats.

"Tiger called my room, said he'll meet us all here. I think he's a little tied up. He said they slept all afternoon after they got in this morning." Fletcher laughed. "He made me swear not to tell you who he brought with him to Paris. He wants to surprise you. Angie and I didn't know until we met up with them at JFK."

"Do I know her?" Michael asked.

"Tiger said you would 'recognize' her. Let's leave it at that."

Their discussions continued as they quickly finished the first bottle of Nebbiolo Barolo wine, a magnificent red from Piemonte region of Italy. "You can almost taste the oak barrels," Samantha said as she put down her glass, "We have to get a case of this for our cellar at home."

"I'll have to ask Alex if it's alright. He approves anything that comes into the cellar now." Maybe it was the wine, maybe a feeling of relief, now that he and Samantha had reconciled and opened up about at least some of their indiscretions. It was a rare slip for Michael, always so careful with his words. He hoped his laugh made it apparent that he was joking. He noticed a puzzled look on Fletcher's face. He watched for a reaction from Samantha. He knew the demonstration in the wine cellar of the virtual Alex had upset her. They had rarely spoken of it since, another of the many dark secrets that had been allowed to seep into their marriage over the past year. The secret he was determined to reveal. This one, he knew, needed more preparation, more groundwork, before revisiting with her.

Fortunately, Samantha let it go.

Just as Michael was about to lift his glass for a subject-changing, light-hearted toast, his cell phone rang. He looked at the screen, subtly hiding it from Samantha's view. "I'd better take this outside. This place is too small in here to speak. I'll be right back."

Michael noticed that Samantha looked perplexed as he rose and walked out of the restaurant and onto the quiet sidewalk.

As he put his ear to the phone, he heard the sultry, familiar voice—and before he had any idea of what would transpire on the call—he was already wondering what he would say to Samantha when he re-entered the restaurant.

"Michael, I just want you know that I'm good now. I know it had to end. But we had a good little run. I don't have a great track record with men, in case you haven't noticed. I think I've killed more of them than I've loved."

"*Sindy*, where are you?"

"I'm taking a vacation in Europe. I needed to just get away. You know, after the shooting, I went right from the stadium to the St. Regis, got my things and took the next flight out of JFK to Venice. I always wanted to see it. It's beautiful. I'm going to travel for a while now. I couldn't afford to have the cops questioning me. Once they started digging into my past and things that happened back at school, it would have snowballed out of control. So, I had to just get out of the stadium, even though, you know, I was just trying to protect you from that madman."

"And what about Sharkey ... have you—"

"Sharkey had a heart attack."

"A heart attack?"

"After I put a knife in it."

"Oh, God." Michael knew she'd murdered him—but hearing how she did it made it oddly real.

"He's out of your life, Michael. I took care of it. I made a deal. The Vatican guys are not going to bother you anymore either. They gave their word. For whatever that's worth."

He was listening so intently that he was jolted when he felt someone from behind gently tap him on his shoulder. He spun around, the cell phone still in his ear, to quite a surprise. "Sindy, hold on for one second. Don't hang up, I'll be right there."

Michael took a step back. It was a sight to behold: Tiger and his voluptuous girlfriend. Although she was clearly quite younger, they made a colorful couple. She was wearing a very short, simple, red dress, which left nothing to the imagination of any of the Frenchmen who were turning their heads back to look fifty feet up the street. Michael remembered seeing her before, briefly, at Mario's.

Tiger had the broad smile of an expectant father, "Michael, this is Chambers Galore, she was in a lot of those big films." She was giggling. It was obvious they had both stopped for drinks on their way.

"My face was also on a lot of detergent boxes and my legs were on hair remover jars too," Chambers Galore proudly proclaimed as she planted a greeting kiss on Michael's cheek. Looking at Tiger, she continued, "He's so sweet. I'm too discreet to mention the films. I don't want people to think, you know, that I'm unapproachable or anything like that. Please—go back to your call. We're going to head inside."

Michael watched as they entered the restaurant, joining

Fletcher, Angie, and a now, for at least another few minutes, preoccupied Samantha. He turned his attention back to Sindy.

"Sindy, you saved my life at the stadium. I realized he was there to kill me." Michael said, intentionally ignoring the call from Alex and his warning that it was Steele who would murder him. "When he saw you, it must have disrupted his whole plan," Michael said, not wanting to have her think he knew she had planned to murder him. It seemed safer not to let her know that he knew the truth.

"When he saw me reach for my gun," she said, "he knew I'd shoot him. But he had his out before I could move. That's why I had to jump onto the field. I didn't think he'd be crazy enough to try and shoot me in the middle of the goddamned game on the field."

It all fit together, just the way he and Fletcher had speculated, Michael thought. "This guy must have been working for Sharkey."

"At least indirectly. His real boss was inside the Vatican. He was the guy we saw in L.A. when that photographer was killed. The same one I saw in the restaurant right after in Beverly Hills and way back when you had dinner with Bishop McCarthy at Piccola's in Astoria."

Michael was stunned. He had no idea someone had been following him that long. "What was the guy's name?"

"Frank. It was Frank Cortese," she said. "What difference does it make?"

"None, I was just curious." It was the man Alex had warned him about weeks ago. "Anyway, he's gone now."

Despite everything, Michael knew he would miss the extra security that Steele provided—even if she had been about to murder him.

"I think Cortese may have put a lot of extra work into a simple assignment for his own purposes."

"What do you mean?"

"Cortese was the one who took Samantha out of the bar at the Surrey that night I was with her. I think after he started watching you, he became infatuated with her and wanted to get you out of the way so he could make a play for her. He was forty-something. The guy had never been married. He was sick, Michael. That's why his plotting got so involved."

"My God. It's all so complicated. Do you really think he was hoping to hook up with Samantha after he eliminated me?"

"Absolutely. Think about it, Michael, a person who is obsessed becomes delusional—and will stop at nothing."

Michael wondered whether Steele knew she could have been talking about herself. Did she get the irony of what she was saying? He glanced inside the restaurant; he had to get back inside before Samantha became suspicious and came out looking for him. He wanted to ask her about Rosen and Samantha. Was she telling the truth about them at the stadium—or was she just trying to bait him? He couldn't trust very much that she would say anyway, and he didn't want to engage her any further, so he let it drop.

"What will you do now?"

"I'm headed to Marseilles. It's a great place to get lost—and from there, who knows? Oddly enough, no one seems to be looking for me."

It appeared that Sharkey had "disappeared" and his murder had gone unreported. The Church works in miraculous ways, he thought. He needed to get back inside before Samantha came out looking for him.

"Well, I wish you the—"

"Michael, there's more about me than you know."

"I know." He believed he did. "You mean what happened in med school?"

She appeared surprised. "Well … yes. That too, I guess."

"We know about the bishop."

"Of course. That was actually a pleasure. You know, when work and your passion come together."

"What else? Hightower?"

"No, I had nothing to do with his murder. That was those money guys who, I'm sure, were afraid he was going to turn on them for a plea deal. They have some crazy neo-Nazi fanatic kids do some of their dirty work for them."

"OK, what haven't you told me?"

"When we met in your office, I told you I was a bodyguard. I was a lot more than that."

"Yeah ..."

"Almost since that incident, so to speak, at Stanford, I've been a paid assassin. A professional hit man, woman, whatever."

"Well, I can't say that that's a total surprise to me at this point—"

"There's more. Remember when you said you'd noticed me in the Peninsula Hotel in Beverly Hills?"

"Yes, the night before my speech."

"And the night before Applegarden was murdered."

No, he thought. "But ... how—"

"Johnny Feathers had called me for the assignment. I'd done work for him before. I put a small team together, two other pros. We got into his room while he was asleep. I injected him—right in his groin—he couldn't move or speak. We held a pillow over his face. ... It took a couple of minutes."

"But how did you know it had anything to do with me? I never had a clue Feathers was going to do this. It was a huge misunderstanding."

"Feathers told me just enough. He said he was doing this as a favor for the brother of a friend of his—obviously Alex—who'd been murdered. I did a lot of Googling and figured out you were the brother. He said for him it was a freebie, so he actually paid me less than I usually made on a job. I was infatuated with you, your background and everything, all so different from your brother and the people I deal with now—so I tracked you down. I realized later that you didn't have any idea what Feathers really did—or that he'd act on what he thought you wanted."

Her mood then appeared to change. Michael had seen it before, as though she reached back into her mind or memory and found something there that she'd buried.

"The problem is, Michael, sometimes I kill the ones I love."

He didn't know what to say. He was afraid to go deeper. He needed to get back to Samantha.

"How will I contact you?" After the words were out, he knew it was a question fraught with problems, he wished he could pull it back. Just in case he was ever questioned, it was probably even better that he didn't know. Maybe even if he was never questioned.

"Michael, you don't need to contact me. You just need to be careful. But, most of all, you need to go back to your family."

There was an extended silent pause. Michael checked the screen on his cell to see if he had lost the connection.

"Sindy—are you still there?"

"Yes, Michael, just be well."

He felt relieved. Until he heard her voice again.

"Don't worry, I'll find you."

Chapter 93

Saint Paul de Vence, France

"Bertrand Rosen was a shit and I hope they have thoroughly cleaned the sidewalk so there is no trace of him in Paris," Catherine Saint-Laurent pronounced.

Michael detected an audible sigh from many of the nearby patrons on La Columbe d'Or's outdoor terrace, so it was apparent that they were all eavesdropping on the famous actress' every word.

Catherine was as beautiful as ever. Even more radiant now, he thought, with her career on a rebound.

"Michael, how could you have done business with such a man?"

He began to answer but since no one at the table would dare interrupt her anyway, she continued. "I'm only sorry that he didn't live on a higher floor so that he could have had more time on his way down to think about what awaited him. He ruined so many people. He lived like a king—mansions, yachts, helicopters—on everyone else's money."

Saint-Laurent then turned to Samantha, "And, you know, he was a creep. He was not an attractive man. He had money, that's all.

Actually, he only had the money of the people who trusted him. Many of my good friends lost everything because of him."

Samantha, showing neither emotion nor expression, looked down and straightened out the white linen napkin resting on her lap. Michael, sensing her unease, thought about Sindy's bewildering announcement that she had seen Samantha enter Rosen's apartment. He had not been able to dislodge it from his mind but had chosen not to ask Samantha about it. He wondered whether it was true or had Steele made it up in a desperate attempt to turn him against his wife. And, after all, he thought, he was no longer in any position to pass judgments on issues of fidelity.

Catherine continued, "He was screwing around left and right. Even the hotel maids where he stayed weren't safe. His wife left him, but they had an arrangement. She lived another life, with an apartment in the sixth in Paris, she did everything she wanted to do—and he paid for it. He had no choice. She knew too much."

"But wasn't he considering financing your movie before Alex jumped in?" Michael asked, recalling that Catherine mentioned that to him when she advised him to be leery of Rosen.

"He said he was interested—but all he was interested in was getting me to the bedroom. He wanted to be able to say he made love to Catherine Saint-Laurent. He was a terrible man."

Michael noticed that, several times, as Catherine spoke about Rosen, Samantha would reach over and gently touch his arm. Perhaps just a casual gesture of polite affection, he thought, yet, he couldn't recall any such gestures recently.

But once the discussion of Bertrand Rosen was over, everyone seemed to relax and take in the beauty that was all around them. "Life is good, my dear friends," Catherine said as she raised her glass of champagne.

And, indeed, for Michael, as he took in the view of the mature trees, the twinkling lights, the large canvas umbrellas, and the garden's contemporary sculptures, the world appeared to have calmed down.

The cuisine, his own simple skirt steak with shallots, and Samantha's perfectly prepared sole surrounded by fresh, locally grown vegetables, was artfully orchestrated on each plate. The candlelight on the table bathed everyone in a soft glow, making the attractive beautiful, and the already beautiful ravishing.

Jennifer Walsh looked fresh and tan, like the fantasy all-American beauty, in her low-cut coral cotton dress. Her cleavage showed a slight touch of perspiration, glistening like a fairy-dust sprinkling of Swarovski crystals. As the French diners stole discreet glances toward their venerable star, Catherine Saint-Laurent, Michael knew that none would imagine that the fresh young American beauty beside her, known in the American tabloids as the "hairdresser to the stars," was her lover.

Jennifer looked at Catherine, "We are so excited about the movie. Catherine is dying to tell you both the latest."

Michael and Samantha, simultaneously, called out, "Yes, yes. Of " course."

"We just completed shooting last week." Saint-Laurent said, beaming. "I believe that *Mirror Image* will be my triumphant return to the screen." Then like the great actress she was, her expression quickly turned melancholy. I'm afraid though that people will use the horrible C word when speaking about me."

Momentarily shocked, everyone else was about to protest when Catherine waved her hand dismissively, smiling. "I mean that horrible word, *comeback*, of course.

Although it seemed a lifetime ago, Michael recalled the first time he met Jennifer Walsh, the day she revealed that she had been Alex's mistress and disclosed the existence of his secret Apple laptop. It was Jennifer, Michael thought, as he watched her across the table, who'd brought him closer to his brother than he had ever been while Alex was alive.

"You know, Michael," Jennifer interjected, "the story is one that should interest you. It takes place in the south of France. It's about two brothers, one who is very straight, a corporate guy, and his brother, who is the exact opposite, involved in organized crime and stuff."

"I can see the obvious similarities but Alex was never involved with organized crime. He liked to organize his own crime," Michael said, hesitant to pursue the topic further.

But Samantha was definitely curious. "What happens to the two brothers?"

Before answering, Jennifer looked to Catherine who turned solemn. "One of them dies," she said.

"Well, which one?" Samantha asked.

Catherine, carefully watching Samantha's expression, must have sensed it was time to rescue the brash Jennifer. "Oh, do not worry, my dear Samantha. It is merely a script, fiction; it is just our Hollywood. It's not real."

"Thank you, Catherine. I know you are trying to spare me any discomfort but, I am curious, who dies?"

"It is the older brother, the bad boy, the one involved in all the illegal businesses. Too many women," she glanced at Jennifer, "perhaps too many at one time too, yes? Let us say that he lived a very unhealthy life, not unlike our dear Alex, I'm afraid." She then turned to Michael. "But there is a surprising secret twist to the story, which, unfortunately, does *not* follow real life. I am not supposed to reveal it to anyone." Ever the actress, she then proceeded to pick at her dinner.

Samantha looked ready to leap out of her seat. "Catherine, you are terrible. You *must* tell us!"

"Very well then, I will tell you. But you must swear never to repeat it."

Almost in unison again, Michael and Samantha shouted, "Yes."

Catherine took her time, obviously relishing the drama—or the attention. Finally, she looked up from her dish and revealed her secret.

"The dead brother may still be alive."

Samantha closed her eyes, "Oh my God, no." It was the *last* thing Samantha wanted to hear, Michael thought.

Unfazed as she picked up her fork again, Catherine whispered, "Unfortunately for my dear Alex, life does not always imitate art."

Author's Note

Death Logs In is a work of fiction. The names, characters, places, and incidents described in this novel are the product of the author's imagination or have been used fictitiously. Any resemblance to actual persons, businesses, events or places is purely coincidental.

Acknowledgements

Many thanks to my editors, Peter Gelfan and Debra Ginsberg, for saving me from myself.

Thanks also to the great professionals at The Editorial Department, including Morgana Gallaway and her team of cover designers, notably Pete Garceau. Also to my many friends and readers, including Kay Kopec, Sherry Moran and Bill Finan,

A special appreciation goes to Donald Luciano, who, despite his prior commitments and busy schedule, provided invaluable creative ideas and a thorough and painstaking review.

Finally, my loving appreciation to Andrea and Danielle, who tirelessly read my drafts and offered their brilliant advice, solicited or not.

Preview
DEATH LOGS OUT
Fall 2015

Chapter 1

Westport, Connecticut

It's never good news when the phone rings after midnight.

"I have your precious Sofia here."

Michael Nicholas knew he would hear from her again. Her voice carried through the telephone receiver and seared through his chest. He didn't have time to speak before she continued.

"Michael, I told you I'd find you."

Michael hoped it was a cruel joke, but he knew Sindy Steele— and therefore, it was no joke. His daughter, Sofia, should have been safely tucked away in quiet Chapel Hill, for her second year at the University of North Carolina. However, she was now in the hands of the woman he wanted, yet feared the most.

"Sindy, what are you doing?" He couldn't keep the sense of desperation out of his voice.

"Soon you'll know what it's like to love someone with all your heart – and not be able to have them again. Michael, you're going to experience that never ending emptiness that comes from loss, terrible loss."

Fifteen years ago, Sindy Steele, a brilliant, beautiful—but

troubled—medical student at Stanford University, poisoned her live-in lover. She did so expertly, using her new found aptitude for pharmacology. Due to the fact he had just dumped her, the police strongly suspected foul play, however they couldn't find evidence of anything to explain his sudden death. School officials also found the circumstances to be, 'problematic'. In exchange for Sindy voluntarily leaving Stanford, they provided her with a substantial payment. In a round about way, that turned out to be Sindy's first paid 'hit'.

That instance inspired her to use her talents for profit—as an assassin for hire. It was how Michael Nicholas met her.

"Sindy, please, don't touch her. She hasn't done anything to you. What do you want? What do you want me to do?"

"There's nothing you can do. It's about what you've *done*, Michael. What you've done to *me*."

"Sindy, there's got to be something I can do. Please. Let me speak with Sofia."

After a momentary silence that seemed to last forever, she answered, "Sure, I'll let you speak with her—as soon as I can get the duct tape off."

The line went dead.

For previews of upcoming books by E. J. Simon, and more information about the author, visit www.ejsimon.com

E.J. SIMON is the author of *Death Never Sleeps,* his debut novel.

He is the former CEO of GMAC Global Relocation Services (a division of GM) and the Managing Director of Douglas Elliman, the largest real estate company in New York.

He is from New York City and lives in Connecticut.